HELEN'S HOUND

Rawle C. Eastmond

Holford Johnson Publishing Inc.

Copyright © 2006 Rawle C. Eastmond and
Holford Johnson Publishing, Barbados

All rights reserved. This publication may
not be reproduced, in whole or in part,
by any means including photocopying or
any information storage or retrieval system,
without the specific and prior written permission
of Holford-Johnson Publishing Inc.

Cover and Layout Design:
Digital Stealth Studio
http://www.digitalstealth.com

Print Production:
A & A Printing
Tampa, Florida

Published by:
Holford Johnson Publishing, Inc., Barbados, W.I.

ISBN: 976 - 8215 - 15 - 1
ISBN: 978 - 976 - 8215 - 15 - 4

DEDICATION

To the memory of:

Muriel Christie
Bob Shaw
Joseph St. Clair Yearwood
Andrew Alphonso Bend
Lionel Cummins-Jones
Ernest Rocheford

and

The greatest respect to:

my mother Lucille Eastmond
Mrs. Sybil Leacock
Teacher Colin Payne
Egerton 'Max' Archer
Neville Phillips
Norman Daniel
Winston Gibson
Adonijah
Elombe Mottley
Carol Pitt

all of whom have provided inspiration.

This book is a work of fiction. Names, characters, places and incidents are either the products of the author's imagination or are used fictitiously. Any resemblance to actual events or locales or persons, living or dead, is entirely coincidental.

Table of Contents

Foreword vi
CH. 1   The Beginning... 1
CH. 2   One Who Looks Promising 9
CH. 3   Celebration After All 19
CH. 4   Sou-Sou 28
CH. 5   Truant 39
CH. 6   Wayward Youth 49
CH. 7   Times in the Regiment 59
CH. 8   A Priest Arives 71
CH. 9   Seminary 80
CH. 10 The Ranch 91
CH. 11 Another Priest Arrives...............................100
CH. 12 Hester and Drugs 107
CH. 13 Debate on Homosexuality 119
CH. 14 A Cooperative Could Evolve 128
CH. 15 Church Council..138
CH. 16 September 11th 147
CH. 17 Counselling Session..................................159
CH. 18 The Credit Union.......................................171
CH. 19 The Fair...182
CH. 20 Counselling Twist 193
CH. 21 Occult Ritual 204
CH. 22 A Proposal..214
CH. 23 Old Talk 223
CH. 24 Recovery...234
CH. 25 Lecture in England....................................246
CH. 26 A Motivational Session 258
CH. 27 A Truly Sick Man 270
CH. 28 A Peculiar Sermon 281
CH. 29 Death 288

FOREWORD

"Helen's Hound" concerns itself with questions to do with morality, religion, social advancement, the nation and its development in a changing environment.

Eastmond has a proclivity for constructing credible characters. It is these characters that help infuse the work with much of its power. There is a certain clarity and transparency within the narrative. But this (apparent) directness is an authorial device. It serves as an ironic commentary on the shady nature of social relations within crucial arenas of Caribbean society. Chapter titles indicate important movements within the text's plot, but these titles also mask other latent issues that permeate the work's sub-text.

Eastmond has created a novel of considerable intrigue. There are several layers of meaning within the work. Here is a craftsman that understands the rudiments of literary construction. His is a shrewd mind. "Helen's Hound" is not only about a single island, it also has broader reference. One reading of the text produces many moments of jouissance. The public will want to read this work a second time as they go in search of its other "hidden" pleasures!

Dr. Curwen Best
Senior Lecturer (Literature and Popular Culture)
UWI, Cave Hill Campus, Barbados

Chapter 1

THE BEGINNING

THE BABY STORMED INTO THIS WORLD screaming at such a volume that the three who witnessed this event were clearly alarmed.

Midwife Isalene jumped back. In all her years she had never seen a human being so large at birth. Drawing in a deep breath she looked upon the child who continued to cry at a pitch entirely inconsistent with its age. She moved towards Sarah to complete the bodily separation of infant from mother.

Sarah's feelings blended together as joy at seeing her new born, relief from the pains of labour and confusion brought on by the deafening noises coming from the shrieks of her son. Sarah's eyes met those of her husband of twelve years and the fact of his bewilderment did not escape her.

"Miss Sarah, it is a boy and he is a very, very, big boy."

Sarah could hardly hear the words of the midwife as the male infant 'bawled' as some West Indians, especially Trinidadians, would have said. The midwife, discerning that Sarah did not comprehend what she had sought to communicate to her, repeated:

"Miss Sarah, it is a boy."

What was clear to Zaccky was that on this occasion the words of Isalene, the midwife were softer. How, Zaccky thought, could she feel that his wife would hear her on a second occasion when her voice was softer than on the earlier occasion?"

Always respectful of others, it was Zaccky that marvelled

more that at first Sarah either did not hear or could not hear when the words appeared to him to be louder and just when the new born was crying even louder, the midwife could decide to drop her voice. Zaccky did not want to be judgmental, but was it that there was such an air of astonishment?

Isalene was one of a few remaining midwives practising their profession privately. Under an Ordinance akin to the Nurses and Midwives Registration Act of a nearby island known as Bimshire, trained midwives could deliver babies without a confinement in a hospital. In modern times, as most midwives in private practice grew too old to carry on, and increasingly more mothers were opting to go to hospital to have their babies, Zaccky and Sarah, Catholic and Conservative to the hilt and devoted to the norms of their grandparents, decided that Sarah should have her baby at home.

One of the things about Zaccky and Sarah was that they studiously observed the teachings of their church, respected their elders, and clung fast to the standards, beliefs and practices passed down to them by their ancestors. Both Zaccky and Sarah were nurtured by grandparents even though their own parents were available to do so, but it must have been that the parents themselves were willing to delegate many responsibilities to their own immediate parents.

Their village did present a charm brought on not just by its location at the foot of a hill but also by folkways which permitted licence to grandparents to act *in loco parentis*. This meant that grandparents were accorded a most interesting role. There were scores of instances in which a young married couple would have no difficulty having their parents live with them although the cases of some young husbands resenting their mothers-in-law seemed to be on the increase.

Zaccky looked in Sarah's direction. He did realize that she was looking at him. Zaccky could not work out the true character of the expression on his wife's face. Then he became worried and turned to the midwife.

"I see the boy. He is very, very big. He is making so much

noise that I am beginning to get a headache."

By now the midwife had decided to take a seat in a small chair next to Zaccky.

"Tell me, Miss Isalene, is my wife alright?"

Isalene looked in Zaccky's direction asking:

"Why? Do you think that she is in difficulties?"

"Just now, Miss Isalene, when you said something to her, she did not even blink and earlier you did look in her direction and you tried to speak to her but she did not respond."

Isalene now moved towards the bed. She too was starting to feel headachy; not because her work of assisting with the delivery of the baby was eventful or stressful, but because of the noises the infant was making. Babies cry. In cases when babies enter the world too silently a slap on their frail bodies is enough to start them crying. Babies do cry. It was obvious to the three adults who were present in the largest of the four bedrooms of the house that the noises being made by the newborn alternated between shrieks and howls—growls even. The largeness of the child registering in every cell of her brain served to wake up the midwife to the reality that each baby is different. But while she owed it to Zaccky to ensure that Sarah was in good health she, Isalene, a midwife of thirty-seven years experience had never seen a baby so big or capable of creating such a serious din.

"Mr. Zaccky out of his undying love for you wants to know if you are feeling well."

"I am okay," Sarah whispered in the softest of tones, "but the baby's different noises are troubling to me. Do tell my husband that...."

Just then the new born went quiet. "Yes, do tell my good husband that I am alright."

Sarah's voice was now noticeably stronger. The relief she was now experiencing was due as much to the fact that Zaccky was interested in her well-being as it was to the reality that the infant had suddenly gone still. This period was used to breast feed the new born. Thereafter Zaccky moved close to his wife

3

and child. Isalene assured the two of them that she had done her best, checked on mother and child, and left.

The baby went to sleep. Zaccky and Sarah looked at him and at each other. They could not decide who the child resembled. For days and days they simply could not work out who the child looked like. Then one day:

"I have come to congratulate you. I understand you and Miss Sarah have a new baby. Wish Miss Sarah well."

Zaccky, having opened his front door, realized it was Matthias and became aware of the odor that accompanied this man's breath almost each time. It was about 6:15 in the morning and Zaccky was thinking that Matthias must have kept back some of his favourite substance from the night before or found someone just like him prepared to indulge him so early in the morning. Zaccky, however, was unsure of the exact brand, but quickly speculated to himself that it could have been puncheon rum, the favourite of every typically addicted drinker.

"Now, Mr. Zaccky, when is the christening? I am ready for the christening. Will it be next week or two weeks from now?"

"Mattie," Zaccky started, then stopped .

"Yes, Mr. Zaccky," Matthias loved whenever anyone called him by any name connoting affection but his favourite friend as he would say, was Zaccky and oh how he gloried in being called Mattie by someone of Zaccky's standing.

"Sarah and I have decided not to have a christening right now."

Zaccky understood that by 'christening' Matthias actually meant the party that most folks in the community held to commemorate the birth of their babies.

"But, Mr. Zaccky, you still have to give your child a name."

"Oh, that will be done within a few days at St. Ignatius but there would be no feasting, at least not right now," Zaccky said firmly, but politely.

Then the two looked at each other for a short while. By now Matthias had actually crossed the threshold having come past the door.

"Sit down, friend," Zaccky invited Matthias.

"Just now, Mr. Zaccky, I saw you looking at me and you were saying nothing."

"Oh, to be truthful I was thinking of how I can do my best to rehabilitate you. I really want to be helpful to you. I wonder if you would start to come to church with me."

"No, Sir, No, Mr. Zaccky, I cannot see any church taking me."

"You know that we would welcome you at our church," Zaccky assured.

"I doubt it," Matthias said with a mild retort.

Then Zaccky asked him, "Why would you not want to come to church?"

"I feel so bad about myself," Matthias lamented. Zaccky became even more sensitive to Matthias' lament.

"Surely you have done so much labour work that you have money to buy clothes?" Zaccky insisted.

"Man, I have some clothes, but not enough. The rum and the women."

Without judging Matthias, Zaccky could easily figure out the types of women to whom Matthias referred, though the number of such women were declining. Zaccky said to Matthias:

"I can hold your money for you and when it is time you will get more than $1,000."

FOR SOME time Sarah and Zaccky continued to have highly ambivalent views about their son's moods. Cindy, their first child was frequently the victim of the aggression demonstrated by Aaron towards her.

There were occasions when Zaccky actually accused his wife of not being firm enough with their son. For there were instances when Sarah did indicate that Zaccky was too harsh on the boy. Zaccky had on many occasions come very, very close to telling his wife that she was spoiling Aaron. Her love for her son was strong, and surely from time to time when he did wrong she had failed to confront him. Sarah knew that that very strong bond that kept her family together could be undermined when her husband became so flustered that he actually lost patience with her and she would concede – to herself – that if her marriage and family life were at any risk it was the impact of Aaron's behaviour on Zaccky which was responsible.

Zaccky would always remind her how on one occasion three years earlier, just after Aaron had snatched Cindy's food before she had half completed it, he scolded the boy. Aaron, resenting his father's intervention, tried to push him away. Sarah would remind Zaccky that their son did not succeed and that in any event the incident should be forgotten or at least forgiven.

"If there is a threat to our family life," Zaccky would tell her, "it is the attitude and conduct of this boy."

Zaccky and Sarah were devoted to one another and their enduring hope was for them as husband and wife to live in harmony, and for all of their family peace, love happiness and unity. Then Sarah decided that she really had to break the ice.

"Honey, be assured of my love. I want here and now to discuss this matter of Aaron's behaviour so that we can find a solution for the good of our marriage."

"This way we can and will settle our differences." Zaccky suggested.

"My problem is that you seem to pick on him." Sarah said.

"No, darling. That boy came close to assaulting me. You must remember that he tried to push me to the ground." Zackky said.

"Zaccky, are you not sure that you are not being very harsh

on him?"

"Let us look at Cindy. Children will be children. But I could not and cannot even see Cindy trying to assault or beat her father."

"I love my son," she insisted.

"I love him too, Sarah, but he tends to be rude, greedy and disrespectful."

"Let us together in Cindy's absence have a little gentle talk with him," Sarah suggested.

"Alright, we will talk to him. But my fear is that he would not listen. I do not believe in spoiling children. My belief is that he is aware that he is big and strong. He may be thinking that his strength of body will make him so powerful that he can do as he pleases."

"Let us try with him," Sarah repeated.

"Sarah, my love for you will end at death, but remember that for months after his birth you and I were shocked at his screams and looks. He does not look like you nor me nor anyone I know."

"We did not even keep a christening party and the village was very, very disappointed. Some were hurt that we held no party and no one in this village could understand why we did not celebrate just after he was born. If we can get him to behave well for two straight years, allowing a little concession for boyish pranks and mischief, I, Sarah Ruth Fromgence nee Sarah Ruth Epilette will join you, my only husband, to keep a party for his tenth birthday. To you and me it will be the 'Deferred Christening', love."

Zaccky loved his wife intensely and there was an aspect of that affection that required him to give in to his wife from time to time.

"Okay, Sarah. I will do what you want. I am not being henpecked, but you can lead me on this one."

"You know, Zaccky you are the model husband and I am sure that you see me as the perfect wife. But you and I have to live down the early shock of our son's large body at his birth and the tremendous noise he created when he arrived. We also have to try our best with him for I must admit that I am concerned about his moods, his aggression and of course his greed."

"I love you, my wife. I still wonder who in our family tree Aaron resembles in looks and in behaviour. Are you sure that you checked your own family tree carefully?"

"In the interest of peace, Zaccky, I must confess that I will have to speak to Aaron sternly about how to treat Cindy!"

"This is the first time that you are making such an admission, Sarah."

"Zaccky, children have to be properly trained. I will search my heart for any weakness that might have been controlling my attitude to our son."

"Sarah, I love my son, but you have to get Aaron to love his father."

"Are you unsure and insecure in your dealings with our son?"

"To be honest, yes, Sarah. I am assured of Cindy's love and sense of respect for both of us but there have been times when I am sure Aaron complained to you about me. I now feel," Zaccky was saying, "that some children are smart enough to divide or cause splits between their two parents. He is young but he is no fool and I am sure that he knows your weaknesses and your soft spots and in the past he has driven something like a wedge between you and me."

"I will do my best to correct that situation, honey."

Sarah moved towards Zaccky and planted a kiss on her husband's lips.

"I shall do my best," said Sarah, "to get Aaron to behave and to cooperate with the three of us, Cindy included."

The two agreed that harmony was now fully restored to their relations. Sarah was sure that she could persuade Aaron to behave. Zaccky felt that Sarah was the one to show the initiative in the matter. She would take the lead and he would follow with all the support that he could muster.

Chapter 2

ONE WHO LOOKS PROMISING

FREDERICK WEISENBERG WAS BORN IN COLUMBUS, Ohio in the U.S.A. The first of three children of Mary and George, Fred grew up in a state famous for its agriculture and in many areas of the state, its curious blend of religious and spiritual teachings. Mary and George brought up their three children in a conservative manner, insisting that the three respected all people, practiced cleanliness and proper hygiene, and stayed away from bad children. These two parents, who could be said to have come from middle America, were generous people who insisted that Frederick and his siblings should always show kindness, love and patience to others.

One hot summer day after Frederick returned from school George asked him:

"Son, did you remember to show any kindness to any of your classmates?"

"Yes, Dad, little Jim told me that he had forgotten his lunch in his parents' car."

"What did you do for Jim?" George inquired.

"I gave him half of my lunch, Dad."

"Very good, my son," George observed.

"Yes, Dad, it is true and Jim thanked me," Frederick said.

"Frederick, the lesson which I want you to learn from the assistance which you gave to Jim, is always try to be nice to all persons, especially the unfortunate."

For a short while Frederick said nothing, but two clear thoughts went through his mind. That his father seemed very happy to have learnt what he had done and that there must be some very important thing about giving up what was his to another needy person. While Frederick was pondering on this, his mother Mary, herself a schoolteacher, came up to them and said:

"Now what are you two up to?"

George told her that he had just learnt that Frederick had helped a friend in need. Then Mary said:

"Although my son, you will notice many different things in your life, some of which are going to be bad, do your best to be good, value all you learn in school and continue to like your Sunday school."

Mary and George worshipped in the Roman Catholic church in their neighbourhood and always took along their three children with them. In the event that something prevented them from attending their church they sent their children to church with Pat, another devout catholic. In addition, the three children attended Sunday school every week and what made things interesting for the three youngsters was that their parents took time, in turns, to read them Bible stories. Frederick noticed though that some of the children in their area, though sent to school, never attended Sunday school. Later that evening at dinner, Frederick said:

"Mum and Dad, tell me why some of my classmates don't come to Sunday School?"

Mary replied:

"Good question. I guess that either those children's parents do not go to church, do not understand what church is about and just do not understand the importance of Sunday School. It is also possible that those parents who do not send their children to Sunday School did not attend church nor Sunday School when they were young!"

Frederick turned to his father questioningly.

"Daddy, what happens to those children who never go to Sunday School?"

"These are some of the possibilities, son: first I think that they never learn to walk with God, especially if they learn nothing of God in their homes and at school. I am beginning to think that many of our schools in the United States are already moving away from teaching young children about God. Governments in America are often taking the pressure off schools by allowing them to teach secular things more than spirituality. Many parents do not have faith and trust in God and cannot see any value in religion nor the teachings of the church and therefore do not even keep Bibles nor religious books in their homes. But let me tell you, son, Christ is the head of my household. I myself was taught spirituality. My late father was a follower of the Oxford Movement and my mother was a strong believer and in addition they were very strong Catholics."

Frederick listened carefully. Already he sensed that being kind and obedient were qualities which Bible and church would require of all persons. Thinking of his Sunday School days, Frederick could easily remember that his two Sunday School teachers would teach him messages about goodness and also about God's mercies. Frederick was aware that the adults he knew held different occupations: carpenters, farmers, teachers and librarians but he always wondered if priests and nuns were normal workers. As he was sleepy he did not ask his parents if the leaders of his church could be called workers nor did he question them about the way of life of the clergy and the sisters of the church.

Frederick took a very special liking to school, went there willingly, and was nice and friendly to his peers. He knew the eight or nine children in his class who lived near to his church who never attended Sunday school, but never asked them why they did not come to Sunday School. To him they were different but he still showed them love and respect. A bright child, Frederick frequently helped them with their school work, especially during the lunch break. He also developed a tremendous interest in Sunday School and often encouraged Frank and Elizabeth, his brother and sister, to come along with him when these two showed that they did not always want to go. There were times when his brother and sister were not too keen to go. Frederick looked forward to hearing the Bible stories read to him by his parents and asked many questions, some of which would normally be raised by much older people.

Just after he went to High School something happened which both influenced Frederick and played an important part in what he was to become. One of his classmates fell ill and had to be in hospital for months. When Greg first collapsed in school and was taken to hospital, Frederick told Mary and George about what had happened and begged them to allow him to visit Greg. Having no difficulty securing his parents' approval, Frederick would visit Greg no fewer than four times a week and always prayed by his bedside. This impressed Mary and George immensely and one day Mary inquired of George,

"Darling, what do you think Frederick will become when he grows up?"

"Not quite sure, Mary, but I feel he will become a member of one or more of the caring professions," George predicted.

"That would be nice, George, I trust our other two children will follow suit."

In high school Frederick was a top student, excelling in all subjects. He took a particular for Math, Language Arts, Literature and Religious Education. When he was fifteen, one day his parents called him to a meeting while the other children were away from home.

"Fred, your mother and I feel blessed by God that we have such a nice family. We both love all three of you just as we as parents love one another. We have chosen this moment to speak to you privately." George said.

"Thank you, mum and dad."

Fred, without even knowing the real purpose of this meeting, could think nothing negative. He knew he was not in trouble and so he simply sat and waited for events to unfold.

"Fred, George and I feel that at your age it is not too early for you to think of a career," said Mary encouragingly. Smiling, George asked:

"Have you ever considered what you want to do in the future?"

Without being disrespectful or hasty," Fred said, "Do I have to give an answer right away?"

"Take a few days, dear," his mother advised with love.

Back at school Frederick made up his mind to continue to excel in all his school subjects and to help as many of his classmates as he could. He felt extremely happy when Greg was well enough to return to school and during the first week of Greg's return, rather than play at lunch time, he took Greg aside and went through with him the areas of school work which his friend had missed. Frederick was so busy helping Greg that he took no time to think of a future outside of school. Greg realized that in Frederick he had a true friend and felt good that the latter more than anyone else had visited him when he was in hospital and now he was simply delighted that Frederick could help him catch up with his school work.

After ten days or so working with Greg mainly at the luncheon break, one day out of sheer curiosity Fred asked Greg if he had ever thought of the world of work and a career. Greg said that he could not make up his mind if he should prepare to be a doctor, dentist or engineer and enquired of his best friend whether he had made any decision.

"I am thinking of something by which I can truly help people," Fred replied.

"The best thing I can advise would be a career in medicine," Greg advised.

Though very good at the sciences Fred did not like the idea of being a doctor and indicated to Greg that he would spend some weeks and months, if necessary, before coming to a decision. One evening at dinner while being under no pressure of any kind from Mary and George, Fred told his parents that he still needed time before coming to a decision on his future.

"Do not worry unnecessarily," George advised encouragingly.

"I have the American dictionary of Occupational Titles and in fact I left it in my room in case you wanted me to look up some job titles with you. If you want to look at it all by yourself that is okay with me."

"Dad, my homework for tonight is quite heavy and I sense that tomorrow night it will be no different. How about looking at it on the weekend?"

Back at school next day at 2.30 p.m. a lecture was to be delivered to the school by Father Valence Clark who was scheduled to speak on the topic: Lessons from the scriptures. The Priest began:

"By scriptures I mean the books of the Holy Bible. The Bible contains over sixty books and is divided into the Old Testament and the New Testament. In many ways the Old Testament speaks to aspects of Jewish history and does contain considerable inspiration. The first book of the Bible is Genesis which both speaks of how the world began and the story of the first people, Adam and Eve. Genesis is followed by some books of which the first few are Exodus, Leviticus, Numbers and Deuteronomy. I do not have time to discuss all of these books of the first part of the Holy Bible but I can tell you that Deuteronomy 27:10 says: *'Therefore you shall obey the voice of the Lord your God and observe his commandments and His Statutes which I commend to you today.'*

When I was a very small boy in school, believe me we had to learn Exodus 20: vs.2-17 where the ten commandments are set out. These ten commandments forbid the worship of false Gods, swearing, disobedience to parents, murder, cheating, stealing and lying. The lessons you can get from these commandments are to be true to yourself, your neighbours and your God and to obey your parents. There are other important things about the Old Testament and if you attend Church and Sunday School enough, you will learn important lessons. I wish that your parents will tell you about what the Old Testament offers.

The New Testament makes promises and gives us hope. It brings the Good News of how God sent his son on earth to help and to save us. The four gospels are about Jesus Christ and his work. Christ preached obedience to God and made a very strong comment to us to love our neighbours as we love ourselves, Christ also showed in Matthew 5 vs. 12 which persons shall be blessed and in Matthew 6:9-15 you can find the Lord's Prayer which I encourage you to know and above all to study and understand. That prayer is a classic.

I also want to tell you about the personal relationship each of us should have with God, our Maker. God is all-powerful. God knows everything and everybody. Each of us must try to be very, very, good. We have to avoid hate, jealousy and greed. We have to control our tempers. We must pray. We have to love all, not just our families. We have to do works which will honour and glorify God. We have to keep away from all evil. We must place our Hope in God. God is our Hope and Strength. In all things we have to trust God!"

After the lecture ended, Jim had a question:

"If there are two or three lessons to be learnt from the scriptures, what are these?"

"Trust and love," replied Father Valence.

"What do you mean by trust and love?" Greg queried.

"It is not that easy to describe trust. I take it that you understand what love is. So I will try my best to help you discover what trust is. If I speak of Hope I mean that for us as human beings, there is always a chance for goodness, proper providence, good fortune—if you wish—to come our way. If a person is hopeful such a person expects something. So hope and expectation go hand-in-hand. There is always some uncertainty in life. In the midst of uncertainty if we put our minds on the good things we can get we are hopeful. The future is never certain. Indeed the future is never ours. However a belief that all will be well and a strong positive feeling of hope is a part of trust. Now in life when we as children wake up we hope for breakfast, safe transportation and in fact we hope to have a good day. Our parents provide the breakfast which we expected. Day by day many, many children come to feel sure that their parents will provide breakfast and find means of transporting them to school.

Those who look forward with a feeling that what they want will come to them, are hopeful and when they get to know that there are willing providers on whom they can rely, they learn to have confidence in those who provide for them. When this happens there is a trust—a strong feeling of confidence in human providers.

In my field, religion, we believe in an all-powerful, all-knowing Provider who represents the force of total goodness. Just as humans provide, just as there is confidence in those who provide for all people to put confidence in a Provider and to hope that this provider will supply, is to practice trust. It is not easy to define trust but it is a kind of hopeful confidence mixed with a belief either that all will be well or that there is one much higher who will make sure that all will be well.

Not to have any confidence in someone or something is to say that you do not trust that someone or something. I find it hard to separate trust and confidence from hope. I also find it hard—although some people do believe in themselves—to think that a person can have trust without having a belief that some superior or Supreme Being is and will be looking after the person who is hopeful or practising trust. I will speak very briefly above love. Love is a genuine and strong and unselfish caring for others. Love is almost always expressed in generous kind thought and words for other people and even for animals as well. The best love though is love of the Almighty who has given us all that we have or expect to get which is good and wholesome."

Frederick, thinking that he should not rush to ask questions, decided to wait until all of his peers had put their questions to Father Valance.

"If you had to advise us on what good we could do when we become grown-up what would you say?"

"A very intelligent question," Father Valence remarked.

Then, looking at Frederick with perfect eye-contact, the Parson offered these words of counsel:

"If you mean what good things you can do in a job or career, my advice to you would be to work as directed, obey your boss, never be dishonest, nor disrespectful, and try to use your job to be of service to others. If you mean that in daily living outside of normal work—if you mean what good you can do in community and society—I would give you the advice that my father forever gave me when I was much younger. Influenced by a group known as the Oxford Group my dad would repeat to me time and time again that in all my dealings, I should practice: absolute honesty; absolute purity; absolute unselfishness; absolute love. If anyone can seriously make the practice of those four virtues the philosophy by which he or she lives, such a person would inch closer and closer to God with close to a 100% probability of experiencing the sunshine of the Spirit."

Then Frederick asked Father Valence:

"Sir, could you tell us what being a priest is about, what your daily life entails?"

"I wake up each morning and before doing anything else I thank God for another day and ask him to guide my day's work. I ask God to make me an instrument of his peace. I check to see if I had left anything undone from the previous day. I pray for the protection of my community and my country. Before 7.30 a.m. I spend about twenty minutes meditating on God's perfect law, on the order in the universe. Just after 8.00 a.m. I go out to the shut-ins and the sick. There are those who are unable to attend church and I go to them, reading passages from the Bible. I offer Holy Communion to those persons who want the sacrament but are prevented from leaving home either through old-age or illness. I get back home most days by 12 noon.

Now I must tell you that on some week days I do hold a short mass in my church. In the afternoon I counsel persons who have problems and who have arranged to see me. I love counselling those with special needs. As a member of the Franciscan Order I have pledged my life's work to serving and helping others. I try as far as possible to finish my day by 8.00 p.m. so that I can get lots of rest. In my Ministry which is often extremely challenging, rest is important because it helps to keep my energy levels high."

"If I wanted to play a big part in the church as counsellor, what advice would you give to me?" Frederick was curious.

"It all depends on how far you want to go. If you want to live completely selflessly, if you want to put the interests of others above yourself, you can consider—I know I cannot force you into leading a life of purity, poverty and chastity —putting the things of the spirit before all else. You can train as a priest in the Catholic Church but you have to be strong. Three of the best known orders in my denomination are the Dominicans who specialize in preaching, the Jesuits who are an order devoted to teaching and my order is the Franciscan order which is famous for pastoral work which includes counselling."

A little bashful, Frederick then asked: "Suppose I was interested in becoming a priest in the Franciscan Order would you speak to me privately at the end of this session?"

"Of course."

At the end of the session, Father Valence sat with Frederick and spoke to him for close to an hour. Frederick's mind was made up. When he returned home that evening Frederick proudly announced to his parents:

"Mum and David I want to be a priest in the Franciscan Order and I intend to apply to go to Theological school very, very soon."

Chapter 3

CELEBRATION AFTER ALL

THEY STARTED TO GATHER JUST AROUND 4.30 in the evening that Sunday. Already persons like Packa-wow, Henri, Merle, Ismay, Agnes, Leonard from Bimshire and the Martiniquan Gregorie had arrived. Sarah, with Zaccky's help, had laid out the tables and chairs in their spacious yard. Grateful that their son had reached ten years despite their concerns about him, and pleased that they possessed a solid four bedroom house and a large yard, the couple had invited the village to attend this anniversary. Ten years ago this boy had been christened Aaron Isaac Zacariah Ezekiel Fromgence.

Occasions like this one were special events all over Helen Isle. Rich and poor alike put together resources, often with the help of relatives, friends and employers to stage a party, almost all of which were renowned for love, warmth and friendship. Food and drink were served in abundance. Cooked tanias, yams, green bananas, rice, fish and pork were served. Puncheon rum and some Mt. Gay were also provided for those who were inclined to imbibe spirituously and many of the characters of the village, even the few who did not attend St. Ignatius would attend christenings even if they got to them on their own personal invitations.

The typical Helenite christening was an institution. It provided occasion for thanksgiving, a recounting of stories in patois and congratulations to the parents of the new born. Many christenings started in the evening with religious songs, hymns and recitations, but for those which lasted past 8.30 p.m. secular songs were played, sometimes made available through the kind cooperation of village minstrels who with tambourine, guitar, recorder and drums would play to enliven the spirits of invitees. In a land with a rich creole history and culture, the christening held its own special place and the new parents were proud that their neighbours could savour their hospitality. Zaccky and Sarah had put back Aaron's party by ten years. There were those like Packa-wow and Leonard called the foreign Baje from Bimshire who were reported to attend christenings every week, any place, so long as they could be assured of a plentiful supply of food and rum.

Inside the house, Sarah was very busy putting the finishes and touches to the preparations. Dasheen and breadfruit abounded, roast pork properly peppered, large chunks of chicken, all types of fish nicely fried and giving off a pleasant aroma, were spread out on long tables. The vegetables, like the other dishes were carefully laid out in large containers kept hot by neat glowing flames beneath them. Zaccky himself, no real drinker, with the help of Packa-wow and Matthias for whom he had time on many an occasion, had erected a temporary bar outside under the canvas.

Occasions like the birth of children, funeral wakes and weddings brought together nearly a whole village and even persons from outside. Simple and humble though most folk were, they loved a good party and pooled resources to ensure communal happiness. The Dutch party in Helen Isle was special where nearly every individual either brought a dish or a bottle.

Though this was no Dutch party, the friends of the parents of the child whose christening was to be celebrated years after, had made hefty contributions in kind. Fishermen and butchers had brought fish and meat for Zaccky and Sarah. Other persons donated the puncheon and Mt. Gay, the coconut water and the soft drinks.

To the east a serene hill overlooked Zaccky's house down

in the valley. Not a cloud in the sky, the night promised to be cool. Close to the hill sparrows and blackbirds chirped merrily as though sensing some special festivity. Slowly more and more guests were arriving. About 60 were now there. It was now 6.15 p.m. when Stella, one of two midwives in the village arrived.

The moment she arrived there were very loud cheers–cheers of congratulations at having delivered her 105th child a couple days earlier. Cindy seemed excited at seeing so many people, all of whom were in her eyes quite big and appeared shy because she was not in the habit of seeing so many adults in her home.

Many of Zaccky's guests appeared deeply philosophical, and keen to follow the ways of the Epicureans. As the evening progressed Packa-wow turned to Henri and said:

"Today, we celebrate the naming of the second child of Sarah and Zaccky years after. From my Sunday School days I remember that a Sarah was a good wife and mother but help me for I cannot remember who was that Sarah's husband in my days in Sunday School."

"Abraham," Henri advised.

"Yes, Abraham," replied Packa-wow. "A good man who was the father of good people."

This represented the full extent both of Packa-wow's knowledge of Sarah and Abraham, but one sure truth was that whatever people as a whole thought of Packa-wow, he had enough in him to respect Zaccky and Sarah and some other elderly people.

"Hey, what are you drinking?" Someone shouted to Packa-wow. Unsure of who was addressing him, Packa-wow replied:

"Garçon, it is still early so I am having a glass of coconut water."

Then Henri and Packa-wow realized that it was Easyboy, a tall thin fellow who never missed a good party especially when the food and drink were free. Then Packa-wow continued:

"On this evening we come here to celebrate the birthday of the son of Zaccky and Sarah. God parents have already given a name to the second child of Miss Sarah and Mr. Zaccky."

Packa-wow was now trying to be very formal.

"But it is not only a celebration. I have personally come here to show full appreciation for Zaccky and his wife. After they were nice enough to invite me it would have been rude and disrespectful if I had refused to attend…"

Cutting Packa-wow short, Henri, after realizing that three other people had joined them including Isabel and the midwife, Isalene, made a special pronouncement.

"In this Island bananas flourish. People are poor. But we take pride in hard work, coming together as a community and supporting each other. Lots of us depend on the land and live off the land. We grow and eat plenty ground provisions. We do not have large houses, nor expensive vehicles. Our wages and incomes are low. But I feel that better days are coming. If only our farmers and fishermen could be catapulted…"

Henri had more than a smattering of education and was popular not only because of his good ways but also because in a community of simple folk, he knew how to use language without being snobbish nor ostentatious.

"Better days are coming. I like the good example set by Zaccky who respects others and works hard. I trust that Zaccky's children….. There are two now; would make his name proud."

Henri paused to watch Easyboy, who did not necessarily have to be invited to a party to be present, go over to reach out for a glass in which he poured a sizeable puncheon snap. Then having gulped down his glass of puncheon, Easyboy asked:

"I wonder, when Zaccky and Sarah will present their young son." Then Easyboy, no fool by any stretch of the imagination, waxed as philosophical as can be.

"Our country was taken by Europeans. The early opportunities for our people lay in growing bananas. Our people were used for their cheap labour and they were poor.

Few of us have really known money and in a way our standard of living is low. In the late 1950s and 1960s, the Europeans allowed many of our people to move to Europe. But most of us remained here. The good thing about Helen Isle is our culture, meaning that our way of life and community spirit are high. We are fond of each other. If someone is very poor we give them food and clothes and a place for them to have some rest. If we do not have horse we use cow. So if my grandmother has the cold and has no money for the doctor she drinks bush tea, like 'sersie bush', 'cure for all' or avocado leaf. We know no caviar but we have breadfruit. We know no posh wines but we have puncheon and can get Mount Gay. We know no wealth but we know love, we feel love and we have love. Imagine this evening that I can come here and benefit from Zaccky's love. I can benefit from Sarah's love because although they did not see me in time to invite me to the party, I have still come, knowing that they will accept me. I know too that their fine guests will accept me. In fact their guests are accepting me now.

We do not have a lot but we have tanias, yams, potatoes, coconut water, rice and breadfruit. Some day a brighter sun will rise and it will get brighter still, if we increase our love for each other and find ways to turn back our poverty. And in all our affairs God loves us as we love each other. May we stand up with each other. Let no one turn his back on us or refuse our way of life."

Henri had never heard Easyboy speak like this and felt tempted to think that the substance Easyboy was drinking bore considerable responsibility for the poetic way in which he was speaking. Then suddenly out of nowhere Matthias appeared. Rocking unsteadily, Matthias must have been off work and must have spent several hours in Gros Islet. Matthias had many reputations: a labourer, he was known to work hard and if he did any work in his off time for poor people he served them well and charged them little. He also had the reputation of being so clever that despite his obvious shortcomings of intellect, he was so street wise that he could either manipulate or trick sensible people, especially women. It was believed that politicians used his skills. Above all, when he was not working Matthias drank copious amounts of alcohol and it was believed that he tampered with other substances as well. His many reputations forbade anyone, even when he was drunk, from either snubbing him or cursing him for his drunkenness.

Ismay, already present at the party for forty-five minutes brought a chair and invited Matthias to sit down.

"Garçons, today is a special, happy day," Matthias blurted out. "We have a lot to celebrate."

What made people listen to him was that most of them were bound to hire his services at sometime in the future, coupled with the fact that whether Matthias was drunk or sober, Zaccky and Sarah always had time for him. Zaccky even got him to attend a few services at St. Ignatius. One of Matthias' qualities, too was that even when he got drunk he never even used foul language. If only Matthias could sit quietly and eat and doze off there was a strong probability that there would be no disturbance.

"I have already seen the child," Matthias continued. "He is so big that he might grow into a heavyweight boxing champion or outstanding sportsman."

Since a few of the guests at this evening's deferred christening party had not been yet very familiar with Aaron, many of them looked forward to seeing him. All wanted the best for him. Matthias, shortly after he sat, kept repeating that he had known the child from the time he was an infant.

"He is a big strong lad. Real big. He has his own looks. I have been tempted to ask him to do some labour work with me. I have never met a stronger child of that age."

Then there was quiet. It was clear that Matthias had started to doze off. Ismay, noting that Matthias was sitting very quietly now and was not interrupting nor making any loud noises, said:

"It is so good that we can have a coming together."

She was as popular in the community as Theresa and Henri and since she always proved herself highly discreet, was able to attract a considerable respect among those who knew her. She was also considered to be a good street debater and was usually fully informed about the happenings in her neighbourhoods.

As more persons arrived dressed in their Sunday best the evening took on an atmosphere of conviviality and even some expectancy. Some persons assembled in small groups of two or three and although the yard adjoining the house was spacious no one was really far from the others. There were those who did not only come for the party. These persons awaited the moment when Sarah and Zaccky would come out to present their son, no doubt with Cindy also standing with her parents. Most of them could recount what it was like when Cindy herself was presented years ago.

Then Henri decided to tease Easyboy who was now standing quite close to where Matthias sat. Easyboy's glass was full once more. As Henri moved in the direction of Easyboy, Ismay, satisfied that Matthias had properly dozed off, also approached Easyboy when Leonard also came up and said:

"Easyboy I heard you a moment ago and you spoke words of wisdom."

"Yes," said Gregoire.

"Was it that the drink made you speak so well, Easyboy?" Before Easyboy could reply, Henri said.

"I do not think I will easily forget what you said, Garçon." I like what you said about the love that exists among us and how we make out. You even predicted that some day we will find a way out of poverty. If truth be told, the way these our people of this small island live, the way we smile and laugh, the things we do to assist each other give the lie to our poverty. By metropolitan standards we are not wealthy but nearly all of us demonstrate a faith and an optimism that better days will come. Above all nearly every single individual in this island has been a firm believer in the Almighty. One of our characteristics is not only our capacity to improvise but we share with each other. A person who owns a coconut tree will freely give his neighbour coconuts. In a situation where one of the ways in which we tackle poverty has been growing vegetables and ground provisions on any available land we could access, and within entire villagers, people would pool resources not for selfish gain but to help neighbours and friends."

The Island was one which took great pride in the extended family. Helenites would count up to 60 or 70 people as family even where these people were distantly related. Little children were sent to Sunday School and most children were seen as the children of the whole village. There was but very little selfishness.

Then the moment came. Out came Sarah first followed by Cindy. Zaccky appeared and their son came out.

"Good evening, my friends and garçons," Zaccky started, "Ten years ago this son of ours was born and as all of you may have already known was delivered by Isalene one of our midwives. Today Sarah and Cindy join me in thanking you for coming. God bless you. You know that I am Zacharias Fromgence married to Sarah. You know Cindy and without calling his whole name, this is Aaron I. Z. E. Fromgence." There was loud applause and persons held up their glasses and said

"Cheers."

"Now, my friends, the food is ready," Zaccky announced. "May you all eat to your heart's content. Enjoy this wonderful evening."

In parts of the yard where there were still empty spaces soon more tables and chairs were put down. The bar was now fully opened and the party was now in full swing. Henri made sure that he pulled two tables together so that eight persons could sit and among them were Merle, Theresa, Leonard,

Isabel, a young lady called Bridgette and Easyboy. It was not so much that any division or separateness was being created it was more for the convenience of sitting down in the comfort of chairs. Packa-wow was allowed to join them. There was definitely an aura of warmth, love, festivity and happiness.

"You know, friends." Henri started to observe, "A short while ago I was about to congratulate Easyboy on the statements he made so eloquently. I feel that our country really has love backed up by a faith that we could beat the odds. I too agree that we are not rich when it comes to bank accounts or owning wealth in companies but our people work hard…."

Packa-Wow, who would have deviated time and again in the past, was listening. Easyboy was feeling quite good and was proud to be accepted. Lionel, a foreigner, was all ears.

"You know my friends," Henri concluded "In addition to all that has been said about us, we are a proud, God-fearing people who live in such unity that we practice social solidarity. May we work together for the benefit of us all. Let not one person fail or refuse to be a part of our movement upward."

Chapter 4

SOU-SOU

THERESA AMELIA FELICIEN LA FORTUNETTE was an upright woman in every sense of the word and the single parent of three children, including a child-hood prodigy called Jerome. For seven years Theresa, familiarly known as Auntie Theresa, ran a sou sou spanning one hundred and four weeks. Many knew of this very, very special, but 'informal' savings club and those who never got the chance to join, hoped to do so some day.

Some residents of Castries, Choseil and Dennery, belonged to Auntie Theresa's sou-sou. Some who lived in Micoud had joined this savings club mainly because Theresa's son, Jerome had encouraged them to take part. One person, in this case Theresa, would take responsibility for managing collections and disbursements. Each week or other agreed time like a fortnight, or a known number of times per month with a fixed amount of cash, a pool of funds would be formed, and every week or at agreed periods, a different member would "draw" their turn. For example, if twenty persons each contributed twenty dollars weekly the arrangement would last for twenty weeks and each week somebody else would be entitled to receive $400.

In the case of Auntie Theresa's sou-sou there were 104 members, each putting up $20 per week so that each week individual members of Auntie Theresa's would get $2,080. These small informal savings systems were popular all over Helen Isle and right there in Theresa's village there were another six or seven run by other trustworthy persons.

In an island where many persons worked in agriculture as labourers or pursued occupations that attracted unskilled labour, wages were small and their standards of living low, persons led very simple lives and most of the population of Helen Isle were engaged in battles to overcome poverty. Indeed in the 1950s, 1960s and 1970s there was still some illiteracy in Helen Isle, not because the people were foolish or backward, but because resources did not allow either a proliferation of schools nor an abundance of wealth. Of note in the late 1950s and early 1960s was the fact that many citizens of Helen Isle migrated, many to the United Kingdom, some to Bimshire Isle, and some to the North America, while a few made it to the United States Virgin Islands, Tobago and to mainland Trinidad. Migration to 'better-off' lands offered the hope of higher incomes to those who left Helen Isle, eased the problem of unemployment and to those relatives left behind at home, offered prospects of remittances of cash and the receipt of parcels and boxes of food and imported supplies shipped back by the emigrants to their loved ones.

Within Helen Isle there were many debates about how best to tackle poverty and overcome want. In the rumshops and at street corners, persons repeatedly talked of better days for themselves and for their children. Most of the people of Helen Isle were God-fearing and prayed. A sizeable number of them worshipped in Roman Catholic Churches. Many citizens made 'gardens' growing carrots, lettuce, beets, and beans. The sizes of these gardens varied and those who were fortunate enough to have a quarter of an acre or more would grow yams, potatoes and eddoes. Many kept domesticated animals too. The larger and more prosperous farmers grew bananas and fruits related to bananas like plantains and figs.

The economy depended heavily on bananas and coconuts for many years. Banana plantations abounded all over Helen Isle and these larger farms provided employment for hundreds. Yet there was unemployment and in the midst of it all, a yearning by hundreds to confront and beat the consequences of unemployment, underemployment and small incomes. This is where the sou-sou came in. Guaranteeing participants a lump-sum at different times of the year, they used the proceeds which they drew to buy or make deposits on things they needed. Some of this money bought school uniforms, some paid debts. Some of the money was down-payment for gas stoves, refrigerators and furniture. Where large sums were drawn they were invested in lumber and with voluntary help, men gave their labour to do household repairs, fix leaking roofs etc.

From after the end of the second World War those involved in politics tried to offer help, give assurance and fight poverty, but as finance was scarce even to Government, the battle against poverty was always intense in the households and in the communities. Ismay, who saw herself as the typical Helenite, possessed a philosophy which was shared by many. Work hard, never waste and when things were scarce, see if resources could be stretched. Her friend Merle was always critical of those who lived above their means and believed that even in the midst of poverty, each individual was responsible for their own happiness and that one could be happy even if one did not have a large amount of money. Their friend Theresa possessed leadership qualities, which explained why some persons followed her lead to mobilize savings through the sous-sous.

The three were in conversation. They were in one of the local buses and were coming from View Fort to Castries. Ismay turned to the other two and made the observation:

"I have learnt of some plans to get the cocoa business going again. Scattered in many places in island have been some cocoa trees which as you know take a long time to mature and bear. I did not go to school for very, very long but my feeling is that years ago there could have been a cocoa industry."

"You mean, Ismay," asked Theresa, "That the idea is to grow and sell cocoa overseas to make money for our island?."

"Don't ask the question like that," insisted Merle. "A good way to put the question is if farmers would be encouraged to grow cocoa in large amounts—volumes which can earn foreign exchange."

"Why…" Ismay started to ask the question, "…have you put it that way, Merle?"

"I think I understand what Merle is getting at," Theresa started to say.

"Well if you understand, Theresa," Ismay said, "tell us how you would express it."

"Over the years on account of the importance that bananas have held even though it was known that we could produce cocoa here, only a few growers, some by pure chance, actually grew cocoa and never in enough quantity to export it. The recent news is stating that so much more cocoa is to be grown that its producers will be able to have sufficient to sell abroad, and through this arrangement they will be making for the sale of the cocoa, our young nation will be paid in US dollars or other foreign currency." Theresa observed as though she was in the business of teaching.

She had spoken loudly enough to attract the attention of other passengers on the bus. Those who heard her were quite interested.

"I hope that our country could get some real good benefits so that we can have cash to be used to better the welfare of our people," Merle wished confidently.

"You know, speaking of bananas," Ismay, intervening once more, said. "Bananas have been to us what I believe sugar cane and sugar have been to Bimshire. You know, girls, sorry, sisters, if our island was three quarters as flat as Bimshire and had been taken by the British in the very years around the time they took St. Kitts, a large amount of sugar cane would have been grown here."

"Do you mean…" queried Merle, "…that if we had a very flat island and the Spanish or French had owned our land continuously for three hundred years there would have been no sugar cane?"

"I am not saying that," Ismay sought to clarify. "What I really mean is that with flat lands and stability our island would have been a sugar producer in the days when the Europeans owned these lands."

"I feel," Theresa came in, "that there was a lot in common among the English, French, Spanish and even the Dutch as far as their attitudes to these islands were concerned. But getting back to bananas, I am hearing our younger people say that the future does not look good for bananas. I hope that our banana business can survive. I know we sell most of our bananas to Europe but we still do keep back some here. I love to see our school children eat ripe yellow bananas. I trust that whatever the future of bananas will be, that for all time they would be around so that those of us who love green fig and salt fish will continue to be able to enjoy this wonderful food. Those very rich people in far away countries can take and have their steak but I would rather my green fig and salt fish any day. Hear me?" There was a noticeable pride in Theresa's words.

"Yes, we owe our green fig and salt fish to our banana industry."

"You know," Merle was now speaking again. "I never think of what we do not have. I always make use of what we have."

A young man sitting near the front of the bus heard the words. These words registered in his mind because many minutes ago he had been involved in a heated argument with another person whose position was the very large buses owned by Government should have been made available to the people of Helen Isle. The fellow who was in favour of big expensive buses had remained back in Vieu Fort. The youth on the bus turned over Merle's words in his brain.

"Never think of what we do not have... make use of what we have." Unknown to Merle the youth was fingering his long shining locks, which almost reached down to his waist.

"Yes," Merle continued. "Like many citizens of our wonderful nation I have had to make do. I never go around trying to keep up."

The young man in the front of the bus continued to listen. Then Ismay was heard to say:

"I would like all of the young people of our country to know that there has been a lot of poverty here. But a determination to live has seen our people work hard and do various things to help themselves and their families. Hard work has done it for us."

"For my part," said Theresa, "I know that even though a lot of us have gone through very hard times we have never given up. In our culture we have found ways to eat and even to make money."

The young man had now realized that there was a vacant seat very close to the three. He ordered the driver to stop the bus and to the driver's astonishment, moved around to the left side of it and jumped in to sit close to the three women who were chatting.

"What has meant much for me is my experience growing up in my village. I want all to know," Theresa declared, "that here, the village, next to the family, has for me helped to raise me and make me a full woman." She said these words after noticing that a person who could only be a Rastaman had suddenly moved to sit close to her. Uninvited, this man said:

"I have been listening to you all. I do not know if you were watching me but I just jumped out of the front of the bus to get close to you. You have been having a very, very interesting conversation. I heard one of you say. Never think of what we do not have. Make use of what we have.

Another of you said that even when times are hard we should not give up and I have also heard a statement pointing to the important role of the village. Now ladies, I have been studying the ways of our African forefathers and I have also been looking at our culture. I want to tell you, ladies, that you have spoken a mouthful. Your conversation has meant so much to me that I had to get close to you. Don't you see that I have now come and put myself in between you.

I have heard somebody mention of making merry. When I heard you talk of making merry my mind quickly went on some of our festivals. In the days of slavery the opportunities for celebration were few. The oppressors forced our forefathers to toil and labour but on occasions like at the end of a harvest on some estates, slaves were permitted to make merry. In recent years right through the Caribbean our carnivals have been big events and times for celebration." Then he said rather philosophically,

"Those who are forced to toil and labour do merit opportunities for relaxation, fun and frolic."

The love that the three women had always practised for others required them not only to listen to this youth but to welcome him to their conversation.

"I would not swap my country for any other although my knowledge of the Caribbean countries does allow me to understand that there is such a thing as a shared Caribbean culture, for even Suriname and Haiti, though outside the English-speaking Caribbean, do show traits of culture that do not differ to any significant extent from that of the former British colonies."

Ismay turned to the other two with that look in her eyes that revealed an admiration for the stranger. Just then he introduced himself:

"I live in Choiseil now and my name is Ras I-Win. As you can see I am a Rastaman and I do my best to learn of my roots as the descendant of proud Africans. I adore our local culture and I also admire the way of life, folklore, music and art of the Caribbean. I did study at Mona, Jamaica and I have qualifications in sociology," Ras I-Win said modestly.

"I was born right here in this lovely island. I grew up here. The very first island I saw was Trinidad. I am yet to see Tobago. Then before traveling to another six islands close here I did live in Jamaica for three years. Oh I loved and still love life in Papine. I often walked on long walks from Mona down past Campion College and as far as Half-Way-Tree and often stopped to speak to those interesting people who inhabit Jamaica."

Not only Ismay, but Theresa and Merle as well, were admiring the way in which this obviously bright young man spoke. They loved his way of delivering his words and they were attracted to his content and substance as well.

"I must say," Ismay started, "that you must be a true and real Helenite first, as well as a genuine Caribbean person."

"I agree," Theresa stated.

"Boy, if I can call you that or 'garçon' if you wish, you have been talking a whole mouthful. We like your style of speech and the meaning you are giving in your words." She continued.

"You know, ladies...." The driver who had at first wondered why he was forced to stop to allow this man to run into the rear of his bus was listening.

"Before we left Vieu Fort a fellow who was critical of how things are down here in our country tried to argue with me that we should have bigger buses. 'Real buses', he called them, such as which run in Trinidad and Bimshire but I told him that we both have to use what we can afford and provide livelihoods for small working class businessmen who are now permitted to operate public transport services as entrepreneurs. I contended that with the right support, these people who own what the fellow called 'vans' or 'pick-ups' in a very pejorative manner, would not only provide good reliable transport but many could in the foreseeable future actually become bigger businessmen. My grandmother told me that there was nothing wrong in starting small. Now back to culture: When I was quite young I became aware of a festival which I am sure you know called 'La Marguerite'."

The three females started to laugh almost simultaneously.

"Why do you laugh, my friends?"

"You should be bright enough to know why we are laughing

and why we will laugh together."

"Ladies, I almost said 'girls' but my grandparents taught me to respect my elders—respect for elders being a core African trait—do tell me why you laugh."

"We laugh," said Theresa, who to Ras I-Win did have the bearing of their leader, "because we three know each other well enough to advise that we ourselves were socialized to take part in late August in the La Rose Festival."

Conciliatory, with a wish to enrich the incipient friendship, Theresa assured. "No hard feelings. We adhere to the Rose; you to the Marguerite, but from today onwards we should still be friends."

Merle then provided information on what she knew about the feast known as La Rose. "I feel this very festival has been known as Santa Rose in Trinidad. In Mon Che, La Rose has been a big thing and people from elsewhere do take part. I wish to say that years ago La Rose came to Helen Isle to celebrate the canonization of St. Rose of Lima, Peru who was if not the first new world Catholic Saint, definitely among the early Catholic Saints of the world which Christopher Columbus was reported to have opened up and revealed to the Europeans."

It was now Ras I-Win's turn to experience and feel a strong sense of admiration for this lady who was—as the other two no doubt were—definitely a Helenite through and through. "We here and our neighbours in the Caribbean may not have riches in abundance—at least not a majority of the people, and certainly not most working class people—but we do have a strong culture," he observed, a kind of patriotism affecting his voice and feeling. "Now look I have gone past my destination but our conversation is worth it. You know all of us, whatever our estate, do have a contribution to make."

"Yes," Merle agreed. "We may be of lowly estate like Blessed Mary Ever Virgin, Mother of Jesus, but we each have our contributions to make not just to our families, but also our communities including our wider communities."

"In all this," Ismay was cutting Merle short, "I remember the example set by a man called Bousquet. He can be considered to be a person who was to a typical Helenite. He came from very, very humble origins and never became any University Professor nor top professional. But he loved people and he loved this island. He proved that hard work brings success. He also proved that a low social class at a person's birth will not necessarily keep a person down. I would want all of our young people who today are gaining more opportunities than the people of Bousquet's days, to work hard. But I want all of them also to remain real Helenites—no foreign accents, no foreign ways of life."

The bus was now approaching Castries and the four were about to disembark. As Ras I-Win was about to bid the others farewell, he turned to Theresa and asked.

"And friend what are you doing for your community?"

"Me? I work mainly as a domestic but my pride is my sou-sou."

"I am not sure who started the first sou-sou in our island but for me the sou-sou are very important."

The Rastaman then tried to trace the origin(s) of the sous-sous.

"It would not have happened during slavery. The reason is that slaves earned no money. Even after 1838 wages were so low and remained so up to about 1940 that I doubt if sou-sou could have taken off well, while wages remained low. Yet there is some possibility that even between 1900 and 1940 there could have been arrangements like these. The point is though, that nearly everywhere in the Caribbean sou-sou exist whether as 'Pardners' or as 'Meeting Turns'."

Smiling, Theresa declared: "I feel so good having my sou-sou. All the members are honest and realize that there has to be trust and support among us."

"May all good things come to your sou-sou members and of course to you three fine ladies. Goodbye."

Ras I-Win then left them with these words:

"May the peace of the Most High in terms of Psalm 91 remain with you and may you all abide beneath the shadow of the Almighty."

Chapter 5

TRUANT

NEITHER SARAH NOR ZACCKY slept the night before. They knew that their only son was not unintelligent, but Zaccky was very, very wary of Aaron's moods. In fact, whatever confidence and love Sarah held for her son, there were many times when Zaccky was deeply troubled by his second child's indiscipline. After all, both parents often faced the fact of their son's disinterest in his homework and were not always convinced that he was telling the truth when he came home in the evening declaring that he had no homework at all.

His teacher Mr. Epson had more than once informed Zaccky and Sarah that although there were days when no homework was set, the norm was that there were more evenings when his class was given things to do at home, than those on which he had given them a break by not setting homework. The comfort that Zaccky and Sarah drew was that Mr. Epson always assured them that Aaron was indeed a child possessed of innate intelligence. Mr. Epson had spent the whole of that day coaching his students and doing his utmost to provide encouragement for them.

A teacher at primary level for the better part of thirty years, Mr. Epson was loved, even adored by his students. A staunch Catholic whose parents had made every possible sacrifice for him, Devion Epson was the doyen of the teachers at his school. Having benefited from exposure to teacher training both at home and abroad, Epson was renowned for many things.

He arrived for school early every day. He never had to resort to inflicting corporal punishment, not even on the rudest and most wayward children. He never missed class. He mastered every subject in school, got most of his charges to apply themselves and always got excellent results. He encouraged his pupils never to look down on anyone. At his insistence, agricultural science was introduced to the curriculum of his school. He found time for slow-learners. Whenever he did extra-classes on evenings after school, he did so without fee or charge.

The day before the 11+ Exam he said with love and encouraging advice:

"My children, tomorrow is your big day. It is the day when you have to do the Examination for Entrance into secondary school. Do your best. Above all, place your faith in God. Speaking about God and his love and power, please bow your hands and observe some moments of silence as you say your prayers quietly to speak to God about all your needs and in particular your desire to do well tomorrow."

Sixty-three seconds passed. To Aaron this time was like an unpleasant eternity and during it, his mind roamed all over the place. Aaron said no prayer.

Then Mr. Epson asked the children to repeat after him:

"Heavenly Father whose Grace and Power are matchless, look down upon us with all your mercy. Bless us with your wisdom and knowledge and guide us in all we do especially at this time. Help us to achieve our aims and make us thankful to you for all you are doing for us. Amen."

The outstanding primary school teacher then gave his students a powerful motivational talk designed to inspire them to do well. He ended by encouraging them to be relaxed, to reach the examination room early, to check the instructions carefully and to read over. Aaron was not listening.

ZACKKY AND SARAH, having seen Cindy succeed in her examination for admission into secondary school, were understandably anxious and agitated over the fact that in a few hours their only son was due to face his test which would have an enormous impact on his future. They knew that Aaron was intelligent; but they sensed, based on the moods he demonstrated regularly, that he could be unpredictable and uncooperative. The feelings his parents experienced towards Aaron reflected the fact that they did not trust him completely although Sarah often accused Zaccky of judging him too harshly. Sarah asked Zaccky:

"How did we act when Cindy was writing her examination?"

"My memory is not bad," replied her husband. "We were a little nervous but we did sleep and what we did too was let Cindy walk to the Examination alone so that the walk could relax her and it worked."

"I hope that our young man would be relaxed too. He has shown a good understanding of English and I am sure his Mathematics is even better. Aaron should have no difficulty passing. He is no fool." Sarah observed.

The two chatted and chatted and they fell asleep around 4.00 a.m. Meanwhile Aaron had gone to bed on the instructions of his parents around 8.00 p.m. He slept for seven hours and came awake at 3.00 a.m. He did overhear his parents chatting about school, education and himself. They were unaware that he could hear them, although he did not always make out exactly what they were saying. Whatever it was they were discussing, he hoped that they were not comparing him with Cindy. Boys ought not to be treated like girls or made to be like them. Aaron was aware that most students knew the importance of the coming Entrance Examination but in his heart he could not understand the fuss.

Aaron felt that persons like Mr. Epson and his parents had the wrong attitude to children and he did not like how his parents were behaving and talking to him in the days preceding the examination. He had known that there were students who could not possibly have passed their Entrance Examination and who still gained admission to good secondary schools. So why the fuss? To Aaron, surely Sarah's name was so good that she could persuade a Principal to allow him membership of a secondary school and if he failed, there could be no doubt that Zaccky's reputation would entice any headteacher of any school to accept him. Then Aaron's mind was cast back to the last two weeks of preparation and the ill-concealed excitement there was among his classmates. He did not appreciate why his fellow students and moreso their parents got so worked up about the Examination. Aaron felt that the parents were old enough and should have been sufficiently mature and wise to act differently.

From 3.00 a.m. until 6.00 a.m. he tossed and turned and did realize that beyond a certain point the talk which he had been hearing between his parents had ended. Aaron dozed off just about 6.15 a.m. and was interrupted by three loud knocks on the door of the bedroom. It was 7.45 a.m. The examination was due to start at 9.30 a.m.

He was now dressed. His parents spoke to him about the need to be relaxed. To them he could best relax if he was allowed to walk to the Examination Centre. It was not a far walk but was enough to allow any normal child to relax. Aaron was delighted that his parents permitted him to go alone. There were times when he definitely resented his parents, but on this occasion he was quite happy at their gesture in giving him licence to travel alone. He was sure that on this day many other parents in their nervousness would either have walked with their children or even hired transport at great personal sacrifice. It was a special day.

For weeks Aaron could not understand what made the Common Entrance so important. To his mind the excitement and expectancy affecting parents and students were very badly misplaced. There were times when he felt like striking his peers whenever they referred to this Examination. Aaron was on his way to the Examination Centre to do a test in which he had no interest. His idea was that one day and one test should never hold the type of importance they did, and he calculated that if such a test had been in existence all these years there must have been students who missed it though their numbers would have been quite low. His belief was that those few who had missed the examination would not have died for missing it and probably did not become failures as a result of not doing it.

He was about eight minutes away from his destination when the thought struck him forcefully that there was little point in writing the Examination. In addition he was in no mood to see his classmates nor students from other schools who would be attending the examination centre. Aaron had heard the term 'playing truant' and understood what it meant. He always had a secret admiration for those students who played truant but had never absented himself from school before.

He made up his mind. Today he was going to play truant, the only trouble would be where to go and how to pass the time. Clearly it would not make sense being anywhere too close to the Examination for after all someone would see him and report him to the authorities or to the Police. Aaron therefore decided to walk and walk and to go as far away as possible. So rather than take the road which led directly to the Examination Centre, he went off track and decided to walk to Anse-la-Reye.

This fishing village was some distance away and a walk there and back would see him reach home long after the Examination had ended. What would he tell his parents? What would Mr. Epson think when he realized that Aaron had refused to take the Examination? What would his classmates think? No doubt some of them would see him as a rebel but the possibility was that to a few students he would be something of a hero. The hardest problem was that he would have to give an explanation to his parents. A long explanation if not backed up properly would not go down well. A brief explanation would be better but would cause shock. Aaron's parents had never been in the habit of regularly inflicting serious punishments on him. In fact his mother, to the dismay of Zaccky, had frequently spoiled him.

Aaron had made up his mind. He was both going to miss this Examination and admit to Zaccky and Sarah that he simply did not feel like doing it, and he would face the consequences. Meanwhile, he set out for the very long walk to Anse-la-Reye. It was a good day and if he walked briskly there would be no real discomfort since the temperature of the day was on his side. But if he walked too quickly he would have too much time on his hands. It was cool with some possibility of rain. What if the rain caught him in an area where he could not shelter? A funny thought hit him. What if someone who knew that he should be writing the most important examination of his life to date, spotted him and went and brought his parents to see what he was doing? For a short while, Aaron ruminated on these matters and then decided that he would still go to Anse-la-Reye.

He set on walking briskly. He thanked his lucky stars that on this day it was not necessary for him to wear his school uniform. He calculated that he was walking at the rate of about twenty minutes per mile. He had been to Anse-la-Reye four times before and even though not quite able to fully appreciate the quaintness of this wonderful fishing village, from the first time he had been there he had seen fisherfolk in their element. Yes, he thought to himself, he would go and pass away the time in this village.

After he walked for about three miles, by which time he calculated that the first paper, the one in English Composition and Comprehension would be finished, a car drew up close to him. Before he could look inside of the car he trembled momentarily in the fear that he was being found out. Then to his amazement a person who clearly was a tourist, asked him the way to Anse-la-Reye.

"If you let me come into your car I will show you."

Aaron was happy that he had met a good Samaritan and the tourist invited Aaron on board the small yellow mini-moke.

"Go ahead you are on the way," Aaron announced proudly.

The tourist, for his part advised to be careful, did observe Aaron's size but also noticed that the physique and appearance of this young man carried a face that presented tender years.

"How are you?" The tourist queried.

"I am alright. I have to go to Anse-la-Reye.

The two travelled up hill. The moke, clearly well-maintained, proved equal to the challenge of the hills along the way.

"What are all these plants?" The driver asked.

"They are bananas." Aaron replied proudly.

Despite his youth Aaron was clearly in the habit of deriving considerable pleasure whenever occasions allowed him to exhibit his strength or knowledge."

"The lovely trees bear fruits. Actually, sometimes there are other trees looking just like the banana trees that bear figs and plantains. But most of what you are seeing are banana trees.

"Why so many bananas?" His new found friend asked.

"I have learnt that for more than ninety years, probably even a hundred years bananas have been the biggest crop here in this island," Aaron said with an air of triumph.

"What do your people do with so many bananas?"

"We sell them to far off countries," came Aaron's reply.

The tourist accepted this answer for it was clear that Helen Isle grew so many bananas its population would have been hard pressed to consume all of the bananas grown. Then they moved up another hill.

"Stop here." Aaron commanded.

The tourist had no reason to fear being hijacked or ambushed but wondered why the young man gave the order. The mini-moke stopped. Aaron then said:

"Follow me up this grassy hill." The tourist complied.

To the north lay a promontory and beyond it across the blue ocean lay another land.

"Look, there is the French Island, Martinique."

The tourist was impressed. After all initially he did not quite know where he was going and by a stroke of good fortune met a youth, a friend, who was proving to be something of a tour guide.

"Look down on your right." The tourist saw more banana trees.

"Do you not see something rather different?" Asked Aaron.

Up until now the tourist was sure he had seen Martinique in the far distance to the north. He did see other hills but saw nothing spectacular about them.

"Look down in the valley, my friend, to your right. Not too far away. Look right down."

An old building presented itself.

"What's that?" was the tourist's question.

"An old sugar factory." Aaron felt like an educator.

"I have already told you about our bananas. Bananas are our main crop. Our lands are hilly and it is not possible to grow many plants that like flat lands. However for some years on some of our flat lands we planted and grew sugar canes."

Before Aaron could continue, his guest observed with the best possible sincerity, "Oh I find you an intelligent young man."

This was this visitor's first visit to Helen Isle. In fact it was his very first trip abroad. He was from England.

"There are many persons who have no idea that you and your people are intelligent. It is amazing how ignorant we tourists can be. Tell me some more. I find you well informed." The tourist observed gratefully.

Flattered immensely, Aaron, behaving more like a schooled professor than a truant was careful to speak about sugar.

"The grass, sugar cane, used to be planted and when it got

ripe it could be made into molasses, syrup or sugar. What I am showing you is the old sugar factory of the area. It does not operate any more. It has closed been for years. Sugar cane and sugar were never very important in our island."

Impressed, the visitor mentioned that he had never seen a banana tree nor a sugar cane plant at which point Aaron directed.

"Let us go. I must show you Anse-la-Reye."

They reached their destination. The mini-moke was parked and Aaron took the visitor on foot through a few parts of Anse-la-Reye. They walked past an old Catholic Church twice and then the tourist inquired of Aaron,

"What's that sweet smell?"

" I feel that it is fish being fried. You can get plenty of fish down here although in the night or weekends the fish fries are known to be important. By the way, Sir, we are in Anse-la-Reye."

It was now around 11.15 a.m. and just then Aaron remembered that he had refused to do his Examination and for the first time it occurred to him that if he could not provide a proper explanation his parents would be quite angry and let down. Yet, as he thought about what would certainly be a problem for him, a strong sense of indifference had enveloped his mind. He knew that his parents did not believe in corporal punishment, even after on one occasion he had actually nearly slapped his father for speaking to him sternly about a misdeed he had done. In other words, Aaron felt sure that he would get away with little or no punishment for failing to write the examination and believed that his parents, especially Zaccky, would be able to find a place for him in a secondary school if that was their desire.

Aaron himself had never felt up to this point in his life that the schooling he had experienced would give him the wealth, power and standing that he wanted.

"What is that over there?" The tourist pointed out a small area to the north and Aaron unsure said:

"I can walk with you so that we can see."

A quiet figure appearing subdued and preoccupied was painting portraits of some simple houses, some trees and banana fields. The tourist stopped and spoke to the artist, then pulled a wad of foreign money bills and paid them to the artist after taking three pieces. He then offered Aaron £100.

"Take this. You are helpful."

"What else can I do for you? If you want me to show you the way from down here to the city, I will be happy to do so!" Aaron offered.

The two then boarded the open top car and drove back towards Castries. Not much was said especially since Aaron did not want to play his hand and the tourist was not intent on being too inquisitive.

"Stop here," Aaron ordered.

"Thanks, I am getting off here."

On his way home Aaron found a story which after careful invention he felt he could sell to his parents. On reaching home Aaron admitted that he did not write his Examination. He said that he was vomiting so much he did not want to disturb the Examination.

Puzzled and disappointed, Zaccky and Sarah decided that they had to approach an influential person who could pull strings to have their son admitted to a good secondary school.

Chapter 6

WAYWARD YOUTH

SENT BACK TO HELEN ISLE by Dora and Daniel to Isabel her grandmother, Hester Isadore returned to Helen Isle just when she was twelve years old. Sure that she could nurture, raise and maintain Hester, Isabel read her night time stories, prayed with her, sent her to Sunday school and church and did her best for this young girl. Isabel, in a manner typical of Helenites set out to engender values and norms that spelled out: frequent attendance at the local Catholic Church St. Ignatius; self-respect; respect for others; feminine decency and morality; keeping proper company; and hard, honest work.

Aware of why she had to return to Helen Isle, Hester, who was no fool, decided initially to tow the line with her grandmother, both because she could not return to her parents and also on account of the reality that Isabel appeared strong in every respect and that if a careful line was towed, she and Isabel would be able to put up with each other. Hester therefore resolved to be discreet even if she had to be super-clever to do so.

"You hear me?" Isabel would ask Hester. "Your parents sent you to me that I could care you and raise you to be a lady."

She ensured that Hester was tidy at all times and met no resistance on this matter. In the home in Helen Isle, Isabel would set out to train her only granddaughter to be decent.

"Young girls must grow up into fine, educated hard-working young ladies who must not knock about, flirt nor be slovenly," Isabel admonished.

Hester, bearing in mind that at twelve she had few options after having been deemed by her English school to be disorderly, disruptive and devious, and after being abandoned by her parents, did make solid efforts for about three years to be careful. She feared that it would never be easy to win with Isabel. She knew no other relative in Helen Isle who would accept her and come what may, she sensed it would be dangerous and senseless to lose a roof over her head. In any event, Isabel gave her more than her own parents did, and it never occurred to Hester that her grandmother was so self-sacrificing that while she was growing up, the older woman literally donated much more to Hester than she kept for herself.

Yet Isabel was by no means rich. She worked as a labourer like other Helenites tending banana trees. In her spare time she did odd jobs like babysitting for tourists or washing and pressing the garments of better off people.

"You know, Hessie," Isabel would say fondly to Hester. "These days are different here in Helen Isle. Years ago there was poverty but little crime. Off and on certain men would get drunk on puncheon rum or Mt. Gay from Bimshire. But we hardly had crime. We had no drugs. Prostitution occurred in Rose Hill but our communities were safe and women carried decency with them. Hessie, you see drugs. Promise me never, never to get involved in drugs? Anyhow I see it, drugs is crime. Never, never you do drugs. You are big for your age so men will tempt you. Always be careful. Promise me to be careful. Swear to me to be careful."

"I swear , grandma."

"In the olden days, in fact, up to a few years ago women here hardly drank heavily. Very few women ran wild. Women raised children in the fear of God. Nearly every child went to Sunday School and Church. People had little but they tried hard to save. What today's young Helenites need are standards, yes, standards!"

Hester, possessed of native intelligence, and bolstered by a clever use of the Queen's English which she learnt in her years in England did give the grandmother an ear but wondered how she could blend grandma's advice with the way she had planned to learn the ways of the street.

Neither Dora nor Daniel had ever thought of taking Hester to a psychologist and so far Isabel saw nothing wrong with the girl and herself had up to now never heard of a psychologist, but in her quiet moments Hester found her mind harbouring thoughts of making money, of being rich and famous, knowing that people who had met her and heard her speak marvelled that Hester thought like a grown up and was of the build of a grown-up. To date Isabel held no proof that Hester was 'too big for her boots' or 'womanish'. Like many of the other children, Hester walked to school on her own.

Shortly after returning to Isabel she had been admitted to Helen's High School and was placed in the top first form. She struggled to behave herself, but had her own private notion of what constituted her rights. She was comfortably the biggest child in her form in which she had a special presence. The smaller children wisely avoided any contact with her. At lunch and breaks Hester socialized with fourth and fifth formers, including a very few senior students who had already gone astray. Astra, Hazeen and Tara were such students; all too willing to share all types of stories and escapades with Hester.

Hester adored these three friends and though she could not verify the stories these girls told, a strong bond developed among them. Hester, after finding out where Hazeeen lived, decided to introduce her to Isabel.

"Grannie here is my best school friend, Hazeen."

"Miss Hazeen, welcome."

Isabel, as pleased as punch, grinned. "How are you?" She enquired.

"Very well thanks; grandma," Hazeen obliged. The three spoke briefly about life at school before Hazeen said she had to go. Isabel did take note that Hazeen was about 6 inches shorter than her granddaughter and concluded that the two secondary school students were in the same class grouping. When Hazeen departed, Isabel told Hester.

"Your friend is good looking. I bet that she is bright."

"Yes, Grannie."

"I feel she is a decent girl."

"Yes, Grannie, and she comes from a decent family," Hester muttered.

"Well, Hester, she is the kind of friend you should have. Well, granddaughter, what did you do in school today?"

Carefully assessing Isabel's level of education, Hester calculated that she could fall in a trap if she only mentioned that she did Spelling, Hygiene and Religious Education. And since she was at secondary school, a privilege that her grandmother had never had, she had to mention areas of study with which her grandmother was too unfamiliar to ask probing questions about.

"Today we did Algebra, Geometry and aspects of Botany and Zoology," Hester lied.

"Very good," Isabel congratulated, although she herself had never heard of those four subjects and in her ignorance, Isabel was prepared to accept that anyone granted the opportunity to study such things must be bright.

"And I trust that you behaved well."

"Yes," declared Hester truthfully. The hard fact was that Hester was too busy with thinking if Tara, Hazeen and Astra really had achieved the types of adult experiences of which they boasted. In any event she found that despite very many thoughts and temptations, school in Helen Isle was not as unpleasant as in England and so she hardly gave trouble at school. In addition, Hester felt that as the biggest student in her class she had to set an example to those other students who, to her, lacked maturity. She developed a special admiration and liking for her male teachers and detested the female ones. So Hester was telling the truth when she said that she behaved well.

The next day at school Hazeen took Hester aside and bragged that after she left Isabel's house she went out into the country for a drive with a handsome young man and returned home at 7.45 p.m.

"You know, Hester, believe me. I can teach you a thing or two and introduce you to some interesting people."

Hester was clearly interested, but told Hazeen that she feared that her grandmother's attitude was one that would not easily allow her to be as free as Hazeen.

"Do you want to know how to get over your grandmother?" Hazeen inquired.

"Yes," replied Hester.

"You have to make your grandmother trust you. Volunteer to do as many things as possible for her. Run errands for her. When she gives you money do not spend all and every two weeks let her know how much you have saved with the view to showing her you are responsible. Come over to her as respecting older women and after a while you will notice that she will trust you. Most of the older folk frown on teenage pregnancies and loose behaviour by females and object to drugs, vandals and beggars," Hazeen admonished.

Hester, after listening carefully, thought for a while.

"I am thinking about what you have said and I am now studying the ways of my grandmother," Hester told her friend.

"There is a young people's party coming up in three weeks and I want to take you with Astra, Tara and me and you will have fun." Said Hazeen.

"How can I come?" Hester asked.

"Make no mistakes at all at home on the days before the party. Show respect to your grandmother. Be seen doing your homework. Say some of your home work aloud, run errands for your grandmother and she will believe in you and I will speak to her and get her permission and even tell her that you will get back home safely."

Hester, eyes wide open, looked Hazeen in the face and declared:

"You are a true friend. Tell me, are Tara and Astra like you?" Hester was curious. Hazeen, taking Hester into her confidence, said:

"Between you and me. They are good girls and they are getting more experience each week, but I am their leader and I set examples for them."

Before Hazeen could end, Hester had decided that she would do her best to stick to these three girls and to share in the fun and pleasures which they had obviously been savouring for a while.

On returning home Hester noticed that Isabel was not home and that there had been a dirty saucepan and two dirty plates in the kitchen. She immediately set about washing these things and having finished, took a look at her grandmother's bedroom and promptly tidied the bed there. After doing these things, she took out some school books placed them on the small kitchen table, stood up, stretched and sat down and then she heard a knock on the front door of the small house. Without even looking to see who it was, Hester opened the door and saw Isabel.

"Very good evening, Grandma," said Hester.

Oh what a polite granddaughter she had, Isabel thought pridefully to herself. She made her way to her tiny bedroom and noticed how the bed had been made up.

"Granddaughter, thanks to God for you, because I know it was you who fixed the bed."

"Thanks, Grannie," Hester offered with the greatest humility. She then went quickly back to her books without saying anything else. Isabel sat on her bed and started to look through the large, old Bible which she had had for years. She turned to the Book of Proverbs and read Chapter 2, verses 5-10. '*Then shalt thou understand the fear of the Lord, and find the knowledge of God. For the Lord giveth wisdom: out of his mouth cometh knowledge and understanding. He layeth up sound wisdom for the righteous: he is a buckler to them that walk uprightly. He keepeth the paths of judgment and preserveth the way of his saints. Then shalt thou understand righteousness, and judgment and equity; yea, every good path. When wisdom entered into thine heart, and knowledge is pleasant unto thy soul; Discretion shall preserve thee, understanding shall keep thee.'*

After that she took a quiet peep in the kitchen where Hester was doing her homework. Isabel, feeling that she should not disturb her granddaughter, decided to lie quietly in bed until after Hester had finished. She waited for a long time before Hester paused. Going towards Isabel's bedroom, Hester was heard to ask

"Is there anything that I can do for you, Grandma?"

It was as this question was being aimed that Isabel noticed that the kitchen wares she had left were as clean as a bone.

"Hester, you mean that you cleaned the saucepan and the plates?"

"Yes, Grandma."

"Now, Hester, I was just reading the Book of Proverbs in the Old Testament of the Bible and the simple story from the Second Book of Proverbs is that if you trust and depend on God, you will gain understanding. So Hester, trust God and you will be bright in school and you would do very well."

"Thanks, Grannie," Hester said with ostensible gratitude.

If a person versed in the Bible were present he or she would have explained to the two that the words of Proverbs 2:5-10 resembled those of Matthew 6:34 whose message was also captured in Psalm 91.

"Can I read the Bible with you tomorrow night?" Hester inquired.

"Yes, my dear loving granddaughter, I would not force you to read it tonight because you have worked hard this evening."

Then Isabel who was delighted at how her evening had passed asked Hester to kneel in prayer:

"Heavenly Father, we thank you for a good day. We thank

you for bringing us safely to the end of another day. Protect us through the night and ensure that everyone in our village is safe. Save us from fire, house-breakers and bad weather, may we rest well and awaken to your glory, tomorrow."

"Grannie."

"Yes Hester."

"Today is the 15th of the month. My friend Hazeen wants to come to see you around the 24th or 25th of this month."

"Okay, dear, I will see her." Next morning some howling dogs and bleating sheep awoke Hester around 5.30.

She went to the kitchen table and took out a book called Huckleberry Finn and started to read it. When Isabel did get up, having not heard the noises of the animals, she marvelled at how Hester was again doing school work aided by the light of a lamp whose shade was marked "Home Sweet Home."

Hester quickly finished reading and picked up a broom and started to sweep.

"Oh Hess, do not work too hard, darling." Isabel demanded.

"It is alright, Grannie. I want to sweep the floors of every room before I get ready for school." came the reply.

The next day at the lunch break Hazeen received an account of how Hester was putting the advice rendered by the older girl into action. Hester not only kept her promise relative to sweeping and tidying but also helped in other areas. Sure that she had her grandmother on her side, one evening after school, Hester took Hazeen to speak to Isabel. After Hazeen told Isabel about the up-coming social event, the latter agreed that her granddaughter could go to the party.

Prior to the party, Hazeen, with help from Astra and Tara, prepared Hester for the occasion and told her about some of the things to expect including advances from members of the opposite sex.

"For a start be careful with men. We will show you how to deal with men in the future."

The night of the party came and the four school girls showed up early. Some time after the start, the place filled up with scores of energetic youth. Outside of their school uniforms the quartet passed for grown women and the manner in which they danced, confirmed their ostensible maturity.

After quite a few dances, Hazeen introduced Hester to a tall youngster who gave his name as Kevin. Kevin told Hester that the night would be more enjoyable if she drank a stout and suggested that there were a couple of other things which would be available.

"Yes, try a stout," Hazeen advised, "but be sure to drink it slowly out in the open air?."

Determined to be part of the crowd, Hester sipped the dark substance from a small plastic cup slowly and cautiously. Witnessing what she had done, Kevin inquired of Hazeen and Astra if she was ready for the real thing. Hazeen and Astra walked a short distance away and engaged in a brief discussion.

"This is her first night out with us and she is young," Astra cautioned.

"Yes, but if we introduce her to it now rather than in the future she would grow accustomed to it at an early stage." Hazeen insisted.

"Plus she is so naturally intelligent she might be able to attract some sales for us. I think the hardest thing is to get her home fairly early in one piece and on her feet. I feel she would do whatever we want. She is already good at keeping secrets too."

Hazeen was sure Hester was no misfit and would do all that they wanted. Astra then declared that she would agree with Hazeen to expose Hester to the high now that she took the stout on condition that on this occasion there would be no sex at all for any of them. Hazeen quickly went back to Kevin leaving Astra to coach Hester on what was to follow next.

A roughly rolled reefer. This is the best description of the cigarette that Kevin presented to Astra, Hazeen and Tara who each inhaled mightily from it. They were clearly taking turns.

Then Tara invited Hester to have a 'drag', first demonstrating to her how to inhale effectively. The effect of the stout, still making her experience a sensation she had never known before, the youngest member of the group did as told and shortly after, felt her heart beat faster, her lips become numb and her head begin to grow. At first the thought hit her that the two substances she took were drugs but as she wanted to be one of the girls and in the swing of the party, she felt obliged to follow the others.

"You will get better at it," Tara declared.

"And in the future you will learn to handle yourself in these things."

Fearing that things could be spoilt if Hester over indulged, Hazeen handed the cigarette back to Kevin after taking it from Hester and herself pulling on it. Kevin took a pull too.

"Okay, let us go back inside to dance."

Once again Hester obeyed and notwithstanding that she did feel rather weird, she danced with the first young man she encountered on returning to the dance floor. Meanwhile, Hazeen, Astra and Tara met outside, agreed that Hester was doing well though she was new to the 'club' and that while things were still going right they should take her back to the place where she lived. Kevin provided the transport and the other three accompanied them to Hester's home. After but two knocks on the front door Isabel opened, and happy that Hester returned fairly early with her friends, the grandmother told them how glad she was to see them and how thankful that they brought her granddaughter home safely. She bade them goodbye as Hester went to her room. She slept for no fewer than eleven hours.

The next day Isabel requested a report on the party and all Hester narrated was that there was good music, mainly reggae, good food and excellent dancers. Hester, feeling slow and rather down was to have spent all day in bed trying to read but found it hard to concentrate.

Chapter 7

TIMES IN THE REGIMENT

AARON WAS NOW TWENTY YEARS OLD and judging from the way he felt about his parents and what he required to feel good about himself and be seen as a person of power and prestige, he responded to an advertisement inviting young men to join their Island's militia. Helen Isle had a small militia. Indeed it would be better to call it a Regiment. Yet it was the Defence Force for Helen Isle, recently attaining the status of an Independent Nation and lacking the resources to deploy a sizeable army. As an island in the open Caribbean sea, in days of old it had been attacked. The Island changed hands and just before Independence, was a British Colony. But it used to belong to France. There was a need to defend the Island both on land and at sea. The Police would be the internal defence. The Militia would support the police and offer a type of coast guard service.

Among those recruited at the same time as Aaron to join the militia nicknamed by many St. Cecilia, were Georgie Smith, Arthur Charles and Theo Anthony. Georgie Smith was a close relative of Packa-Wow. Georgie Smith was Packa-Wow's first cousin. Georgie did have a strong sense of discipline and honesty, yet shared an excellent relationship with his first cousin whose personal traits in no way resembled those of Georgie Smith.

In these times, women were not yet allowed to join the militia. In Helen Isle it was only very, very recently that females who were unmarried could bear children and maintain their jobs in the Government teaching service. Naturally, the early private schools run by religious institutions would have been originally responsible for staging the moral stance that clear proof of fornication acted as a bar to functioning in a respectable position. The military training itself consisted primarily of physical exercise, map reading, weapons' training, the recognition and dismantling of bombs with a very, very strong emphasis on disaster-preparedness and responses to emergencies like hurricanes and aircraft accidents. There was coast guard training as well. To the extent that the local fire service was a part of the St. Cecilia's militia, fire-fighting was part of the curriculum of the institution. Trainees lived in, and had the option of going home on weekends and public holidays.

Questioned by Georgie Smith as to why he would have wished to embark on a military career, Aaron, after hesitating for several moments during which he nearly rebuked his fellow recruit for not minding his business, replied:

"Soldiering is good discipline. It provides strength and character."

In Aaron's heart though one reason was the power Aaron would derive. Georgie, however, felt that Aaron's huge imposing physical structure was the principal factor.

"But Aaron, you seem so strong that I feel it would be natural for you to become a soldier."

Not taking kindly to this exchange with a youngster whom he thought was clearly nosey, barely restraining himself from requiring the questioner to mind his own business, and a little confused as to if a genuine compliment was being tendered, Aaron enquired sarcastically:

"Mr. Smith, am I the only strong big person here? And besides, you are in the funny position to be the smallest male member of your magnificent family."

Georgie, not fully appreciating how sardonic Aaron had become, said in all earnestness:

"Listen, Aaron all who know you, garçon, feel that you are

a tremendous athlete with a fine frame."

Not enjoying the conversation, Aaron started to hate Georgie but yet with some cool told Georgie that he could not talk to him anymore and had to leave because he was given permission by the Colonel to go to View Fort. Georgie remained just where he was just outside of the gym and what entered his mind as Aaron left him behind, was that Aaron was so big and yet so fit that it was already clear who the best recruit would be. Just before leaving the gym to go to the barracks, Theo Anthony came up to Georgie:

"Georgie I noticed as I was coming here, that Aaron Fromgence walked away."

"Theo, I do not think that he left because you came. In fact I doubt that he saw you. He said he had to go to View Fort."

"How can you be so sure?" Theo asked.

"Tell me something, Georgie," Theo demanded. "It has only been a couple weeks that we have all been here at St. Cecilia, but give me an honest opinion of that fellow, Aaron?"

"You know, garçon, that Aaron's father Zaccky is a very, very wise, hardworking man known for his honesty and Christian ways. A kind man. Until I can see otherwise I am prepared to judge Aaron strictly as Zaccky's son."

"I do feel," Theo said, "that if to be a soldier a person has to be tough and strong, Aaron would be the perfect soldier."

The two walked in the direction of the barracks. Yet Georgie started to wonder if Aaron really had to leave the compound and if Zaccky's son felt offended by his queries. In the barracks Georgie and Theo had a long discussion on why they chose military training but Theo constantly cautioned Georgie that the person they felt would be best turned-out recruit had an air about him, a manner and a persona that were difficult to describe with any proper degree of accuracy. They spoke and spoke until they both fell asleep.

The next day all of the trainees had to get up at 4.30 a.m., run ten miles and return for their baths and the day's briefing and orders. Colonel Sargeant had decided that each new recruit had to repaint the outer walls of the barracks before they could take a break. Aaron was put in charge of the day's work. The barracks were old. In an island in which rainfall was plentiful, rain water had beaten upon these barracks for many years. First occupied by the colonial regiment, these barracks could hold about eighty adults.

A cold and miserly gray was the colour chosen in recent years for the exterior of these buildings which had been erected neither with the small brown bricks from which many buildings in England were made nor with the concrete bricks which were the materials of choice in many Caribbean countries. Stones known either as soft stones or saw stones boasting a limestone core provided the material from which these barracks were erected. Winds and sun had conspired with water to weaken the colour outside so that once every year it was necessary to repair the outer walls of the barracks. Fortunately, the interior walls never craved regular maintenance and the trainees in the militia provided the workmanship necessary to give the outer walls a boost. The trainees could not charge for their labour and maintenance costs were low, partly on account of the fact that the astute leadership of the militia ensured that generous amounts of paint donated by the business community were procured for the repainting efforts.

After Colonel Sargeant departed, leaving Aaron in charge of his fellow recruits, all of the recruits set about their tasks energetically. Initially Aaron kept his supervising to a minimum. In the early morning before the morning's break the fellows worked well without over-exerting themselves. It was if they were pacing themselves. At break Aaron was allowed to see Colonel Sargeant in the latter's quarters.

"Sir, I want to report that after 2½ hours all on duty have done well. But the sun is hot…."

Colonel Sargeant interrupted. "Son, hot sun is no excuse….."

"Sir, please permit me to finish. I was about to say that if any of my fellow trainees has been so affected by the sun that he cannot finish his assigned area in time, I will voluntarily assist because I am not tired at all and this morning's exercises did me well."

The Colonel was struck. For in his thirty years in the military in Germany, England and Bimshire he had never had to meet such a courageously driven request. How could a recruit a mere few weeks in training dare to appear to want to relieve colleagues and what motive did Aaron have for wanting to do additional duties?

After the break, Colonel Sargeant accompanied by Captain Gregoire returned to speak to the group.

"Once again good morning all," the Colonel greeted.

"Good morning, Colonel," the soldiers in training replied in unison.

"At this hour in the company of Captain Gregoire I have come back to you to see your work and find out for myself what progress has been made.... I would like to see these barracks painted up so nicely that all who continue to occupy them will do so with pride. On occasions like these it is the normal practice to have a member of staff do the supervising. But today young Aaron, as you know, has been put in charge. I want all of you to continue to obey his commands and he now carries authority—authority granted to him by me—and he is to report all acts of disobedience and non-cooperation to our High Command. In the unlikely event that Aaron proves a bad leader, be sure to inform me."

At these words Aaron grimaced, for in Aaron's mind how could the Colonel think that he would be so irresponsible to abuse those under him or otherwise prove himself a bad leader. Colonel Sargeant and the Captain departed.

Then Aaron ordered Georgie Smith to take the biggest of the ladders around the other side of the building, some one hundred yards away. When Georgie returned, Aaron, who in his own mind was chief orderly, got Georgie to take the second ladder to the north of the building. When Georgie obeyed and returned, Aaron despatched four trainees to the west and sent four others to the north. He then commanded Georgie to position the third ladder to the east of the building, a few feet from where all had originally assembled. Aaron then demanded that Georgie take up three cans of paint and to put them on the large ledge below the windows of the first floor.

This done, Aaron walked around the building giving instructions to individual members of the group. Within fifteen minutes all had settled down to performing their tasks. Somehow Georgie Smith felt that his area was the largest and another ladder was needed.

"Aaron," Georgie shouted.

"Yes!" Snapped Aaron. "First thing, young fellow you were wrong to shout at me like the way you did. I have been put in charge of this operation and you should not have shouted at me like that. You should know that in any army your superiors should be shown respect. From today onwards I want you to see me as your superior in every sense......"

"Come on, Aaron, clearly you are not my superior, you have only been chosen to be our leader for as long as this job is to last. As a temporary leader of no higher rank than any of us the most you can be is a type of prefect, but do not think that you are our captain."

Aaron was offended and if it were not for the rules of the militia he would have given Georgie a beating or at least would have threatened him. How could Georgie Smith see him as a mere prefect and less than a captain? Could it be that since Georgie had been a form captain in a school that he was pulling this one on him?

"Look Georgie, show proper respect. You already are disrespectful and to make matters worse it seems to me as though you do not want to work."

As Aaron was uttering these words he was thinking about how to punish Georgie if he could. This nosey Georgie had before asked him embarrassing questions; now he was proving disrespectful and it seemed too that he did not wish to cooperate. Oh how he hated Georgie.

"All I want from you Aaron, is another ladder and two more men to assist. My area is definitely the biggest area." Georgie came to the point but Aaron was liking nothing of it.

"I repeat," Georgie spoke up with air of defiance. "I want your cooperation Mr. Aaron Fromgence to get another ladder and additional assistance."

Aaron immediately sensed that Georgie's use of 'Mr' was actuated more by sarcasm than genuine respect and decided to demonstrate his status to Georgie.

"Listen Georgie, I have been put in charge of this operation. As you know or ought to know, Colonel Sargeant and Captain Gregoire chose me as the leader of this activity. You must know that Colonel Sargeant is your superior. You must know that Captain Gregoire, though lower in rank than the Colonel is your superior...."

"They are your superiors, too, Aaron," Georgie pointed out anger building up in him. Aaron would have none of it from Georgie.

"Georgie Smith, I find you rude and crude. You are acting as though I have no power and authority over you."

By now Aaron's voice had been raised several decibels. Other trainees had noticed that he had stopped patrolling and was stationed by Georgie for what seemed to be a very, very long time.

Neither Aaron nor Georgie had realized that the loudness of their voices had so attracted the attention of some of the trainees that almost all the preparations and the painting had stopped as those involved in these activities were concentrating more on the argument between Aaron and Georgie than on work. Aaron moved closer to Georgie, hate intensifying in him as he did so.

"You are trying to undermine me, you Georgie, you have done nothing so far today and you seem to think that I am afraid of you...."

"You, Aaron Isaac Zachariah Ezekiel Fromgence are provoking my spirit. You are lucky to be in charge of us and power has gone to your head...."

Nobody had ever spoken to Aaron like this. Calling out his whole name in a loud aggressive manner and hinting that he was power drunk was too much for Aaron. He moved closer still to Georgie and it was only the fact that four trainees made their way so close to the scene as to be seen by Aaron that put a halt to Aaron's further forward movement. Not intimidated at all, Georgie shouted.

"No point in advancing towards me, touch me and you will see!"

The other four moved quickly between Aaron and Georgie. In this militia it was the practice that the real superiors always insisted that those in training should have their eyes so open to fractures in discipline as to report them forthwith or do all in their power to suppress them before they got out of hand. Knowing the rules and realizing that witnesses were present, both Georgie and Aaron calmed down, chiefly because four mouths taking the news to the High Command saying the same thing, could land these two antagonists in trouble.

Curiously, Aaron walked away and made off to the north of the building and put himself out of the view both of Georgie and the other four. Beneath a huge Samaan tree, Aaron sat reflecting on what had transpired and planning revenge against Georgie and if necessary anyone who had reported them to Colonel Sargeant.

Strangely, neither Colonel Sargeant nor Captain Gregoire heard what had transpired, but what they learnt was that all the trainees definitely needed at least another six hours to complete the job. More strangely still, the High Command did not think that the amount of work done to date fell short. Their decision was that the task would be completed next weekend under a different leader, not because Aaron had not done a good job but to rotate responsibility. Rotating responsibility and leadership functions was a great feature of this militia. The next week another trainee would be in charge. Despite knowing the practice of the rotation of roles, when Aaron heard that someone else, yet to be named, would be in charge of supervising when next the painting resumed, he was furious. He felt he had lost power.

On the Friday, the day before the paint job was to be completed a memorandum was sent to each trainee informing that Georgie Smith was to lead the completion of the paint job. On hearing this news, Aaron decided that he would be sick from early Saturday morning. All those who started to paint under Georgie's supervision could not help but remark to themselves how Aaron's illness coincided with Georgie's assigned role. By this time nearly every trainee had come to the conclusion that there was enmity between Georgie and Aaron.

While work was proceeding in good order in the barracks, Aaron was in his room plotting against Georgie. He felt that he owed it to himself to do something to gain revenge against this Georgie who clearly was his adversary. He longed and hoped for an opportunity to deal with this 'upstart'. He thought long and hard. He could find no easy plan by which he could hurt or destroy Georgie. Aaron was becoming uncomfortable with himself because of his difficulty in finding a strategy by which Georgie could he humbled. Should he move to ensure that he found the best possible favour with Colonel Sargeant? He thought. Then the idea came to Aaron that at the end of their training, there were bound to be prizes and trophies for those recruits who excelled in different areas. Aaron smiled to himself at the thought that he stood an excellent chance of being best recruit. But this would not be enough. After all, it was one thing to receive the top award. But all things considered, Aaron opined to himself, there was some possibility that Georgie could get some prize too.... Just then Aaron heard a knock on his door which was not locked. The door was pushed open and in walked Colonel Sargeant.

"Good day, I have come to see how you are feeling. Should

I call the doctor or our volunteer chaplain/counsellor?"

"Good morning, Sir," Aaron answered very politely. "I am not well, but I feel I will feel better after some rest. I do not feel I need the chaplain who is our Training Camp's counsellor. I would not say that I have any personal troubles bothering my mind! Sir, a few days rest and I will be fine. But, Sir, I really want to thank you for coming to see me. Your coming to see me means a lot to me, Sir. I feel like if you are my father, Sir. I do not think that you had to come here to see me so I thank you for going out of your way to see me...."

Colonel Sargeant sat in one chair in the living room.

"It is alright, Son. So far you have really been excellent in your training. I feel that you will make an excellent soldier. By the way, before I forget, Son, in the field of military studies there is a position known as military police officer."

Interrupting, Aaron asked:

"What is a military police, Sir,?"

"Aaron, such a post in an established army is one where a person is both a soldier and a policeman, usually with the highest investigative skills; it involves a combination of skills. Here in the Caribbean there would not be many such persons at this stage but I believe that in the aftermath of events in Grenada between 1979 – 1983 there would have been some who had to be military policemen so that order could have been properly restored after the unfortunate manner in which many died, including Mr. Maurice Bishop."

"Sir, I would like you to tell me some more in the future when I am better able to understand."

"Okay," complied Colonel Sargeant.

"You know, Colonel Sargeant, I love being here and you are an excellent leader. I have no doubt that your excelled while at Sandhurst...."

Aaron was about to embark on a strategy of flattering the Colonel. Much as the trainees were not informed as to the level of training of their superiors nor the institutions which they attended, Aaron's ruse was to establish Colonel Sargeant as one of the greatest and he was going to do so there and then! Colonel Sargeant pretended that he did not hear Aaron's reference to Sandhurst though feeling very, very elated that Aaron could feel that he was Sandhurst-trained. He managed to show no emotion to that fine shot that Aaron had fired on his behalf.

"Sir," Aaron, without pausing, said: "I feel very comfortable here. You have been an inspiration to me. If you find me an eager trainee it is because of your excellent example and skilful manner of preparing us. Nearly every single cadet if I can call my peers such, is absolutely impressed with you."

Smiling, Colonel Sargeant interrupted. "I thought that all of those who will soon recruit favoured my style and manner."

"No, sir. Unfortunately not all appreciate your administration."

"What?" The Colonel was caught by surprise. For he felt that he was very popular with all those whom he was training.

"Sir."

The Colonel stopped Aaron short. "You mean, Aaron that I have enemies?"

"Sir, I really should not be speaking like this. I really do not want to squeal on my colleagues," Aaron observed while cleverly pretending not to wish to report news. "Sir, should I say what I really want to?"

"Go ahead, Aaron."

"Sir, it grieves me to tell you that Georgie Smith bad talks you either because of jealousy or because he is a liar. I have known him all my life. We come from the same place. He is bad, Sir, he is bad. Of course he is a liar to criticize you. But you would be shocked to hear that Georgie is a big, big thief too. I never said anything to you before but he is a robber. Somehow those who chose us for the training did not know anything about Georgie for if they did, he would never, never have been admitted here.

"But today he is in charge of duties on the barracks!"

"Never mind that, Colonel Sargeant, Georgie is a rogue and vagabond."

Not being able to bear it, Colonel Sargeant, clearly upset, wished Aaron well and retreated to his office.

Easter Monday, a public holiday, came. Most trainees spent the day away from their barracks. But Aaron and Georgie, who somehow did not see each other that day, were the only trainees to remain on location.

Later that week there were reports that two 9 mm glocks disappeared. The news was very shocking. After charging Georgie with theft, Colonel Sargeant expelled him from the course. Georgie Smith's ambition to be a soldier ended.

Chapter 8

A PRIEST ARRIVES

RESOLVED TO PERFORM HIS MINISTRY through good works to the Glory of his Creator, within less than a fortnight, Father Fred set about to add to his Ministry in the church. Frederick Weisenburg, upon becoming 'Father Fred', had migrated to Helen Isle. He moved around Castries, Dennery and Micaud, and even went south to View Fort and Laborie.

An excellent listener, he was learning faster than normal. He learned that many adults had lacked schooling though in the last decade much had been done to educate the youth. He became aware of an economy originally based on bananas and coconuts that could not absorb the hundreds of unemployed.

Father Fred learnt that the society of Helen Isle was still largely patriarchal, and one in which many women especially the older ones felt that they had to depend on men. Yet single mothers headed most families. He learnt also that some spirituality was present, that Catholicism had been the main religion but concluded that he had to support those institutions which offered hope, including the school system. He had hatched in his fertile mind a programme by which he could engender self-development among many sectors of Helenite society.

In little or no time Father Fred learnt other things as well: that Martinique a French Department lay close to the north of Helen Isle, that Helen Isle itself was under French control before the British took it and that every resident old and young, spoke patois as well as or better than English. His compassionate spirit led him to empathize with the poor and the aged and he launched an outreach programme to ensure that the less fortunate people had food, clothes and hope.

Before settling down to his new calling in Helen Isle, Father Fred was made aware that two of its citizens, Derek Walcott and Arthur Lewis, had won Nobel Prizes. He decided that he would use the achievements of these two great Helen Islanders to inspire his flock and his parish to move on to accomplish. Aware though that beyond food, clothes and shelter, most simple folk were in need of education, work and self-development, an idea struck Father Fred. His church St. Ignatius, had a sizeable outside hall with tables and chairs. If he could find five or six reasonably educated persons in the community he would stage weekly sessions aimed at education, thrift and budgeting and other forms of edification. Even if he could find some not particularly learned nor educated, but willing to achieve progress, he would establish programmes to uplift individuals and their communities.

It was while walking around various villages that Father Fred met Henri.

"Good afternoon, young man, my name is Father Fred and I have been recently appointed to the Catholic Church of St. Ignatius."

Henri himself had been confirmed at St. Gabriel's the Greater, and had recently hoped to resume attendance there.

"It is my intention not only to be a priest in a narrow way but also to do a community outreach programme geared to having the residents of this beautiful island see themselves in a healthy positive way and determined to conquer those things which have held them back for years. I am from Ohio, but I have not come to your island with any preconceived ideas. I do not want you or any of your country-men ever to think that you as a people are inferior to any one. My mission will be to work with the people here and to use any God-given talent and training I have, to ensure happiness among you. Shortly I hope to meet some of you for you to provide information to me about things of which I am ignorant. If you have time, Sir, I would be willing to speak to you right now."

Henri Jean Baptiste Alexander was one of the personalities of the north of Helen Isle. Born in lowly circumstances, like most of his peer group, Henri loved to interact with older people. He would tell his superiors in age that there was no better teacher than experience. Henri loved to read. He played cricket, football, dominoes and whist with his friends. He kept very good company and was loved whereever he went. He was not vain nor arrogant and he felt it his duty to speak to this holy man.

"Father, we are a small island, but bigger than our neighbour to the South East. That island Bimshire about which you must have heard, is tiny. Ironically, Bimshire appears to be better known than Helen Isle. Our people are industrious. Some of the smaller sectarian churches in our midst appear to be growing faster than the Episcopal church or the Catholic Church. By history and tradition we really are Catholic but the fundamentalists are growing rapidly. The Jehovah's Witnesses are growing rapidly. I feel that they have an effective marketing programme and they make good business people too. There is something about our people. There is a kind of social intimacy among us. Our family structures do not see people relating only to their own small nuclear family. My family is my mother, her sister, her half sister, my grandmothers, any one else related to my grandparents and the children of my sisters and brothers just to mention a few. In our culture if a child was unfortunate enough to be an orphan, the community will take care of that child. Believe me, Father, do not be surprised if many people come up to your home without any appointment at all to see you and bring you potatoes, yams, tanias..."

"It has started to happen already," came the quiet interjection of the newly arrived priest. "Your people are kind!"

Feeling good, Henri continued. "Oh Father, I must say that our people cultivate gardens and raise animals. I must tell you a little anecdote about those who keep sheep, goats, rabbits, pigs and the like. For short some people call these 'stock'. A possibility is that the word is the last part of 'livestock' but few actually use the word livestock regularly. In your country certain investments are called "stock" and are seen to be investments and such investments bring additional resources. Which one really explains why our peasant and subsistence farmers see their animals as 'stock', Father?"

"Both. I find your explanation to be cute to put it like that," Father Fred mused.

"I was to tell you, Father, that recently some of our educators and social workers have been advising on the teaching of Black Studies in our schools. Time was when there was a Euro-centred approach to culture and education at the formal level. Parallel to that, though, were always our local dances, songs and sayings. Yes, there are those who would wish to promote things like African History, African Dance and African Culture so that our people can relate to their true roots. All over our region, largely as a result of our colonial past and the results of the triangular trade, there have been developments aimed at extolling our roots."

"What was the triangular trade?" Father Fred was curious.

"To make it easy for you, Father, that was the trade by which African slaves came to this region. This was responsible for importing West Africans and bringing them to the Caribbean to work in the plantation systems."

"I understand."

Explaining further and being overjoyed to do so, Henri pointed out:

"The triangular trade pushed the slave trade and by this route West African slaves were brought to the Caribbean to provide their labour for persons called 'Massa' which means master."

"It must have been frightful."

"Oh, yes," Henri continued, "and slavery was a pillar of early colonialism. Father, with no false pride or boasting I want to tell you something. I have read and have encountered accounts about colonialism, exploitation and mercantilism..."

"What is mercantilism, I have never heard of it?"

"I trace mercantilism to the Navigation Acts of the mid seventeenth century. The metropolitan colonizers would target colonies as markets for their goods and services. The colonies would be used to produce primary goods for dispatch to the metropolis. The metropolis would often process these primary goods like sugar for example and make huge profits. But above all, each colony was so bound to its metropolitan owners that it could not as a colony ever trade with countries other than its so-called mother country..."

"Interesting." Father Fred's eyes were wide open.

"Father, would you from my brief account label mercantilism as a form of economic integration or should I suggest that on balance, the extractive, agricultural stage of production was needed by the metropolis and the colonies did not benefit to the same degree as their European colonizers. The trade was definitely tilted in favour of Europe. Eric Williams proved that in his Ph.D thesis. Walter Rodney wrote of it in How Europe Under-Developed Africa."

Father Fred was impressed by the innate intelligence and knowledge of this young Helenite. Only if every single other Helenite could follow his lead, then education and training would abound in Helen Isle and would provide the basis for people's development. In Father Fred's mind surely there must be others like this able young man.

"Yes, Father, there is a definite interest in Black History here. Some of our people know of that brilliant black intellectual Angela Davis, of H. Rap Brown, of Stokeley Carmichael among those of us old enough to have learnt of him, of Muhammad Ali who was much more than a boxer and who has inspired pride among many of us. As blacks in ex-colonies we have to remain sensitive to the historic struggles that persons of the black race have been driven to endure. I refer to nothing military, Sir, but the battle is not over. I trust you understand Father.

Dick Gregory was another outstanding black who made many stories and anecdotes. He held a tremendous sense of humour. Talking about sense of humour when you settle I will introduce you to tapes of stories of Paul Keens Douglas. I do not wish to be funny. But we blacks do have a sense of humour. We have a sense of humour. With it too we have to have a sense of culture. Have you ever heard of Derek Walcott and his outstanding, most outstanding contribution. Walcott is a world-great, Sir.

Here, Sir, in the Caribbean we have had heroes who battled for our people's self-determination, for their identity, for their independence. I would like you, Holy Father, as soon as you can, to trace Caribbean History and to learn of the outstanding contributions made by persons like Dr. Eric Williams, Norman Manley and his son Michael, of persons like George Charles and others.

Down in Bimshire there have been astonishing accounts of the difficulties Grantley Adams went through to bring democracy to his country. In fact, I should have told you that coinciding with the World's Great Depression of the 1930s, there were riots in nearly every Anglo-phone Caribbean country."

"Riots, why?" The priest sought clear information.

"In the 1930s, one hundred years after slavery was supposed to have ended in the English speaking Caribbean, there was no true democracy. There was oligarchy. There was psychological slavery. There was rampant poverty and privation. The masses of people were poor and dispossessed. Conditions for them were unbearable. Dilapidated housing; slumocracy."

"What? What? Tell me what on earth is slumocracy?" The priest demanded raising his voice somewhat.

"Sir, that is where slums abound. Father, where slums abound, there is poverty. There is poverty of body, mind and spirit. You, Sir, may speak of ghettoes, a word no doubt coined in your country of origin. Ghettoes are slums. Slums are societal institutions that dehumanize, Sir.

You would agree that if my Sunday School classes have taught me correctly that man was born in the image and likeness of God, mankind ... sorry, Sir, humankind should not dwell in slums. There are no slums in Heaven. Surely, Holy Father, there can be no slums in Heaven!"

Father Fred was astonished. He had never heard anything like this and these words emanated from the heart, mind and spirit of a third world citizen. Deep philosophy, Father Fred thought. He paused to resume his breath.

"What is your name young man?"

"Do feel free, Father Fred, to call me Henri," came the honest reply.

"Before I let you speak some more, I want to say to you that on the matter of Black Studies I have myself read of Booker T. Washington and George W. Carver, two great black men. I have also been attracted to the work of the late Martin Luther King who met an untimely death around 1968, during a decade when it became fashionable to assassinate. Martin Luther King was killed. His work, ministry and legacy have to live on! I just wanted to include that. I am doing this to advise that I am ad idem with you, Henri.

Ad idem are two Latin words which literally mean "towards the same thing" but are best translated as either being of one mind or simply 'being in agreement'." The priest suggested, without any hint that he was teaching Henri something.

"Next Saturday afternoon, not this Saturday but the following one, the 14th of the month at my church hall in St. Ignatius I am staging a Self-Awareness and Self Development Session. I want you to be there Henri, if you can find the time. It starts at 5.00 p.m. Let your friends know that refreshments will be served. I am confident that you will invite your friends."

TWO WEEKS after, a representative cross section of persons from Castries, Dennery and some from the Rodney Bay, Gros Islet area attended a meeting which they had heard was about self-awareness and self-development.

"Good evening everyone. First I want to thank all of you for coming. I feel good to see you. I want to thank everyone whom I have met and who has been good enough to make me feel welcome. Some weeks ago I was a foreigner. This evening I must say to you that I feel that I am already a part of you and see no difference between yourselves and me: neither difference based on race nor difference based on status. There is no social or other distance between you all and me. For I am your humble servant. Any questions?"

"Sir, could you delay a little bit? Don't start yet, Sir, I know someone who is coming. In fact more than five of my relatives are coming. Could you wait please?"

True humble servant as he was, Father Fred agreed to hold on for a few minutes.

"The first thing I want to say is that God made us intelligent, capable of reason and creativity. As a religious leader my first duty is to honour and obey God and in glorifying God I must thank him for creating you all and me in his image. Secondly, I want you all to aim for perfection. Do your best in all you do. Aim high without being haughty. Tell yourself deep down that the Creator, perfect law and perfect God have moulded all of you into bright people."

There was a giggle. Father Fred ignored the giggle but understood instinctively that when many, many people are told that they are bright or intelligent, they are amazed.

"The typical person does not like anybody to call them a fool, yet on occasions like these still seem surprised to be told how bright they are. One problem many people have is a low self-esteem based on feelings of inferiority. You are not inferior. You are a bold, hardworking, proud people."

"Stop, Father, last Sunday my pastor said words to the effect that proud people are not really good people. Now you have me confused," a woman whom no one in the room could remember seeing, but who must have been invited by someone not yet present, lamented.

"How, Father, pride can both be a good thing and a bad thing?"

A broad smile came back at this interested lady.

"I must tell you what I mean by pride, my dear lady. By pride I mean self-worth good enough, deep enough for anyone to respect oneself. By pride I mean a very strong sense of being so good as not to disrespect or dehumanize oneself. This form of pride gives one dignity and such self-respect that one would veer away from nastiness."

"Go no further, I understand but is there another pride, another kind of pride?" The extroverted lady at the back asked.

"False pride, my sister," Father Fred stated, "is based on arrogance, conceit, vainglory, boasting and too high an opinion of oneself where one is trying to prove oneself as being higher and mightier than others. Do you understand?"

"Yes, Father, last Sunday my pastor did not explain it but obviously meant the second and lower form of pride you mentioned."

The class, as Father Fred called it, continued for just over two hours and his audience learnt how to think clearly, how to be positive, how to be assertive without being unruly and how not to hurt others, among other things. He also advised the people never to squander their opportunity to do God's will which he aptly described as a willingness to love and help others in God's name.

Present among the people was H. J. B. Alexander who thoroughly enjoyed this session.

Chapter 9

SEMINARY

THE DEHAVILLAND DASH 8 was clearly approaching land. As he looked out of the porthole, Aaron could see a relatively long stretch of land some eight or nine miles away. He marvelled at the white coastline, the dreamy trees and the flat land in the distance. He did not recognize one hill, far less a mountain. Coming from an island with many elevations including the two majestic pitons, Aaron wondered what kind of place this Bimshire would be.

"Fasten seat belts. We will be landing shortly," the sole flight attendant requested. The way she said it appeared more like a sweet plea than a firm order.

Aaron fidgeted with his seat belt thirty five minutes after he had had to be helped putting it on! Oh how angry he was with his parents for not having provided him with the means to travel before. He had known a few in his age group including two females who had travelled by air and more than once.

'Imagine two girls being allowed to travel and he was now on his maiden flight', he thought to himself. The stewardess moved towards him.

"Fasten seat belts, please…"

Once again she helped him to fasten his seat belt, smiled with him and then made off towards her tiny seat. He gazed at her and wondered who she was. She in turn noticed that he did not thank her either while she helped in Helen Isle nor now.

"Your pilot speaking. We are approaching Adams

International. On behalf of the crew of this the Little Island Air Tours Flight 87, I would like to thank you for making it L.I.A.T. Hope to see you soon. Always fly with us."

Despite being just some months before the top soldier graduating from military school, Aaron, having lost his confidence, felt more a green cadet than an achiever. Uncertainty gripped him just because he did not know what to do when he left the aircraft. No fool by any means, he elected to walk behind all the other passengers to see what they would do. Four of them went in businesslike fashion up to the Immigration counter after a relatively short walk. The first one presented a white card. Then Aaron reached into his pocket for the document which the flight attendant had given him. He looked at it and was surprised to find that all he had to do was fill in information about himself, his place of birth and passport number.

"This thing is easier than I thought," he murmured to himself. When he reached the counter the officer checked the form and said:

"Sir, please sign the bottom of the form here."

He cooperated and then looked up to see where those who had preceded him went. He followed them to a conveyor belt and recognized his suitcase. He took it up, still a little uncertain and a red cap asked:

"Can I help?"

"No."

"Sir, the Customs is over there. Go to the Customs." The red cap advised with a strong sense of encouragement. At Customs, the clerk inquired:

"Anything to declare?"

Aaron looked at her.

"Do you have anything to declare? Sir, let me see your suitcase. Please unfasten the lock."

She looked inside and told him:

"You can go."

Outside of the Customs, Johnson held a medium sized

piece of card bearing the name Mr. A.I.Z.E. Fromgence.

Immediately Aaron recognized the man who carried his name and remarked to himself that not even in secondary school was he ever described as A.I.Z.E. Fromgence. If he had known this man for any length of time, this stranger, he would have been sharply upbraided him. Because this man had been chosen to see him into Bimshire and to ensure that he settled, Johnson got away.

"Hi, Mr. Johnson."

Aaron's innate common sense invoked politeness when it suited him. Clearly this was an occasion for him to show respect. Sarah and Zaccky had repeatedly required their offspring to demonstrate manners and respect and it was only Aaron's ways that did induce him to deviate. If Aaron had faithfully abided by the standards his parents had set, he could have been the perfect gentleman. Though admitted as an undergraduate theological student, anyone, including his parents, would have constantly provided him with many fireside chats to impel him to walk the straight and narrow way.

Johnson took Aaron's fairly heavy suitcase and ushered him towards the car park. As his eyes caught the numbers of the motor vehicles, the priest-to-be hardly saw any of the registration numbers marked 'P'. He did notice that the numbers started with various letters of the alphabet and he did notice that some started with X and O. He said nothing and when he reached the motorcar, a Mazda which Johnson told him was the one which would transport them, Aaron realized that its first letter was 'J'.

'Was it that Johnson could have the licensing authorities in Bimshire commence his licence plate with 'J'? If all twenty-six letters in the alphabet were used by an identical member of owners and Bimshire had more than twenty-six owners of vehicles then how could the system work sensibly?' He wondered. He was debating to himself if to question Johnson about the system when he heard:

"No, man, although you are opening the back door, please come and sit in the front with me and be my co-driver."

Co-driver or not, Aaron's sense of self-importance ruled out cooperating with Johnson.

"No, Johnson, it is alright. I feel to sit in the back."

He was born in a country in which it was customary for a driver who was offering another a free ride or 'lift' as it was called in Bimshire, to insist that a single passenger sit beside the driver and here was this stranger and theological student making a taxi-driver of him, Johnson opined to himself. 'Was it that the youngster was rude or was he a natural upstart?'

"Do you really not want to accompany me in the front?" Johnson's plea was plaintive.

"I tell you it is fine for me to stay right here." Aaron was able to say firmly, not wanting to show Johnson his bad side in words. "I am alright here."

Johnson decided that their relationship was too new for him to be stubborn and so he gave in to Aaron. Aaron sat in the back as though he had won a battle. To say that he was triumphant would have been an understatement. The Mazda made its way northwest, its driver thinking to himself at first then did say aloud to Aaron:

"Man, in this island we do give people lifts and like them to travel in the front seat where possible. When people refuse front seat rides and sit in the back, we tell them flatly that we are not driving taxi."

"I did not know that," Aaron said. "But I will be funny enough to advise you that for your own good either act as if you are my taxi-driver here and now, or act as if I am in the front seat."

"You are calling on me to be a double doer because you have asked me to be an actor in two ways, Mr. A.I.Z.E. Fromgence."

There was silence. Aaron definitely felt offended. He was starting to resent this stranger. The silence continued and it was as if each man were reluctant to break it.

Aaron looked outside. Shortly after leaving the airport he could see sugar cane plants everywhere. Some looked tall enough. A few had a youthful newness about them as if they were freshly planted. These shorter ones were planted under what some residents called force back and were growing not from ratoons but were recently planted.

Then the relatively long silence ended and as though he had done nothing to offend Johnson, Aaron asked:

"Why are some canes so short and some long?"

As it seemed that Aaron was conciliating Johnson said:

"The shorter ones are known to us as first crop canes meaning that they were recently planted in September. The longer ones, a few of which have arrows, spring from roots in the ground left back after having been cut in January or February or March."

The pleasantness in Johnson's voice suggested that he had got over being made to be 'driving taxi' but he was still bemused by Aaron's declaration that he should 'act as if'. Johnson was a friendly man who made his living as a baker. In fact he operated his own bakery and had been to Helen Isle on four occasions. He had met so many Helenites that one had asked him to take care of Aaron especially in his early days in Bimshire. Johnson loved people and liked to help. He came across very many people every week and had had some problems with difficult people.

His idea now, though, was that he was going to be as genuine to Aaron as so many Helenites had been to him. In the interest of a flowing conversation Johnson asked Aaron:

"What flight did you come by?"

"I came by an aircraft whose initials are L.I.A.T. and some people knickname it Leave Island Any Time but I am sure it was early today."

Aaron was now looking at his right "Hey what is the building over there with what looks like a chimney?"

"It is an old sugar factory and it closed own some years ago," came the reply from Johnson.

"It is not very, very late. We have to travel another seventeen miles to go to the north of the island and since it is your first day in this blessed country and your flight so short I am willing to drive you around for about forty-five minutes before I take you to where you will be staying in St. Andrew," Johnson offered.

Aaron decided to keep the conversation running: "Where is St. Andrew?"

"It is an eastern parish and it is not the same as Christ Church or St. Michael. It is hilly and it has its own soil types. It is quite beautiful. There is the possibility that its hills will remind you of your beautiful island," Johnson advised.

"I would like you to give me a little round trip before we go to St. Andrew," Aaron requested.

"That is alright with me, brother," Johnson obliged.

For a short while Aaron felt that it was much too early for Johnson to see himself as his brother. In fact, judging from the composition of his family, he had no blood brothers and had never given any thought as to what life would be like if he had brothers.

Johnson then made a turn to the left. More cane fields; but after about seven minutes after passing a church on their right, Aaron was curious:

"What is the name of this church?" Aaron asked.

"I think that is St. David's Church. To us it is an Anglican church. The Americans would call it St. David's Episcopal Church," Johnson replied. Within a short time Aaron's eyes caught hold of a very tall building.

"What's this?"

"It is Cable and Wireless External Telecommunications, but I was about to tell you that around the St. David's church is a wonderful old village which together with one not too far, Watts Village, has produced many outstanding Barbadians. The people of St. David's have always valued education. Good people come from St. David's," Johnson said proudly.

The drive continued. From the number and type of

buildings they were either in a city or close to a city, Aaron believed. They were in a place called Wildey.

"Hey, tell me what is Bimshire's national dish."

"We have cou cou and salt fish. Cou Cou is made from corn meal, not corn flour, and okras. Speaking of corn flour at our Independence we make conkies also known as stew-dumplings from corn flour with coconut, raisins and good essence. We do them in the singed leaves of the banana plant. A national dish that is popular, mainly on Saturdays, is Pudding and Souse: there is black pudding and white pudding. In recent years people have been making steam pudding. I will give you all the details in the near future and will indeed provide samples of these things for you.

Oh, we have National Heroes. Sarah Ann Gill, Hugh Springer, Frank Walcott, Garry Sobers, Samuel Jackman Prescod, Clement Payne, Charles Duncan Oneale, Bussa, Grantley Adams and Errol Barrow. Walcott died recently after an outstanding career in trade unionism. He was a typical working class person who went on to be a big spokesperson for working people. Sobers, you must know of, reported to be the greatest cricketer ever. Adams was a Parliamentarian for my area, St. Joseph. He had to fight oligarchy. He mobilized working class people whose consciousness was raised by Clement Payne. Payne inspired resistance, rebellion and revolution. Adams carried on his work and was the founder of democracy in Bimshire. Barrow once said that Barbados is friends of all without being a satellite of any state. His name is associated with free secondary education, independence and modernization.

Bussa had way back in 1816 working alongside Washington Franklyn sought to end slavery. Sarah Ann Gill was a heroine who risked her life in an attempt to educate and edify poor grieving blacks. Oneale was a visionary who early in the 20th century launched a platform for the improvement of our people. Springer and Walcott were pioneers in the labour movement and were associated with Adams in our First Workers Union.

Sobers at his peak was an extraordinary cricketer. His talent is universally known. A person sprung from the working class, the legacy he has left is that 'excellence is not the narrow preserve of the privileged'."

Aaron was impressed. Their conversation continued for quite a while. After many minutes Johnson said:

"You know brother Aaron I used to be a teacher before I decided to start my own business," Johnson declared with pride.

They had now reached the modest bungalow in St. Andrew. Johnson offered to return to Aaron in a few days to take him to the College.

ARRIVED AT the College, Aaron was in the front row of the class. After those who were present each identified themselves, the lecturer Dr. Snaith started by saying:

"I am here first to teach you to think critically. You must know that not everything in black and white is true. I adhere to the Christian faith but I hereby assert that Christianity is not the only religion. I want each of you to have a open mind. You are going to have to cast aside a lot of the brainwashing inflicted on you, indeed injected into your minds by your parents and probably your churches. Part of my mission is to liberate you. My approach is not going to be evangelical nor fundamentalist. Each of you has the potential to be a scholar. No scholar accepts information uncritically."

Aaron was trying to figure out what angle Dr. Snaith was coming from.

"Oh," Dr. Snaith paused. Then he resumed. "I am American. I have written five books in all."

Aaron's mind temporarily drifted to the tall, elegant Royal Palm trees—cabbage cloaked trees as Johnson called them. He thought about Johnson giving up control of students, opting for manipulating dough. Those very tall trees more than thirty of them, imparted a special ambience to the setting. Aaron felt rather poetic as his eyes espied the sea aback of some short hills. Then Aaron was listening to the lecturer again.

"I am seen as an expert in the New Testament but should I tell you something. If it was just the Old Testament we had, there could have been no Christianity."

To Aaron this did not sound like what he had learnt at Sunday School back home.

"Yes, dear students, the Old Testament by itself cannot be considered to be any basis at all for our great religion."

The first ten books of the Old Testament also belong to another religion, Judaism. If Judaism is not the same thing as Christianity a logical question would be how could two entirely different religions share the same basic text? It was not just Aaron that was amazed. The other eleven students were equally astonished. Dr. Snaith stopped speaking. There was silence.

"Are you following me? I bet that you are becoming critical, doubtful, even!" He stood silent before them again.

"Well if you are becoming doubtful and even cynical you are on your way to becoming true intellectuals. My ministry is to impart an intellectually stimulating attitude to your work. To me religion is more about the mind than the heart. Those sectarian preachers spout emotionalism and with it, they may be guilty of hypnotizing the masses. You will be detached and fearless after being exposed to my teaching."

"Can I interrupt you to ask you a question?" came a query from the back of the classroom.

"Go ahead."

"What do you mean when you say that religion is more to do with the mind than the heart?"

"In seminaries like this one even before you as students are exposed to our sacraments and rituals we your tutors try to inspire both creative and deep analytical thinking. You are to be urged and will be directed to question even deeply entrenched doctrines. You must never be unthinking receptacles. You will be exposed to controversies and will be expected to base any conclusions you draw on logic and reason."

"Are you saying then, Sir, that in the Bible there are statements and teachings that are open to question and that by intellectual inquiry a lot of what has been written may not be sound and accurate?" The undergraduate inquired.

"Exactly," the theologian and scholar agreed. "Religion is not an exact science. Indeed it is doubtful whether religion is a science. May I as an authority on the New Testament posit the view that Colossians and Ephesians were not written by St. Paul."

"What?" Four students exclaimed loudly.

"Do not be shocked. True scholars have formed the view that style and vocabulary are evidence pointing to such differences in Colossians, Ephesians and probably 2nd Thessalonians from Paul's turn of phase and sentence structure, that these three epistles could not have been written by Paul. There is a strong probability that these 'letters' were written after Paul's death."

All of the students were clearly shocked.

"I'd better stop there," Dr. Snaith relented somewhat. "I may have given too much in this your first lecture. But before you go, notwithstanding all I have said, this seat of learning will still prepare you to be clerics. You will be priests as long as you pass your examinations.

Before I close you must be told that a priest is a person of many, many parts. You will not be one dimensional individuals glibly pouring forth things from the scriptures, having learnt them only on face value. You will not be blind ignoramuses obsessed more with cursing Satan then bringing your congregations to good Christian understanding. You will even be able to do proper counselling, for you will receive rounded training even in things like psychology. "You will know about psychologists like Freud.

"Who is or was Freud?" Asked Aaron.

"I can only introduce this great thinker to you briefly.

Sigmund Freud is best known for his position that three desires dominate the thinking of man and these are: desire for sex; desire for money; and desire for power."

"Thank you, Sir" said Aaron. "I take it Sir that on these three scores our class can now end."

"Yes, thanks."

Outside six of the new students, Aaron included, gathered under a tree to reflect on their first lecture.

"I wonder if I have come to the right theological school." A twenty- five year old Bimshire student said. Then another person who identified himself as Leon observed:

"I really want to train as a priest but some of the things Dr. Snaith said really surprised me."

A third person said emphatically that he found that the utterances made by the Doctor of Theology were an attack on the fundamentalists.

Without waiting to be asked his opinion Aaron intervened:

"I was shocked. I am still in shock. I feel so doubtful that I am beginning to feel agnostic. I would agree with anyone who says that his faith is shaken. Finally, Dr. Snaith does not sound to be a strict, strict Christian. He seems to have a very, very, open mind. It is clear that he too has some doubts about what has been written. Remember he said that some of Paul's epistles could have been written by someone else. I was also enthused about his argument that a psychologist said that the chief activators in human affairs are sex, money and power.

Chapter 10

THE RANCH

THOSE WHO ATTENDED THE RANCH decided that among themselves there would be a special friendship and in addition the highest possible levels of secrecy.

Beejay held himself out as the owner of the Ranch. Some five or six years older than Aaron, Beejay came back to Helen Isle having travelled and lived abroad. He boasted of several achievements both in the U.S. Virgin Islands and the British Virgin Islands. Many of his achievements awaited corroboration and confirmation. Beejay decided that the upper room of the ranch could be accessed only by a very special few who would gather there for activities that he alone permitted.

A dapper five-footer given both to boasting and priding himself in his achievements, Beejay had always had time for Aaron from the time the latter was about fifteen or sixteen years old. Aaron, who in his teenage years always preferred older company, found a friend in Beejay whose influence on him was greater than that of Zaccky, his father. It was six months before graduating from the Seminary that Beejay had both introduced Aaron to the ranch and to Poker and Tonk.

"My friend and brother, you can use this place anytime. If you want to relax or be in private just call me and I will have it ready for you," said Beejay. Always loyal to his older friend, Aaron agreed.

"When you return from Bimshire I will allow you in this place which I love to call the Ranch. Most times when I open it, it is for the purpose of playing cards, mainly Poker and Tonk. Naturally we have all kinds of drinks available and once a month I stage some esoteric sessions in which I want you to take part when you return for good. If you are interested I will teach you the finer points of our main card games. Next to me in authority in this place is my good friend Pierre whom you will meet in the future."

Beejay then introduced Aaron to Poker, explaining the significance of aces, dueces, kings, queens and jacks and Aaron was immediately attracted to the cards.

"In this place we do not usually permit games that involve throwing dice but we do have a good time. Each person who comes here understands brotherhood and secrecy and we function in unity."

Beejay was aware that Aaron was in training in seminary for the priesthood but knew him well enough to conclude that the latter would never be fanatical about religion nor unwilling to follow any lead that he as his senior in years would set.

"I cannot wait that long for you to return, Aaron, our social activities will be boosted by your regular attendance."

Upstairs the ranch had two sets of lights one set of lights, lights of colour, were clearly intended to cast a hue of semi-darkness and quiet. There was a bar, a brand new air-conditioning system, an emergency exit and several pieces of antique furniture which Beejay said he had imported from various places abroad. Behind a dark brown partition were two beds, which from what Beejay said, could provide rest and relaxation if such were needed. There was a large fire proof filing cabinet, a first aid kit and a safe.

Aaron was attracted to the safe and the two beds behind the partition.

"Oh, we play with cards made in China," Beejay said. "At this point ahead of your return my closest ally is Pierre, a no-nonsense loyal friend who can hold on for me if I am unavailable. Pierre owns three large boats good enough for inter-island travel. He has friends in the local customs and is well to do and kind. When we meet for card games, we often have discussions—discussions of all kinds and we bond in a way where we are loyal to ourselves and keep outsiders out. You will notice that downstairs has more space and in time I will let you know what happens downstairs as I will also let you know about the other five or six special members.

Do know that we do not admit women into our secret affairs because women talk too much. We keep them out of what we do upstairs and we forbid them from being members of our monthly club. Women definitely talk too much."

Aaron saw no need to ask Beejay any questions especially since Beejay had never let him down. Then the two left the Ranch.

On Aaron's return to seminary in Bimshire he constantly remembered the ranch.

"Oh when would these next six months come and go?" he wondered.

Back in the seminary after a one week break, the fifteen priests and theologians-to-be, came together to focus on:
1. Pastoral care and counselling.
2. Episcopal Rituals concerning Baptism, Confirmation and the Sacrament, and The Final Rites.
3. Ecclesiastical Law..
4. Work in the community.
5. Sacerdotal Etiquette.

They had so far done almost three years and all looked forward to graduating.

Leon, an exceptionally bright student from Anguilla was often allowed to conduct Peer Group Tutorials. Aaron hated the idea of a fellow student put in charge of his tutorial group. One day during a tutorial on Sacerdotal Etiquette, the eight member group were looking at the matter of dealing with those who were grieving. This tutorial followed a lecture by Father Teddy who had been careful to explain how to empathize with the grieving:

"Whatever our station in life, at the end of the day we are

human beings subject to sickness, pains of all sorts and to death; pain and death are like levelers equating the poor man at his gate to the rich man in his castle. We here are theologians and shortly everyone in this room will be priests. As priests we cannot be snobbish nor scornful. We have benefited from schooling and education and I believe that in our territories in the Caribbean we will find respect and even reverence. We are called upon to practise self-respect and to lead by example. We should neither make fools of others nor ourselves. We must show that we are God-fearing and we must inspire confidence….."

Aaron was not listening.

"Many persons will trust us because of who we are. We ought not to take those who trust us lightly. We are leaders and not confidence tricksters. Now how does a priest deal with the pain and suffering of others? In a few days all of us will be priests. But bear in mind, "Once a priest, twice, indeed three times a man. We are firstly human beings. We have parents and loved ones. Some of you already have your own families.

We do have experiences and feelings. As human beings we are prone to have the same experiences and feelings of other human beings. There exists a word called sympathy. But very, very closely related to sympathy is a word known as empathy. Empathy is about putting yourselves in the shoes and place of another. If someone is grieving, bear in mind that they are experiencing hurt and pain. When dealing with persons who are weighed down by grief, let us all remember to put ourselves in the same position as those who are grieving, for a day will come when we too will experience grief.

Even when somebody is crying uncontrollably and feeling hopeless any priest who is approached by such a sufferer must show patience and find ways to provide comfort. We have to bear in mind that Jesus is the ultimate comforter."

One student put up his hand.

"Suppose a mother has lost a dutiful son or daughter in a

tragic murder or accident. How do you recommend that we deal with such?"

"Let the person put in words how they feel. If they are crying let them cry. Wait on them. Know that depression is very much a feeling of hopelessness. Give them the assurance that grief does come in the evening but after all joy comes in the morning. It is never easy. But put yourselves in the place of that person who is hurting. Assure them that you understand their pain and the reason for their pain. Know your Bible and supportive literature well enough to read them appropriate passages of scripture. Offer to stay with them for lengthy periods if necessary. Pray with them and for them. Show them love and respect."

IT WAS now the very final day of their last examinations. Aaron had been looking forward to completing his examinations and returning home. Just before the three-hour examination on the four gospels, he reflected on the progress he had made and the fact that it would not be difficult to be posted to a church in his homeland. However, the most pressing thoughts in his mind related to all that Beejay had told him and he did look forward expectantly to writing this last paper and returning home a few days afterwards.

The examination started. Aaron had entered the Examination Room with some understanding of the Gospels of Matthew and Mark and as he did not know enough about Luke and John he was hoping that all of the questions would be set on the areas which he knew well. He read through the Examination paper, realizing that he had to write five essays. Time was no problem for him for he always wrote quickly. The problem was the total of nine questions which were set of which each student had to write five. He was comfortable with the first two questions on the paper and felt he could score heavily on them. Another two, though not so easy, would see him get some marks, but he could not be sure if he could do them as well as the ones he saw at first.

Aaron looked to his left. Close by sat Leon looking studious and prepared. He could see clearly what Leon was writing. Aaron decided to work frantically on those he could master and decided that so long as he was not caught, he was going to do some copying of Leon's work. This he felt he could do, since the invigilator was the oldest lecturer in the seminary and was known to have problems with his vision and eyesight.

He saw a question which invited students to write an essay proving how Luke's gospel and account of Christ's ministry was more thorough than John's; and the final question was to compare the various accounts of what happened in the garden of Gethsemane. He knew that he could easily ignore question four and concentrate on five. Having read back over his paper, he hoped that if he could be sure that Leon was doing the final two he could look on his neighbour's work and arrange his own answers.

Then he noticed that Leon was doing question number nine first and Aaron counted fourteen blank pages in his own answer book and commenced to follow Leon, making changes of words and style, and did succeed in copying the latter's ideas and writing them. Aaron answered question number nine on Pages fifteen, sixteen and seventeen of his answer book. Others in the room were so intent doing their own work that not even Leon noticed what Aaron had done and the invigilator, who was not inclined to stroll around the room, actually observed much less than Leon.

Aaron then speedily went back to Page three and wrote volumes on the first two questions which he knew he could answer. It was just past two hours and two questions remained to be done. As he observed that Leon was doing question number six, Aaron's eyes picked up his neighbour's arguments and with the 'appropriate adjustments' Aaron completed his fourth answer which took up page ten to fourteen. He had now done four questions and felt that he could, on his performance on these, earn a pass.

In view of how he had written the paper, Aaron decided to play strategist. He was alert to the fact that the first two pages of his Examination Book were blank and he titled them 'rough work' and scribbled both of them full of little snippets from what he could recall writing in the body of his answers. Question number five required candidates to show how together the four gospels could be said to lay the foundation for accounts of the early Christian church and its mission. He was prepared to woffle and pad if necessary, but felt that he should begin by explaining what the Christian church was about in its early days. He then made up a workable definition of the word 'mission' and found that he had already written a page and a half.

As tactfully as ever, Aaron ignored mention of the early life of Christ when he was growing up and could recall things that Christ had said in his sermon on the mount and argued strongly that Christ's sermon on the mount, the Lord's Prayer and his healing ministry were pillars on which Christianity had been built. He paused. He took a breath. He knew that if no questions had been raised about the content of his work in a seminary with a low failing grade, that he was bound to pass.

Having arrived back home and assured his family that he felt he would do well he then telephoned the person he wanted to see the most and told him,

"I am coming."

Beejay was awaiting Aaron. "How did you get through with your finals in Bimshire?"

"I feel that I will make it," Aaron answered.

"Well, welcome back home. The first thing that I wish to speak to you about is my fraternity, the Leopards. The Leopards is a secret society which encourages bravery and fortitude, brotherhood and loyalty. For reasons which will become obvious to you in the future, we do not admit women into our society, some of the reasons being that many women prove fainthearted and they talk too much. In our society we

can use the Bible if we choose, but our basic texts are:
1. Chariots of the Gods.
2. The lost books of the Bible.
3. The Da Vinci Code.
4. The dead seas scrolls.
5. The silver cord.
6. The sixth and seventh Books of Moses.
7. Various works of Lobsang Rampa.

We offer various degrees. We have our own secret place for our meetings. We swear all our members to secrecy. I am the boss and leader for life and I set the rules. Nothing to be scared of and I will physically supervise all of your initiations.

Aaron, we deal in the esoteric and metaphysical. I would have briefly raised these matters with you just as you were returning to Bimshire to complete your studies. If you follow me and do as I direct you will achieve progress. In fact you will learn the truth. Several degrees await you, and in time just as my Chief Lieutenant Pierre has progressed, you too will achieve progress and advancement. If you read the literature and learn the rituals and mysteries, you will be a real man and with your background as a soldier you will be absolutely fearless, prudent, wise and strong."

From the time he was quite young Aaron always wanted to be a participant in anything that could make him strong, or rather stronger. Aaron was paying close attention to all that Beejay was saying.

"You know, Aaron, established religion, is rightly perceived to be based on faith, on a belief in things which are unseen."

"Yes, Beejay, I know that."

"One reason, Aaron, why many who attend church doubt, is that they have no way of finding faith, no matter how hard they try. Metaphysics and Mysticism are based on proof and on sight. My philosophy is that if the Bible said everything there is to know, people would be wiser and end up without any fear whatsoever of death. If all there is to know about the nature of self and the influence of the planets on the cosmos, in fact if the character of the cosmos and the cosmic were too widely publicized, people would be so conscious that no religious teacher could drive fear in the hearts of their congregation. If truth, that is objective truth, were to spread all over the place the possibility is that the churches of the world would be empty." Beejay declared.

"What are the Leopards, Beejay?"

"Somewhere Aaron, there is reference to the quick and the dead. The leopards are a society of the quick, yes we are a society of the quick. Not one of us in the society fears death. We are not religious, but our principles are based on fraternity and loyalty. We have signs and we help each other. When you gain admission you will learn our secrets, signs and symbols. When you go anywhere and do your signs, men of similar bent will understand both your signs and immediately know your desires. Should I tell you that worldwide there are priests who are Leopards? It is only the fundamentalists, pious and fanatical that are suspicious of us. Their suspicion is based on ignorance and pigheadedness. My chapter is one of the most respected. If you doubt me, Pierre, who is second to me as Commander-in-Chief will explain our ways. Would you be interested?

"I will join any group you open to me, Beejay, and I want to thank you for the U.S. dollars which you gave me to help me when I lived in Bimshire," Aaron replied.

Chapter 11

ANOTHER PRIEST ARRIVES

THE SHORTAGE OF CLERGY in all the islands including Helen Isle made it very easy for Aaron to be selected as Rector in Charge of St. Gabriel's The Greater. Located not far from Castries, but still nestled in a rural setting, most members of this church were simple working class people who assembled there from neighbouring districts.

What permitted some three hundred folk to make themselves available for Aaron's installation was the fact that he was the son of Zackky and Sarah. It was therefore a packed church that greeted their new parson. In attendance also were the District Superintendent of the Diocese and another church official known as the Vicar Plenipotentiary, both of whom Aaron had met in the days when these two had visited the Military Headquarters of Helen Isle at the time he was training as a soldier. Other members of the local clergy came to see their brother elevated to the leadership of a church.

It was the District Superintendent of the Diocese, his Lordship, Father Gary Jensen who was in charge of installing Zackky's only son into the priesthood. A quiet air of expectancy filled the church building. The service started with the song "Lead us, Heavenly Father Lead Us'. All sang lustily, save Aaron who simply could not sing.

The next item on the evening's programme was a prayer which, by the permission of His Lordship, Father Jensen, was led by the Vicar Plenipotentiary, Rev. Allen.

"O, Almighty Father, our God and King of the Universe,

we your unworthy children this evening look to you as the kindest of shepherds. We your sheep often lose our way and stray down the wrong path. Lead us to all that is aright. Let each one of us here, whatever our condition, state and status understand that you alone are all powerful—you alone are all-knowing. Visit upon us, Lord, your Mercy and remind us that all goodness flows from you. Help us to remember that our bananas, our ground provisions, our animals, our fish have always been provided by you.

O grant us mercy, matchless omnipotent, and look down upon us all here assembled on this occasion to anoint and exalt our beloved brother who, from today henceforth will be named The Reverend Aaron Isaac Zacariah Ezekiel Fromgence. Look down upon him with your grace, good God, bless him and all his family. As our loving Shepherd, guide, care and protect him. Ensure Father, that like you he can shepherd his flock. Strengthen him and ensure that he is equal to the very high calling to which he has this day been summoned. O, benevolent Divine God, nowadays but few come forward to pastor in these lands. Bless this young man who has answered your call to serve and grant him every gift that will make him become a faithful, loving and caring priest.

The next two items were Psalms 121 and 91 whose first lines were respectively, '*I will lift up mine eyes unto the hills whence cometh my strength*' and '*He that dwelleth in the secret place of the most high shall abide under the shadow of the Almighty*'.

Henri, who came to this service on the invitation of Ismay and Zaccky, took note that the first words of Psalm 121 were '*I will lift up mine eyes unto the hills*' and it registered in Henri's mind that these words were appropriate both because St. Gabriel's the Greater was nestled in the hills of the north of the island and that Helen Isle itself was so filled with hills that a special Psalm in the Bible appeared dedicated in a serious way to inviting Helenites to value their hills and to lift their hearts and souls up to Holiest of Holiests. Henri resolved to approach Father Fred for an explanation of both Psalm 121 and 91.

The service continued with '*Our God, Our Help in Ages Past, Our Hope for Years to Come*'. This was followed by the first Scripture Reading taken from Proverbs, Chapter 10, Verse 11 to 20.

At the conclusion of the First Scripture Reading the next song selected was '*Dear Lord and Father of Mankind, Forgive our Foolish Ways*'. This was followed by the Sermon. The text of the Sermon was taken from Acts Chapter 4, verse 10: '*Be it known unto you all, and to all the people of Israel, that by the name of Jesus Christ of Nazareth ... whom God raised from the dead even by his death this man stand before you able*'.

After the District Superintendent uttered these words, he gave a very brief account of Aaron's background, his age and where he trained for the priesthood. His Lordship, Father Jensen gave a detailed account of the resurrection and stressed that Christ's defeat of death signified the basis of the Christian hope.

"Our hope as Christians is made strong by the fact that Christ died for our sins. He is and always will be our Redeemer. Christ's victory over death is important not only because it has shown that God has power to work miracles but all of us have the assurance that if we do what is right we can achieve everlasting life after we leave our physical state."

Some six things which he called pillars of the Christian doctrine were: faith; charity, forgiveness, humility, hard work and empathy. He then spoke of the importance of Evangelism and Missionary Zeal.

The Installation came next and ended with a promise by Aaron to be a serious shepherd of his flock. Then came the Songs: '*Fight the Good Fight with all thy Might*' and '*Immortal, Invisible, God Only Wise*'.

At the conclusion of the service, while the church council took their new priest and introduced him to those persons who remained after the end of the Installation, Patrice, a devotee who never missed a service at this church and was the leader of the church council, waited outside hoping to have word with the Vicar Plenipotentiary, Rev. Allen, Aaron and the Superintendent His Lordship Rev. Jensen.

"Good Evening," Patrice greeted the three. "I am the President of the church council here at St. Gabriel's, the Greater. I am Patrice and have always been a member of the Church. My church council always respects our clergy and I am sure that its members would have wanted to meet our new priest."

Patrice then ushered them back into the church building and just as he said all the members of the church council were waiting. Patrice introduced the Superintendent and the Vicar Plenipotentiary first, then Aaron and all of the members of the church council to each other. He briefly gave an account of the state of affairs of the church with some detail of the number of active members, the normal times of church services and promised to check the bank for the present bank balance. Then the Superintendent invited Patrice to say a prayer for Aaron's ministry.

"Dear Heavenly Father, we assemble here today to give you thanks for what you have done for each and every one of us. Visit us with your forgiveness and power. Bless the Ministry of our new Priest Father Aaron. Guide and guard him. Cloak him with the vestments of humility, pride and hard work. May his work reflect your goodness. Uphold and defend our Superintendent and Vicar Plenipotentiary that they may provide leadership to this, our circuit and diocese. Let them and Father Aaron engender in our worshippers peace, purity and prosperity. Protect us all for the ravages of sin and bring us to enjoy your everlasting glory. We ask these things in no other name but that of our Lord and Saviour, Jesus Christ. Amen."

A remarkable sincerity accompanied the words of Patrice's prayer. It was neither a strong prayer nor one designed to prove that Patrice was foremost among the lay readers at the church.

There were still some persons who had come to the ordination, assembled outside in the church yard in small groups of threes and fours. Inside the Superintendent was talking of the sacrifice a few Caribbean young men were making in opting to work as priests in the church instead of pursuing secular careers. He suggested that Aaron could have, based on his upbringing and education, chosen to be a teacher, accountant, engineer, doctor or lawyer. The Superintendent said that young men in Aaron's position would have had options.

"It is encouraging to notice that our new Priest, Reverend Aaron has turned his back on lucrative careers to follow this vocation which we call the priesthood. You know nowadays youngsters do have more opportunities and with them choices, than in generations of old. In the past ten to fifteen years, there have been improvements in our society. More institutions of learning are available to our people here. The stereotype of the Helenite as a poor illiterate or semiliterate afflicted by ignorance and absolute poverty is undergoing change. Our people are beginning to look up and go forward....."

"And in the midst of it all," the Vicar Plenipotentiary interrupted, "Our people still have time for God."

Aaron sat quietly, listening. In his mind his appointment as the Priest for St. Gabriel's the Greater was one which conferred authority on him. He thought very quickly to himself that authority does always carry some power. The Vicar Plenipotentiary continued.

"Godliness among a people must never give way to greed, lust, envy, false pride, resentment and revenge nor unbridled secularism. Our church and everyone of its members must set a shining example in the community. All our church members must work with people of like mind to promote the spiritual and other welfare of all our communities. Our church must endorse and support worthwhile causes, causes like education and edification, causes that extol goodness and reject evil."

Patrice, comforted, indeed encouraged by the words of

these two denominational leaders observed:

"Things are getting better. Years ago when I first joined this church as a teenager many people did not attend church because they feared that they did not have appropriate clothes to wear to church. There were those too poor to purchase good garments. They sent their children to school barefooted, some of them. I find that some did go to school barefooted but dared not come to this church with their feet exposed. In our church much still has to be done to get more young people come out to our service."

He paused for some moments. Then he continued:

"Our Church Army and Mothers' Union have done outstanding work in bringing in many new members. They have not only gone into persons' houses canvassing and persuading them to join us, they have also permitted some community groups to use our church hall to hold meetings for worthwhile causes."

Then the Superintendent, turning to Aaron, said:

"As a priest, you have to have the interest of your congregation at heart. I am sure that you know the biblical story of the Good Shepherd. You are like a shepherd and your congregation are like sheep."

The members of the Church Council were very attentive.

"When I say that the members of your congregation are like sheep, I do not mean that they are meek and foolish. What I mean is that they are under your tutelage. They are under your care. You start from now by making a decision always to respect and honour them. Do not ever manipulate them. They will find out and it will cost you dearly. Respect them. Do your best that you practice Christian charity and go the extra mile to be supportive of them.

Be prepared to work long hours. The way of life of Helenites is based on trust and respect for God, hard work and community-mindedness. Our people are known to respect authority. Side with every good institution in the community. Good old-time but enduring values have brought Helen Isle far. Ensure that you are seen as the embodiment of these values. In every situation, pray. You can consider a Ministry of counselling and praying for the sick and the infirm.

Even when your own humanity asserts itself, remember the words of the Lord's Prayer, '...*And lead us not into temptation*'. This message was reaffirmed by the Vicar Plenipotentiary with approval from the church council.

"We have to end the meeting now," declared the Superintendent. "I shall do the closing prayer. Father Divine, the Giver of all Goodness, after our Ordination Service we have just ended a short meeting partly to familiarize your servant Father Aaron about what his Ministry entails. Render perfect health and strength to him. Lead him into the paths of righteousness. Bless and enrich his Ministry. In moments when he feels discouraged, energize and inspire him. May those under his charge be guided and may they come to see you as God of all mercy, health and wealth.

Look down on all of us, especially Father Aaron and may his Ministry here at St. Gabriel's the Greater be a beacon for his congregation and for all other priests of our faith. We thank you Father for the opportunity to worship and we do so in godliness and gratitude. Amen."

As those assembled made their way home, Aaron wondered: 'If his church members were like sheep and he their shepherd, what description could be given to Father Jensen and Vicar Allen'?

Chapter 12

HESTER AND DRUGS

PERSONS WHO WERE WIDELY RESPECTED and who could be trusted provided her with their suspicions. She had been noting that things were gradually disappearing from her house. Isabel knew she could trust Ismay, Merle and Theresa. She now knew that she had to abandon her tact and softness and deal with the problem.

Her parents had sent back Hester for her own good and had so trusted Isabel that deep down inside, Isabel thought that she would be failing in her duties if she did not take the bull by the horns. What did hurt her was that she had tried her best to nurture Hester in a proper way and that Hester had been lying to her and deceiving her all along while stealing from her.

If there was any comfort for Isabel it was the fact that her friends cared enough to warn her of Hester's conduct, and secondly, all who knew about the devious path which was being pursued by her granddaughter, promised Isabel their fullest support. Among persons like Stella, Ismay, Merle and Theresa there was a full understanding that Hester's ways were not to be blamed on Isabel, and indeed it was Merle who suggested to Isabel to seek help for Hester.

Isabel could not make up her own mind as to if she had spoilt Hester or if she had proved too weak for her granddaughter. But she worked out somehow that those three girls about whom Hester constantly talked and with whom Hester went around were part of the problem and would have known what she was up to.

'Could it be that the parties Hester went to were responsible for her behaviour and decline?' Isabel thought to herself.

Theresa had notified Isabel more than three times that she had seen Hester in bars drinking stouts and smoking. Stella, who took a hard line against waywardness in young people, had advised Isabel that Hester smoked substances other than tobacco. Stella also told Isabel of her suspicions that Hester frequented the few drug holes in the area and was repeatedly seen in male company, of whom some were known drug-pushers. Merle had seen Hester on many occasions out and about in garments other than her school uniform at times when she was supposed to be in school.

Neither Theresa, Stella nor Merle, all of whom were in the same age group as Isabel, had been known to be given to telling lies and would certainly have had no motive for uttering untrue statements about Hester. What Isabel bore foremost in her mind was that each of her three friends came to her individually and on separate occasions and confided in her, and that they had not discussed what they knew of Hester with anyone else. Isabel knew she had to do something and pondered on how Theresa had said that one or two visits to doctors or psychiatrists would probably not solve the problem. So Isabel decided to discuss the matter with Theresa before confronting Hester.

Meanwhile, Hester had sensed that Isabel's attitude to her was changing. Hester's way of dealing with matters was to do more housework, including cleaning and cooking, but once or twice her grandmother had hinted that Hester's work was not now as good as it was before. Isabel had resumed talking about things like the fact that females should respect themselves, that young girls should avoid sex, and about bad company.

Up to now Isabel was yet to give Hester any kind of 'telling off', although it was obvious to Hester that the grandmother was impatient more now than she had ever been. Having heard some of her classmates recount instances of punishment and severe floggings from their parents, Hester often remarked to herself that never once did Isabel so much as lift a finger to hit her. Hester had no clear proof either that Isabel was aware of the details of her conduct, though concern had been expressed by Isabel that Hester could do better as far as her work at school was concerned.

Isabel waited until Hester had left for school to go in search of Theresa. While she was on her way to Theresa's house, Isabel, who had known nothing about drug abuse nor addiction, did look forward to any help which Theresa could provide. Theresa, like Ismay, had a reputation of always being well-informed. She reached Theresa's place after walking up hill for about half-an-hour.

"Glad to see you," Theresa said invitingly in response to Isabel's loud knock on the front door.

"Come in," she said as she opened up the door for her friend. "Have a seat while I fix some juice for you."

"Don't bother with the juice, I still feel a little full," said Isabel. And she continued:

"Theresa, I have come to you for help. I believe that the things you and others have told me about Hester are true. I feel that Hester is drinking strong drink and using illegal drugs. I believe that she still has much of her health but I want help for her to come off the alcohol and the drugs!"

"Isabel if you take Hester to an ordinary medical person —a physician or even a psychiatrist I do not think you will get results that will last a long time. A physician will probably tell you that there is nothing physically wrong. A psychiatrist will tell you the same thing and if the psychiatrist asks Hester very many questions, she would pick up where he is coming from and lie to him or trick him. Like a few people who live around here I feel that a person who is addicted to drugs or strong drink needs long-term support, especially by working with persons who have a determination to stay free of all addictive substances, both the legal ones and the illegal drugs and substances.

Medical care and advice can help if the victim of substance abuse is so physically and medically sick as to need a doctor. But if a person is well enough to take advice, counselling and support, and really wants to give up the substances, then as long as they are ready for help, they can recover. But they must want help for themselves and not because somebody thinks that they need help.

For example, your granddaughter must want to stop, not to please you, but because she understands that quitting is good for her and that drugs, including alcohol and tobacco are bad for her!"

Isabel was listening very carefully. Although clearly she did not know where her friend Theresa got her knowledge from, the latter was clearly pleased to render advice on how to begin giving up drugs.

"Isabel, I am no expert, but there is a good man, a priest called Father Fred who is very, very knowledgeable in these matters." Theresa said humbly, yet confidently. "If your granddaughter really wants to do something about her problems, I feel that Father Fred who has had some success should be able to help."

"Would it cost anything?" a curious Isabel asked.

"No nothing at all. Father Fred is no materialist at all. He loves working with people."

"Thanks, Theresa, I'll send Hester to Father Fred."

"Make sure that Hester sees Father Fred privately but you can before her first meeting with him tell him everything you have heard so that he will have some idea of the problem."

On her way home Isabel experienced many thoughts, chief among which was whether or not she herself had done anything to contribute to her granddaughter's behaviour. Then she remembered cases of adults complaining that some children do go astray even when their parents and grandparents would have done so much good for them. If only Hester could realize that she was playing with fire. If she could realize that it was not too late to find help and change her ways. If only she could behave like a real school student rather than a 'forced-ripe' woman. In the midst of these thoughts Isabel murmured to herself that what she really could not understand was how Hester was really very intelligent, already could speak English very, very, well and should have had no reason to be carrying on in the way she was. It was also very, very wicked of Hester, Isabel thought, to be constantly deceiving her, playing truant and being seen in very, very bad company.

Isabel was firmly resolved. When Hester returned home later she was going to confront her granddaughter as she had never, never done before.

Later that day Isabel heard a very loud knock on her front door around 5.30 p.m. Without asking who it was she went to the door to see who it was. Hester greeted her, eyes staring wildly and reeking of alcohol and other curious odours. Isabel saw something like blood on her granddaughter's right cheek.

"What is wrong with you?" Isabel demanded.

"Let me get into my bed. I don't feel right," Hester snarled as she rushed into her bedroom.

Isabel attempted to follow her. Then she stopped. She took one look at the teenager sprawled across the bed. Isabel realized that Hester had come home in clothes she could not identify. Hester had brought nothing with her. Where are her school uniform and book bag? Too drugged and drunk to say anything, Hester was fast asleep.

"Surely I have not been raising her to be like that!" Isabel declared to herself. "How did she get home? Did she go to school at all? Did the change of clothes occur after school had closed or before. Where is Hester's uniform? And the bag in which she carried her books and school things?"

Then Isabel soon recalled that Hester had knocked the door to call her attention.

"Where are the keys which I had given her to enter my house?"

Rage, fear, disappointment, hurt and pain descended on Isabel. She reached for a glass of water. She sat at her kitchen table. She thought something must surely be done soon. She had heard rumours and stories. Some circumstances like missing items pointed to the problem. But now she saw for herself first hand.

Somehow Isabel did manage four hours sleep that night.

The next morning as soon as Isabel heard movement in Hester's room, she barged into it.

"Now let me tell you something. You are doing very, very badly. Many good people tell me that you are in drugs, in hustling and probably prostitution. If I had taken a picture of you yesterday you yourself would wonder who it was. Where is your key? I gave you a key for this house and yet I had to open the front door for you as you came in here yesterday evening stoned drunk and totally dishevelled. You have been keeping bad company. Many days you have been playing truant. Your lifestyle is that of a disgraceful, wild wretch."

Hester, never having seen her grandmother behave like this was going to rush an excuse but decided against it.

"You, Hester, have deceived me. You are a liar. You are a rum-biber and drug abuser. Look at me. I have decided to send you to counselling."

Still unaware of why Hester was sent back to Helen Isle, Isabel continued:

"Your parents sent you to me for you to get a good Christian upbringing at the hands of a loving, caring grandmother in a friendly and warm community. You would never, never know how badly you have let me down."

Rather than reply for fear of being thought to be rude and apprehending that if she did not cooperate Isabel would put her out on the streets, Hester decided to wait until Isabel's ire subsided. Isabel paused thoughtfully for a while. Hester said nothing but appeared to be gazing up towards the roof of her modest bedroom.

"Look you hear me, I am sending you to counselling."

"What is counselling?"

"You mean you do not know what is counselling? I believe you know what is counselling in the same way that you know what a truant is. Now you tell me what you think a counsellor is?" Isabel demanded.

"A counsellor would have to be somebody who counsels," offered Hester.

"Listen you know you can do better. Stop being womanish. There is only one woman in this house. Your body is big. But you are still a girl. Answer me properly."

"A counsellor gives advice."

"Yes, and I am sending you to be counselled. You have to change. I am sending you to Father Fred for him to help and advise you!"

THEY REACHED Father Fred's modest manse.

"You wait outside, Madam. Let your young lady read one of the brochures or magazines on the short table next to you and give me a few minutes."

Then Father Fred came into the waiting room and ushered Hester into his study.

"Tell me about your peers."

Pretending that she did not understand this word and intent on protecting the identity and behaviour of persons like Tara, Hazeen and Astra, Hester replied,

"I have four pairs sent to me from England by my mother. Their colours are....."

Before she could finish the description and fully aware of the pranks that person in denial were wont to practice, Father Fred interrupted:

"I am not speaking of shoes, nor avocadoes, let me hear about the friends and company you keep."

Hester was in no mood for cooperating and came to Father Fred only to oblige her grandmother. And she was obliging her grandmother just because Isabel's mood and rage did affect her.

"My friends are very nice people," Hester suggested.

"Have your friends ever got you to do anything?" Before Father Fred could finish Hester interrupted him saying,

"Yes, they share their lunch and toys." She was playing the girl in all this.

"Have your friends ever brought new things for you?"

"Not really," she said.

"Have your friends ever introduced you to new things?" the Priest asked.

"Not really," she said.

"Do you really know why you have come to me?"

"My grandmother has sent me to you?" she said.

"Do you know why your grandmother has brought you here?"

"Not really," said Hester.

"Should I go into the next room and bring in your grandmother for her to explain?"

"No, Sir."

"Should I suggest to you why your grandmother brought you here?"

"No, sir."

"Okay, you are leaving me with no choice but to bring in your grandmother."

"Please do not, Sir."

"Now if I am going to be of any help to you, you have to be honest with me."

"What?"

"When I say that you have to be honest with me it means letting in the truth. If I feel that you are not being truthful, I will have to call in your grandmother."

"Sir, how long am I supposed to be in this meeting?"

"Yes, for me to be helpful you have to be honest with me. If you are honest with me then you will be honest with yourself." Father Fred advised.

"Say what you want to say but please do not bring my grandmother in here, Sir."

"Let me ask you a question. Do you know what to deny means."

"Yes, Sir."

"Do you know what denial is?"

"No Sir."

"Well denial comes from to deny. There are conditions of the mind, emotions and spirit that are so serious they cause people to deny that they have problems. For example, a person is addicted to alcohol. Has to drink first thing on mornings. Has to drink when feeling hungry, angry, lonely and tired. This person gets drunk and loses control."

Before Father Fred could conclude what he was saying, Hester blurted out,

"I do not get drunk all day. It is only the other day that Grannie saw me half-high and half-drunk. I do not know what Grannie's problem is."

Now, for the first time Father Fred felt he was getting somewhere as Hester's denial struck him fully in the face since she was blaming Isabel for having a problem. Gently Father Fred said,

"Should I tell you that people with problems of alcoholism and drug addiction often say that those persons who bring their addiction to those made sick by these drugs – those persons who want to help the drinkers and druggies, are the ones with the problems. The reaction of persons addicted, to those who wish to help them is a mixed reaction of dishonesty and denial?"

"I am no alcoholic nor drunkard but I must say that of alcohol and marijuana I prefer marijuana. My friends tell me that marijuana is better than alcohol and I do like marijuana with stout."

"Pause there, young lady. No alcoholic nor drug-user likes to feel that they have a problem," Father Fred urged diplomatically.

"Now, Sir, even if I did have a problem with these things, how can I face my friends at parties if I go to them and refuse to drink or smoke or refuse to drink the stout? What would my friends think of me?" She asked him.

Feeling that Hester was now showing some kind of courage and that she had forgotten his question of what her friends had introduced to her, Father Fred thought that she was still confused about the issues at hand. He asked her:

"Do you think that you must do as your friends do? Have you forgotten that at the start of this session I asked you about your friends?"

Thinking that she had let herself down by providing too much information to the priest, Hester decided that she would have to be more careful and that she could not risk to expose herself more.

"Sir, my friends are my friends. I get fun from being with my friends and doing things with them," Hester said softly but boldly.

"Do you think real friends would give you alcohol and dope?" Father Fred asked.

"What my friends and I do give us happiness!" she declared.

"You tell me drinking and drugging give you happiness?" he asked.

"I am telling you that I get fun from dealing with my friends."

"Can I take it that you drink and drug because of your friends?"

"No, Sir."

"Hester, can I provide you with insights as to how drinking and drugs affect teenagers and young people?"

"No, Sir."

"Anyway, Hester, although you are definitely resisting the help I want to give you, let me say that using drugs destroys people. Getting involved in selling drugs could lead to unpleasantness, pain, jail and even death. You should not be drinking strong drink nor using marijuana. By the way how old are you?"

"Seventeen," lied Hester, as she stood up making to leave the room.

"Hester remember that very often when we feel we are fooling or tricking others, we are actually deceiving ourselves."

"Bye, Sir."

She left his study and went outside to her grandmother. As Isabel and Hester left the manse, Isabel, not sure how to speak with her granddaughter decided to play it safe.

"How was it, Hester?"

At first it crossed Hester's mind to say something derogatory and even scandalous about the priest but she decided not to be too risky.

"Not so well, I guess." Hester commenced.

"Did you like the counselling?"

"Grannie I feel that counselling will work for me if I can choose my own counsellor from among my people!"

"Do you want another counsellor?"

"Yes, Grannie."

"So how did today's counselling go?"

"He attacked me."

"Did he really attack you, Hester?"

"He did not beat me but his questions were like an attack. The things he said hurt."

Isabel, innocent as ever and inexperienced in the ways of deceivers and persons in denial, did not even think of that popular saying, "the truth hurts." Nor did Isabel attempt, by questioning, to find out why Hester felt attacked. She asked:

"Do you want to try another counsellor?"

"Yes, Grandma."

With proper advice or with sound intuition, Isabel would have contacted Father Fred to ascertain what really had transpired. However, she allowed Hester the liberty of searching around for a counsellor.

"Grandma, I feel that I can find a counsellor who suits me."

Some days passed without either any confrontation between grandmother and granddaughter and Hester did appear tranquil and even hardworking, both with household chores and school homework. During this time Isabel heard nothing more about her granddaughter's waywardness and had not seen Merle nor Theresa. Tara, Hazeen and Hester's friends did not appear at Isabel's house but Isabel still felt that Hester's circumstances warranted positive intervention.

Realizing that Isabel had gone quiet, Hester decided not to irritate her grandmother nor arouse her suspicions. But one Saturday afternoon while Hester was in her books, Isabel came to her with the question of whether Hester had decided on a different counsellor. Being counseled was far from Hester's mind but rather than assure her grandmother that all was well – and from all appearances all was well, Hester promised to do her best to be good while thinking about her next counsellor.

Then about eight weeks after her encounter with Father Fred just as she returned home around 4.30 p.m., Hester, in up-beat mood, announced to her expectant grandmother:

"Grandma, near here are two very nice people known to many as elders, and they are called Mr. Zaccky and Miss Sarah. They have a young son who is the priest at St. Gabriel's, the Greater. If you still want me to go to counselling you can arrange for me to see him."

Chapter 13

DEBATE ON HOMOSEXUALITY

THE DEBATE WAS HEATING UP. This small Catholic nation had not for years experienced so much dissension. Argument followed argument. It had happened that a person of considerable influence in Helen Isle had introduced the idea that abortion, prostitution and homosexuality should be legalized. There were those in Helen Isle who were prepared to treat <u>all</u> three as being morally evil.

Interestingly, during the debate many persons, especially Catholics, isolated abortion as a separate matter so that in many places while there was no talk of prostitution and homosexuality, abortion was the topic of the day. The Anti-Abortion lobby was vocal, using the Catholic Church's known opposition to abortion as their chief attack against "the killing of innocent children." Neighbouring Bimshire had more than a decade earlier legalized abortion but strangely the debate in Helen Isle on Prostitution and Homosexuality raged simultaneously with the controversy in Bimshire over whether or not prostitution and homosexuality should be legalized. It appeared to have transpired in Bimshire that some noted and influential person had suggested that in the efforts to curb the spread of HIV/AIDS, the taboo against prostitution and homosexuality should be lifted by legalising these practices.

In Helen Isle, the issue of abortion was dividing the political class. The Catholic Church was consistent and firm in denouncing abortion. Prostitution, too, had its strong opponents while as far as homosexuality was concerned, there were Helenites as vocal in condemning homosexuals as Jamaicans would.

In the streets, the schools and in the churches these hot issues took centre stage. One journalist, trying his best to be detached, invited Helenites to treat the three as separate issues and to look at the good and bad in each before passing judgment. Naturally, these issues came to the attention of the 200 member congregation at St. Gabriel's the Greater.

Meanwhile in Bimshire, just as the debate on minimizing the effect of HIV/AIDS by way of legalizing prostitution and homosexuality appeared to be dissipating, the word came to Helen Isle about the declaration of the leader of an interest group about his institution's attitude to homosexuality. Ismay, who had read about it, inquired of Henri if he had heard what had just happened in Bimshire.

"Henri, over here in our country we have been having all types of arguments about abortion and homosexuality. I feel that our Government here in Helen Isle will definitely legalise abortion. But I have just learnt that the president of Sperm in Barbados has added his voice to the debate."

"Ismay what on earth is Sperm? And who is its president?"

"Listen, Henri, in Bimshire Sperm is the short form of Society for the Promotion of Equal Rights for Men and its president, from newspaper reports, is an educationist and scholar called Boyse." Ismay advised.

"What?" Henri pressed quizzically.

"Yes, the Society for the Promotion of Equal Rights for Men, declared Ismay. "It seems to me that this is a group that is seeking to put men in Bimshire back in their places," Ismay surmised.

Henri thought for a while, then asked,

"Why would a Caribbean country need a group to promote equality for men. After all in Helen Isle it was the situation that many women depended on men. That in the church, in schools, in medicine and certainly in Government and politics, men were still in charge although in the 1990's it was clear that females were catching up, were setting goals and were achieving in a spectacular way."

"Henri," Ismay scolded, "listen, though highly moral issues have been on the front burner, recently there has been discussion from the Bahamas to Guyana, from Trinidad and Tobago to Jamaica about something called Male Underachievement and Male Marginalization. My feeling is that in Bimshire there are concerns that men have been slipping back, women and girls have been advancing and Sperm has set out to put the males of Bimshire firmly back within the fold of humanity."

"But Ismay," Henri continued, "you and I ourselves are slipping. We are now chatting about male marginalization and the progress being made by women. By the way, is it really that women are taking from men? Is it a clear case where women are moving ahead at the expense of men? Can it be true that if two women press on, two men retire out of sight? Yet I must ask you, my friend, whether our little chat here really started out about conflict between the sexes or about Sperm and homosexuality?"

Ismay started to giggle. "Henri, Sperm and homosexuality?"

"Garçon," Ismay continued, "We may appear to be straying. Yet we are not. The reason why we are not straying nor slipping, is that despite years of being second to you men, we proud West Indian females are now using education and our inbred intuition coupled with brute determination to achieve. Time was in this wicked world when we women were kept either in the kitchen or the kitchen garden, seen only by you men as objects and play things to be bedded by you."

"Ismay," Henri protested,

"You are getting beside yourself. You have been my friend and neighbour and partner in Theresa's sou sou for years and I have never seen such fire in you. Are you a suffragette? Are you a feminist?"

Despite their warm friendship and the respect they had one

for another, Ismay realized that she had come to a moment of triumph, that Henri was clearly forced on the backfoot, and temporarily oblivious of what she had originally intended telling Henri, she continued.

"Henri here in Helen Isle for generations those big rich banana farmers and operators of our copra industry preferred to hire men as workers, arguing that men were naturally stronger than us, women. For years we women could not find decent work. After World War II for about fifty-five years female unemployment here in this island was too high. Women had to get men to support them even when many men were less than men and provided only token support. Many men did not maintain their children. Indeed many men did not even own their children. When women tried to assert themselves, they were abused. Henri, you know the beatings that our Helenite women have suffered at the hands of you, men!"

Hit hard by 'you men' and already on the defensive, Henri grinned innocently. His emotions now kindled, Henri's next issue was how to stop Ismay, then how to control the wrath which was inflaming his mind and of course how to get Ismay back to homosexuality, Boyse and the Society for the Promotion of Equal Rights for Men. He held up his right hand inviting Ismay to pause but she was unrelenting.

"Yes, garçon, for years and years my mother, her mother, your mother, your grandmother toiled in the kitchen, toiled in the house, worked the land—when allowed—raised our children, backed our men and up to now most of the women of Helen Isle who have gone back to their Maker, went back almost naked and penniless! But times are changing. Our women are licking illiteracy. Our women are licking ignorance. Our women are licking injustice."

Henri's impatience and anger started to ease and without uttering one word he felt a mischievous facetiousness as he carefully noted how Ismay was ranting and raving about 'Women licking'. His silence in the face of what he could only consider a chauvinist attack continued and Ismay, uncertain as to whether he was ignoring her or was licked into reticence, blurted out

"Henri, garçon, are you hearing me?"

"Yes, Ismay," Henri conceded meekly.

"Can you agree with anything I have said?"

"Let us get back to our original topic about Boyse's attack on homosexuality," Henry urged.

Ismay proclaimed, "We will get back there in my time." Cleverly, Ismay, reputed in her village to be cautious and very conservative, realized that she held the upper hand. No real feminist, Ismay started to feel both for Henri and a number of male citizens of Helen Isle whom she had known.

"Okay, Ismay," Henri pined, "if there is more you must tell me, carry on."

Henri, a nephew of Merle, had been socialized into avoiding arguments if he could, but socialized more with respecting his elders. After all, Ismay was old enough to be his mother.

"Yes, garçon, Ismay continued. "I really felt that I had to advise you of the problems women in our Island have faced. My only concern is that among the many newly achieving young women, many seem to be haters of men and many young bright women seem to be attracted not to men, even good men, but to other women!"

Henri, feeling somewhat relieved, asked:

"You mean to say Ismay that in our midst there is female homosexuality?"

Ismay paused thoughtfully. "Yes, unfortunately, there are women here liking women."

Henri interjected, "so if women love women that too is homosexuality!"

"Yes," Ismay admitted.

"You know, Ismay, in Jamaica, society takes a very dim view of male homosexuality," Henri observed.

"If we go back to the story of Adam and Eve, Henri," Ismay counselled, "it is very clear that as far as relationships are concerned, proper unions are those between members of the opposite sex."

Henri was a little puzzled that Ismay used the word unions, but he did not ask her why she chose 'unions' rather than 'marriages'. Then he said that it was his opinion that in early times there was little or no homosexuality in Helen Isle and suggested that it was his belief that such a practice came in from overseas. On this there was clear agreement between Ismay and him.

"You see, Henri," Ismay resumed. "In my time as a young child, you had to go to Sunday School and church. You often did not understand everything they taught you, but even at an early age I came to believe that the church was teaching the difference between right and wrong and was trying to make us do that which is right."

"I agree, Ismay," Henri concurred. "In my own life my parents, like yours, believed that the home and church and school could make all of us good."

"We learnt that there is always punishment for wrong-doing and that everyone should avoid evil,: Ismay observed.

"Ismay, I sometimes think about right and wrong. I see some people practising bad behaviour but I wonder when this thing called homosexuality really started and how long ago," Henri wondered.

"Garçon, have you heard about Sodom and Gomorrah?" Ismay asked.

"In a world where to me it should be natural for all people to be attracted to members of the opposite sex, I just do not understand why some men are attracted to men and some women to women. I have heard a few views in favour of homosexuality but I do not understand them," Henri declared.

"What confuses me," Ismay said, "is that very many talented people are openly homosexual, calling themselves gay."

"There is a fellow called James, two years older than me,"

Henri noted, "and James said he once interviewed an artist called Whistler who said that many artistic people are so highly sensitive as to admire and revere their own sex seeing beauty in their own sex."

"I once heard that persons who were badly abused when they were very young, that is, abused by a member of the opposite sex would be tempted to reject the opposite sex and cling to their own," Ismay remarked.

"In some societies, some people treat homosexuality as a serious curse and feel that homosexuals should be alienated and ostracized," Henri said to Ismay.

"It is clear that that is so to many, I feel that Boyse from Bimshire is one of those old time moralists whose idea is that homosexuals should be avoided," Ismay remarked. Then she continued:

"A friend of mine brought a newspaper article to me that seemed to be saying that to attack homosexuals was wrong. That they are firstly human beings and should be treated so."

"Is that how you feel too, Ismay?" Henri inquired.

"Brought up the way I have been, I do have a difficulty encouraging homosexuality," Ismay pronounced.

"What I find most distressing is the talk I hear at street corners that very many young girls in many parts of the Caribbean are allowing men to perform anal sex on them as though that too is not homosexuality," Henri lamented.

"The article I read from Europe gave the clear impression that if someone condemns homosexuals, such a person is narrow-minded, but if we accept them and see them as having equal rights to the rest of the community, then we are broad minded, that article suggested" Ismay continued.

"Clearly I am very narrow-minded and if I am that narrow-minded then there must be many, many more narrow-minded people. What did Boyse from Bimshire say about homosexuals?"

"Boyse is the leader of a group of men who feel that male homosexuals do not qualify to be called men and should be left to themselves," Ismay advised.

"Our Island has no reputation as a place of comfort for such persons, but Ismay, I remember that you said that as many women progressed and achieve, some of them turned to other women for affection. Do you think that this is a serious problem? Of male homosexuality and female homosexuality, which one is more noticeable here in Helen Isle?" Henri asked Ismay.

"Because so many people condemn homosexuality I feel that the few who practice it, do so secretly."

"All except Muscle Martha. Now if homosexuals are talented, artistic and sensitive, I wonder how Muscle Martha could qualify," Henri asked doubtfully.

"Firstly I doubt whether Muscle Martha is really a born Helenite. Then even though in the day he goes around with women bragging about how well he can cook, bake and do pastries, I see no real talent in him and his behaviour is so common that he does not seem to be one who was abused by a woman when he was a young child."

Once again, Ismay seemed to be in the mood for attack.

"No one knows Muscle Martha's mother or father. No one knows if Muscle Martha went to school. No one can prove that he can bake, cook or keep a house. All we know is that he acts like a woman, dresses like a woman and hangs around red-light districts," Ismay narrated.

"Hi, Ismay, do you think that Muscle Martha sells his body? For if he does he would be both a homosexual and a prostitute?" Henri questioned.

"Muscle Martha is so slack he leaves you to wonder if he ever went to Sunday School or to church," Ismay noted.

"It is certainly people like Muscle Martha that Boyse would exclude from the society of men. His wayward, common conduct is such that I can see no good in him. I hope he does not bring his evil talk to me nor to anyone I know," Henri said.

"But Ismay, I think that the troubling part of all of this

is that in metropolitan Europe, the feeling seems to be that homosexuals should be embraced. That is because many Europeans think that homosexuals have the same human rights as the rest of society. But remember that there are European countries that have made prostitution and homosexuality legal. Would we here in Helen Isle ever come to see actions that have for years been seen as immoral and bad made into legally accepted behaviours?" Henri asked Ismay.

"I certainly would not be embracing any homosexuals," Ismay noted rather self-righteously. "My grandmother and great aunt would turn in their graves if they learned that I accepted homosexuals in my life. I also oppose prostitution, but I cannot make up my mind on the matter of abortion," Ismay observed.

"In an Island where there has been poverty and want I believe that we have survived by clinging to our old moral standards, our traditional values and of course the Grace of God," Henri concluded.

"Yes, Henri, if we find that certain standards have worked for us, our families, schools and the church have kept us going, then we should not move away from those practices and beliefs that have served us well. But I have to go to town and I hope to see you soon," Ismay said as she took leave of Henri.

On her way to town she thought to herself that whatever Europeans thought, the people of Helen Isle should be slow to take up behaviours which could eventually lead to licence and permissiveness.

Chapter 14

A COOPERATIVE COULD EVOLVE

"MAMA, I WANT TO TALK WITH YOU about a very important matter."

Theresa was always in the habit of listening to her children. One of the things that stood out about her was that unlike many of her peers she did not believe that children should be seen and not heard. As soon as she finished milking her cow she sat down in the modest living room of her two bedroom house.

"Come, son, come, Jerome," she invited.

"Mama, as you know I went to Bimshire on winning that trip. One evening I went to a lecture on Cooperatives. Many ordinary people were at the lecture. The speaker, a man called Boyse who was a teacher in many Caribbean Islands started to talk about the Rochedale Pioneers who, in order to beat poverty, came together and pooled resources for their benefit in order to tackle poverty.

From what I heard the first thing about Cooperatives is that they teach their members thrift and how to manage money. But they also preach brotherhood, mutual support, empathy, open membership and how to unite and work together to realize their dreams. I heard that there could be Farmers' Cooperatives, Carpenters' Cooperatives, Fishermens' Cooperatives and very important ones called Financial Cooperatives. Mama, I used the opportunity to ask questions while I was at the lecture," Jerome informed his mother.

"Tell me about the Financial and Fishermens'

Cooperatives," Theresa inquired.

Theresa's successful sou sou had made her a kind of working class financial wizard, if such a term could be used. But in an Island in which the fishing community often suffered setbacks and losses, she had always hoped that there could be some organization that would bring together the island's fishermen. She felt that fishermen in the whole of Helen Isle needed leadership, guidance and unity.

"Mama, I worked out that to form a fisherman's Cooperative first there must be rules that would allow fishermen to be members. Then either weekly or monthly, after forming a Committee of Management and a Committee of Supervisors and after people have joined up by paying their membership fees, they could open savings accounts and save every month or week and buy materials for their boats, buy equipment..."

Thrilled at what she was hearing, Theresa asked:

"You mean that our fishermen could form their own club and put up money together, unite and buy what they want all together?"

It took no time for Theresa to work out that if two or three hundred fishermen could be made to save and buy resources in bulk, they could achieve cheaper tackle, gear and resources while saving. Theresa was now all ears.

"The fishermen could put aside money for training, and from among their own membership they could set up a marketing department. They could even buy insurance as a Cooperative." Jerome continued. "If only they could unite, practise mutual respect and rely on each other as a group."

Theresa was thinking. She had seen many individuals both as fishermen and farmers try to operate on their own, only to fail. Then her mind turned on the reputations of three fishermen, Harry, Slater and Fausten, considered the three best fishermen close to her village, how the three were inseparable, walked together, fished together and had stronger boats.

"Mama I got information on Financial Cooperatives. These are savings and lending societies. Members have to agree to save regularly. After enough savings go into a pool for between two years and three years and some of the money is held as a type of special reserve, the rest is lent to members only at a very small rate of interest. Mama your experience in holding other people's money for the benefit of the group should help you understand such a business. The main aim of a financial cooperative is to improve the welfare of its members. The important thing is that members save regularly and borrow only when they have to. Sessions must be kept regularly to do ongoing training, and encouraging the wise management and use of money while promoting cooperation and thrift.

Persons like Maude, Merle, Sarah and Zaccky who have belonged to your sou-sou would be interested, especially since they like other members of the sou-sou always believed in saving and putting money to sensible use."

Ideas, all of them fertile, were coming to Theresa rapidly. She could figure out both how to work with others to launch a financial cooperative and she was prepared to fight hard to bring the fishermen together in their own body to make them as a whole more organized and better off. Even though her mind raced with ideas, Theresa was listening to her second child, a very promising fourteen year old who was filling her with ideas that would definitely benefit many people and even entire communities in Helen Isle. Brimful of courage, overflowing faith and Christian charity, Theresa was sure that with God's help a fisherman's cooperative and a separate financial institution could be set up in the very, very near future.

She was confident that in the same way her sou-sou had succeeded that two organizations dedicated to improving the lot of neighbouring communities would come into being and in the near future at that. She reflected too on how her son had been sensitive to the importance of savings and as she pondered how clearly he had outlined the purpose of cooperatives, she remembered a short passage from the Bible which had declared: 'Out of the mouths of babes....'.

Before she could work out exactly where it had come from, there was a knock on her front door.

"Theresa, Theresa, it is me Merle."

"Yes, Miss Merle," Theresa greeted her friend from inside the house. "I am coming to open the door for you."

"How are you?" enquired Merle.

"I am as good as gold, trusting in the name of our Saviour Lord and risen King," Theresa observed.

"Theresa I have come to pay in this week's sou-sou, along with that of Zaccky."

"You have time?" Theresa asked.

"Yes, I am not busy, especially since I have no little children to look after," Merle noted.

"Look, you, Zaccky and others have for years thrown up money in my sou-sou and it has worked very well. But now I have a new idea. I am thinking of working with others to start up two new groups which if they get going, will help hundreds and assist us in overcoming poverty."

Merle, as thrifty as Theresa and good enough to be Theresa's deputy, sat down in Theresa's old rocking chair.

"Listen, Miss Merle, I want to see a bigger savings society and a Cooperative in our area. If we can join up four hundred people and encourage them to save every week, then after two or three years of honest management, we would have a pool of money out of which members can borrow money. I intend going into town to find out if the Government has any Department which will register this new club and help us with rules. If after three years four hundred people have together saved up $1,000,000, then we can decide to hold back $400,000, and lend out over half a million dollars charging small amounts of interest to borrowers. Even after people borrow, they have to be encouraged to continue saving while paying back their loans."

Merle stopped Theresa. "What you mean is that you intend forming a Credit Union," Merle advised.

"What?"

"Yes, Theresa, a society which arranges for its members to save regularly and to borrow is called a Credit Union. My nephew Andy, who has done some travelling, told me last year that in some countries there are these things, he called them financial cooperatives, in which people save and from which they borrow to buy furniture, educate their children, repair their houses, pay off debts and such like."

"So Miss Merle, you know what I was talking about"

"Yes," declared Merle. "For example, I have heard about a big one that used to be in Bimshire, called The Civic and I have heard from Andy that you find some not only in Bimshire but also in Jamaica, Trinidad and Dominica. In fact Andy told me that some exist in Canada and America too."

"Would you be interested?" asked Theresa. "Do you think we can spread this idea and interest our villagers in it? Do you think that we can also set up a society to assist our fishermen to improve the way in which they operate?"

The two sat thoughtfully. Then Merle suggested that they should go around the village, first to the women and spread the idea and after talking to the women, approach people like Henri and even Father Fred with the view of keeping a meeting to plan a start. They sat quietly pondering how to get things going. They knew that in the many ways the women folk of Helen Isle were the effective guardians of their country's morality, and were also the true and real managers of households. True, many women were locked into relationships to which men did bring money, but when it came to the prudent management of money and effective budgeting within families, it was the women who established a superiority as diligent managers of family finances.

Yet Henri and Zaccky were involved in Theresa's meeting turn and could possibly influence other men. Zaccky was one of the most respected persons in the centre and north of the island and whoever knew him respected him. Henri was seen as a youth of exceptional promise who, if he could be brought on board, could be approached to interest others. He could be used as a speaker at the first meeting(s) to explain the purposes of a Credit Union and a Cooperative. Despite his tender years Jerome could be used to spread the word about cooperatives and credit unions.

To be positively certain that Merle truly understood the aims of the organizations which they were discussing, Theresa reminded:

"Miss Merle the principles which guide cooperatives are: brotherhood or fraternity; the welfare of members; democracy and open membership; working together; thrift and honesty."

Then Theresa invited Merle to pray joining her on her knees.

"Almighty God, Heavenly Father, first forgive all our shortcomings. Help us all, our countrymen, to reject all that is selfish and impure. Use us to glorify your name and to be eager to help others. Bless our intention to do good and give us our credit union and cooperative. We ask these things in your matchless name, Amen."

Then with a tear in her eye, Theresa then told Merle:

"If this Credit Union gets going and we succeed in joining up many members I will have to stop keeping my sou sou."

Moved, indeed shaken, Merle said:

"I understand. I doubt that members will be able to save in more than one savings society." Then Merle told Theresa:

"Trust me. I am going to find Henri and Sarah and tell them about our plans."

HENRI WAS PLAYING dominoes with others under one of the few street lights in the village when Merle approached him:

"Good night, brother Henri, sorry to disturb you. But I have to talk to you right away."

Manny, who was waiting to get a hand in the domino game told Henri:

"Look, Miss Merle wants to talk to you right away."

Thinking that it must be something urgent or at least very, very important, Henri ushered Merle aside. Merle walked away from close to the domino table and Henri followed her. Standing in the dark a good sixty yards from the players, Merle held Henri by the hand. Now Henri knew it really had to be something urgent.

"Listen, Henri, you are a young man with a good understanding and many of us trust you as a leader. Theresa has asked me to speak to you. She and I have an idea. We live in a country with the sea all around it. To many of us fish is important food. But there are times when our fishermen do not get enough catches because of a number of things, including boats that are too small and old fashioned ways of fishing. A few youngsters started to fish and stopped abruptly without learning to fish skillfully.

Like me, Theresa feels that fishermen should be organized into a Fisherman's Cooperative. The purpose of this Cooperative is to improve the welfare, skill and catches of our fishermen. They have to be helped to do better. If we can arrange to have a meeting of all interested persons we can explain to them that a properly run cooperative can increase the money they earn. Some fisherfolk do not even have decent cold storage facilities and if they do not sell or give away the fish fairly shortly after they are caught, the fish spoil and they lose money so their efforts would have been in vain. The biggest obstacle as far as I can see is to bring them together and unite them and have them live and work in unity."

"Merle, I feel I can help, but can I urge you to start by calling on the women who sell fish and the women who fry and cook fish on weekends? I am man enough and aware enough to admit that were it not for our women shopping, looking for bargains, spending sensibly and saving, lots of us males of all ages would not manage."

Merle liked what she was hearing.

"I'll promise you one thing. Tomorrow I am going to

the city to the library to do some research and study of co-cooperatives."

Before Merle could say another word, Henri rushed off excitedly and disappeared in the dark. He had bidden his domino friends good night and went home. Rather than pursue Henri, Merle decided to go to Sarah's house although it was dark and getting late.

SOMEONE WAS knocking Zaccky's front door.

"Who is it?" Sarah asked.

"It's Merle."

"Bless you, Merle what brings you here at this time of the night?"

"Sarah, I want to speak to you and Zaccky!"

"Zaccky, come," ordered the wife.

Zaccky though half-asleep came out in his grey pajamas which had been made by Pytho, the village tailor. Seated comfortably in an old piece of furniture called an ottoman, husband and wife asked Merle to sit in their settee.

"Sarah and Zaccky, I have spoken to Theresa and up to a point, to Henri. The idea is that we could do a lot in the future for our fisherfolk and our wider community. We all here recognize that this state of ours, a former colony known to have been exploited by its colonial masters, has many poor people, some poor not just because they have no great means but because we do not have proper ways of helping each other. We all know how important and valuable Theresa's sou sou has been for us but that is a very, very small modest venture. To cut a long story short, we want to launch a fisherman's cooperative and some kind of large credit union." Merle concluded.

Zaccky asked her to explain what a cooperative was and how it would benefit the fishermen and Merle was able in a simple way to suggest that there is always strength in unity and that the idea was to bring them together along with the fish vendors and other interested parties to pool their resources and work together. Sarah was listening intently. Always proud of their two children who were now young adults, Sarah suggested that Cindy and Aaron, both of whom she indicated were quite educated, could be used to mobilize and educate.

"In all this, I strongly feel that education and training will be necessary," Zaccky pronounced. "To date our fishermen – I do not mean to be unkind – are known to see themselves as small and unfortunate. Many can fish well but most do not see themselves as business people and they limit themselves. They need to be lifted up and kept in unity."

Merle was grateful for this observation and did say that many Helenites need to be helped to think better of themselves. After all, most were hardworking, she thought, and all hardworking people should be properly rewarded and rewards would definitely come if many could lean on each other in unity as they set out to reach their goals and achieve their common aims.

"I feel strongly that Henri has a role in this. I also feel that those women who have both sold raw fish and fried fish do have a role. It seems to me that as far as finances go, the vendors actually do better than those who capture the fish from the sea." Merle said with an air of confident judgment. Then Sarah asked,

"What is a credit union? It sounds like a group which is a borrowing group. How would they be able to borrow?" Merle was happy at hearing this question. Her only current regret was that she did not have Theresa here with her.

"Miss Sarah, from what I understand for a credit union to come about, there must first be a kind of savings club in which members invest savings, for two or three years," Merle added, "Members must make a sacrifice. They must for this period save and not borrow."

"You mean," queried Zaccky, "that for two or three years participants must save up without expecting to borrow?"

"Yes," Merle said. "This is definitely a sacrifice but in

the long run it would work. You see if at the birth of the credit union it allows borrowing before a proper pool of savings is built up, there would be certain trouble. It would go broke!"

"Okay, I understand," said Zaccky.

Then Sarah said: "The hardest part about all this is to get the people interested. Educating the masses is essential. Can you come back later so that we can recommend a committee which can bring the people together and educate them?"

"Yes," Merle replied enthusiastically.

"Henri already is interested and is checking out how credit unions work. In fact I am sure he would be also searching around for information on cooperatives so that help can be brought to the fishing community." Merle emphasized.

Just then Theresa arrived.

"My friends," Theresa greeted, as Zaccky opened the door for her and invited her to sit.

"I feel," Theresa commenced: "That our very, very good friend Merle has been providing information on the plans we have for the upliftment of our people. I have come to support what Merle would have been talking about and to invite you, Zaccky and Sarah to use you strong influence to spread the word about."

Before Theresa could finish, Sarah advised that she was interested and would work hard to get the people interested. Theresa then said:

"Among those whom I would want to see involved in passing around the word are Henri, you Zaccky and Sarah, Merle, my son Jerome, and of course I will try to have as many as possible join up. As far as the fishermen's cooperative is concerned it is my belief that Harry, Fausten and Slater must be approached to work with the fishing community to have a strong fisherman's cooperative formed.

Chapter 15

CHURCH COUNCIL

PATRICE WAS HAVING THE NIGHT OF HIS LIFE. A life-long member of St. Gabriel's the Greater and some seven years older than his parish priest, Patrice's philosophy was quite simple. Be loyal to all those in authority. He felt that if he was to be dutiful to God he had to respect authority. After all, all authority came from God. But the members of the Church Council were on the offensive.

"How could you allow something like that to happen?" asked Sister Agnes.

"I am the Chairman of our Church's Council and I authorize what the Secretary Treasurer does if it seems alright," Patrice said meekly.

"You mean you do not ask any questions at all?" asked Agnes.

The three who were backing each other were Patrice, Hensley the Secretary Treasurer and Jacques a member of the Church Council. But these three were clearly in the minority.

"I have no reason to be suspicious of anyone" replied Patrice.

"You mean you accept everything at face value?" Roger queried.

The meeting of the twelve had been going on for ninety minutes and Patrice, despite being usually the recipient of cordiality and cooperation from his brothers and sisters in the church, was finding that on this occasion nine members of the Church Council were loud and aggressive. Patrice had been a member of the Church Council for years and for the past seven years he was its Chairperson. Getting tired, Patrice started to wonder what error he had done.

"I have not been dishonest. I have not taken the Church's money."

Not satisfied with this, Stella asked him:

"Don't you think you owe us an explanation?"

Patrice grew more uncomfortable. Three people knew the truth including him and Hensley. The majority, some 75% of those present were growing angrier and angrier. Secretly, but deep down in his heart, Patrice hoped that this meeting would end, even if in chaos. The meeting was dragging with the same thing over and over again.

Then, as though Divine Providence intervened, Stella moved a motion to adjourn and all agreed. Patrice, Hensley and Jacques decided to remain behind. Unknown to them, the others agreed to meet at Stella's place. It was now 9.00 p.m.

"Patrice has never, never been dishonest," Stella started. "I am beginning to feel so bad that we attacked him like we did. But this is a serious matter. Imagine how St. Ignatius could improve their church hall and tidy up their church and our church funds are down by $30,000, the people's money, saved up for years!"

"I doubt that Patrice or any member of the church council has stolen that money," Roger noted loudly.

"Friends," Stella resumed, "I would really like to get to the bottom of the problem. Nothing like this has happened in my time in St. Gabriel's, the Greater. You, know whatever outside people may think about us Helenites, we however poor, are honest people. It is my understanding that when our people travel abroad some people call a lot of us ignorant, illiterate Helenites or 'foolish Helenites', but I object. Our people are neither ignorant nor illiterate and it is fairly difficult to find truly dishonest Helenites. Our people are great people. You know recently ganja has come around and certainly there is some dope. Dope makes people bewitched and dishonest. I fear that in these parts greed is beginning to take root too!

This disappearance of church funds? To steal from the church must be stealing from God. Oh, my goodness. I am so sorry that I have started out on Patrice. He must feel bad at how we treated him. I have known Patrice for years. Now we stand to be divided. What or who can divide us? Who is the real thief?"

They sat for a while and stared at each other. One or two stared on the floor of Stella's simple house. Then Yvonne broke the silence:

"You mean that for years our church never had any scandal. People admired our church as a church. True, a few members strayed. True there were some hypocrites. But the reputation of this church has been good. All the Priests we have had here have worked for God and have been excellent examples to follow. True our new Priest has only been here for a short time. But based on who his parents are, though they are not members of our church, quite a few who stopped attending St. Gabriel's the Greater have come back, probably because the priest is young. Our people are loyal and you must note that although his son is now our priest, Zaccky has continued attending St. Ignatius.

Loyalty, years of loyalty does not change. Though proud of Reverend Aaron, Sarah his mother, loyal to Zaccky at St. Ignatius has kept on going where she has gone to church all her life. I wonder what got into her second child to be Episcopal rather than Catholic. I note too that our Reverend Aaron does carry a lonely look yes, sometimes a lean look. He only seems happy when Patrice is with him and without being rude, some young girl or another is in his company after church. But getting back to the point. I am hurt that our church has lost so much money. What has happened?"

Trevor, another member of the church council, known to be

on the quiet side, made the point that if their problem was not solved, they would have to call on the Vicar Plenipotentiary and Superintendent of the Diocese. Trevor further stressed that the best strategy would be to select three members of the Church Council to launch an investigation and report to Father Aaron. Then Trevor back-tracked a bit and said that he was wrong to speak of involving the Vicar Plenipotentiary and the national Superintendent before reporting to Father Aaron.

Yvonne repeated with support from the other eight that it was a very serious matter that the church had lost the money and proposed that before meeting their new parish priest the whole church council should meet again the next week and asked that they end the instant meeting with a prayer which she would lead.

"Great Heavenly Father, O Divine Master whose matchless name is hallowed and most worthy, grant that any personal difficulties facing us may be removed by your power. Tonight, Heavenly Father we here are troubled by a monster of a problem, Dear God; a very hard problem for which we want to find a solution. Help us out of our problem, dear God. Visit not only this little gathering, but our whole church with your cleanliness. Forgive us our sins and steer our church and us in the right direction. We ask these things in your Divine Name, Amen!"

These nine departed to their homes, but the other three members of the church council were still on the premises of St. Gabriel's the Greater. There the three resolved to stand together and since circumstances warranted, try to make peace with the other nine members of the church council. They could not agree among themselves if they should take the majority into their confidence by spilling all. If the truth be told, the nine led by Stella held a firm position that their church's bye-laws be observed and that the very last item of expenditure be approved by the council in full. There was no finance committee and President and Secretary Treasurer did not have any discretion to even buy a sugar cake or a toffee out of church's funds without first seeking the blessing of the full church council.

Father Griffith, Aaron's predecessor, had cautioned that there could be difficulties with a rule necessitating the full involvement of the council in matters of tiny items of expenditure, emergencies and charities. How could Patrice and his side be extricated out of this scandal unless Stella's side were brought on board, cautioned and re-embraced. Would it be that Stella and her cohorts will tell the congregation by having emissaries go through the villages spreading the bad news? How would even a mere quarter of the congregation take the news that church funds had decreased? Patrice tried to figure it out.

He was wise enough to encourage Jacques and Hensley not to say anything to anyone, not even their spouses, either about the disappearance of funds nor the rift that now existed in the church council. Hensley, clearly now getting tired, told the other two that he and Trevor, though now on opposite sides, were friends for years and promised to speak to Trevor to have him soften the attitude of Stella's faction. If Hensley could speak to Trevor convincingly enough he could get Trevor to influence Stella and those of like mind to another meeting of the church council to deal with the potentially scandalous state of affairs, further with the view to saving the reputation of all on the church council and keeping the church in unity and after Hensley met Trevor, he came to the point quite quickly.

"Trevor you and I have been very, very good friends and we do admire and respect one another. I want you to speak to Stella and the others and see if we all on this church council of St. Gabriel's, the Greater could meet again to look at the matter we were discussing a few days ago.

"I promise you, Hensley that I will speak to them and see if we can all get together next Thursday night. If you, Hensley, feel that Thursday night is good get the other two to come along. We have to deal with this problem."

ON THURSDAY night they prayed. They asked God to point the way to harmony among them. Then Trevor started.

"Brothers and sisters what we face tonight cannot be swept under the carpet, but yet we should put the past behind us as we try to discover what caused that $30,000 to be taken from our bank account in a way that we have not been able to trace it."

"Okay," said Stella. "On the last occasion that we met there was some bad blood. Some of us, including I myself raised our voices in anger in our meeting. But before this crisis we have never had anything like this. This grave problem can cause a scandal and possibly create very, very serious problems in our church – the church we love."

"If we agree to proceed in peace I can break the ice. Hensley, Jacques and I, out of a sense of diplomacy did not properly take the whole meeting into our confidence. In a way, some desire not to cause trouble has been behind the position that the three of us have taken. But I shall tell the truth. As you know Hensley is our trusted Secretary Treasurer and this fact is very, very well-known. All of us know this. You also know that the Secretary Treasurer never acts alone. But you will recall that over the years and before Reverend Aaron was appointed to lead our church, the one thing on which this our Council and our church have always agreed is that we cooperate with the leadership of the church and never embarrass it."

The others listened and except for Jacques and Hensley they were not sure where Patrice was heading. In fact, most of them still believed that Patrice was holding on to something which he was unwilling to let go of.

"Yes," said Stella, still somewhat guilty at how she had behaved towards Patrice on the earlier occasion. "All of us have always stressed and practiced cooperating with our leaders...."

Stella hesitated, trying to figure out if Patrice was going to rule her and others uncooperative. She simply up until now could not discern what Patrice was really talking about.

"In our community and church we try to do our best to be truthful and loyal. In this church of ours we respect those in authority over us and cooperate to the fullest with our leaders," Patrice continued.

"A few weeks ago Reverend Aaron approached Hensley seeking to withdraw $30,000 from our church account and Hensley discussed the matter with me. We withdrew the funds and handed them over to our new Priest," Patrice admitted.

There was silence, then Stella gasped,

"Oh, that is what happened?"

Then Trevor observed that there were rules and procedures by which their church's funds were managed. Then Agnes asked,

"You mean to say that the withdrawal of the funds was left to three people?"

"This is not good enough," said Roger.

"We now know what has happened," Yvonne said.

"I do not recall anything like this happening in all my years. Although Reverend Griffith thought that our rules were in need of change, he always followed them," Stella said strongly.

Yvonne, though initially taken aback by the news which Patrice broke, advised that the matter be looked at dispassionately.

"Can all of us here truly say that we know all of the rules of our church?" This question did register.

"I repeat, do we know all of the rules? In fact does any of us have the rule books here tonight?" Yvonne queried.

Not one of them had brought along the non-biblical constitution and rules of the Church of St. Gabriel's the

Greater.

"Now serious though the matter is, let us agree to commence from the start. Do all of us have rule-books at home?" Seven of them had never got hold of their Church's rules.

"Next, even for those who have rule-books have we studied them?" Stella questioned further.

If these church members were going to be honest, individually and collectively, they would have had to admit that except for learning some of the rules from Reverend Griffith, none of them including Patrice and Hensley knew all of the rules.

"But don't we know the rules that regulate money, depositing to and withdrawing from our bank account and spending?" Agnes interjected.

The meeting continued. Harmony returned among them all, for each of them was in a conciliatory mood even if most were somewhat ashamed that they did not know the rules. Then Patrice, sensing that the hostility of Stella's faction had subsided said,

"Can each of us say then that prior to this crisis of this $30,000 we were all guilty of not undertaking a careful study of some of the council's rules?"

To this Stella made the pointed observation:

"One thing is certain. Reverend Griffith, who preceded our newly appointed Priest, seemed to have known the rules very well."

Jacques, though, made this observation:

"But can we not all say that the rule books were never circulated? I sense that a majority of us do not have the rule books."

Trevor intervened.

"What is good about this meeting is the revelation that our new priest asked for funds and those responsible for their management instinctively trusting our Priest, took these funds from the bank and passed them to him. Reverend Griffith used to say that for reasonably small sums the rules could have been adjusted to authorize taking out sums out of the bank without the need for approval by the full church council. In fact rules that require 100% endorsement of twelve people may not be that easy to keep. Think of emergencies. Think of the poor who may have genuine need to go to the Priest directly for funds and assistance and because of our outdated rules the Priest would then have to summon twelve people. What if four were overseas? What if us four were overseas and two were in a coma in hospital? Reverend Griffith always cautioned us about the strict rules, but both did nothing to change them and constantly followed them. Come to think of it I can think of a good half dozen actual emergencies and many other events that really could have been addressed properly if there was some flexibility in our rules…"

"But Trevor," Yvonne interrupted, "we are here talking about rules. But did any of us at all ever give our new Priest our Council rules?"

There was a hush. The pause lasted for very many moments.

"I ask again," Stella inquired, "who among us can say that we took the time to provide Father Aaron with the rules?"

"Well," Trevor declared, "If nobody gave Rev. Aaron the rules he could never have been expected to know them. And if I can make a suggestion. On the basis of the fact that Reverend Aaron did not know the rules along with other causative factors I would have to say that Patrice, the Reverend and our beloved Secretary Treasurer cannot be accused of any wrongdoing. I think that prior to this evening we all should have had the rules and should have gone through them with our newly ordained parish priest."

Chapter 16

SEPTEMBER 11th

IT WAS TUESDAY, SEPTEMBER 11, 2001. Just after 11.30 a.m. news hit Helen Isle that there had been an unusual disaster in New York. Two large airplanes crashed into the Twin Towers of the World Trade Centre. As more and more news unfolded it became clear that the twin towers were ablaze for hours.

Early news reports spoke of persons jumping from the Twin Towers and of brave firefighters rushing into the buildings, many of whom met their death. At the site there was fire. There was destruction. There was ghastly death. For weeks on end the horror topped the news.

Just about four weeks afterwards, Aaron hit on an idea. If only he could persuade his church council, he was going to raise funds to help the unfortunate at the Sunday Service of October 7th 2001, and after getting the nod from his twelve-person council, he chose as the theme for his sermon: 'Helping the Unfortunate out of their suffering'.

"My brothers and sisters," he started. "As you know, recently there was a great tragedy in New York. Many lives were lost. Wives lost husbands. Husbands lost wives. Many young children lost their parents. Many people's livelihoods were rudely disrupted. There will be suffering for some time to come. If we continue to be true Christians we owe it to those who have suffered to help. We need as a serious church to raise funds so that we can despatch assistance to America. All of today's collection and offerings will be stored in a fund and I think we should have at least two fairs backed up by voluntary donations. Yes, brothers and sisters, my church council has agreed that we all should contribute to bringing relief to all who still suffer while we pray earnestly for the souls of the departed."

A sincere empathetic congregation, they all felt it their duty to heed the words of their priest. After this church service ended, outside in the church yard, Girlie Chase, who was born in neighbouring Bimshire but had lived in Helen Isle for fifteen years, turned to Ipsie:

"Ipsie, you would have learnt the bad news."

"Yes, Girlie, on the day it happened I was in Castries and the news spread like wildfire."

Girlie Chase queried, "Ipsie when you first heard, how did you feel?"

"Girlie, I was stunned! At first all I heard just before midday was that two large planes had crashed into the two towers," answered Ipsie.

"I had heard so too and I wondered at first what caused them to crash."

"I could not believe it even though it was real," said Ipsie.

"Then for days all I was hearing was that firemen died, other people died. I saw a picture of people running away from the scene."

"Anyways," Ipsie said, "Reverend Aaron was right when he asked us to pray for those who died and their families and to give money for charity's sake." The two then left for home.

When Aaron reached his own home just after 1.00 p.m. he turned to his charming wife, Elizabeth and said:

"Wifey you are not on my church council, but you have lots of influence in my church and in your community. I want you to get together your friends, all of them, to go through the villages asking for donations and I am putting you in charge of the two fairs I am going to hold."

Elizabeth remarked: "Honey, the cause is a worthwhile

one but much as I want to help, I feel you should have the church council agree to my involvement."

"Elizabeth, listen to me. That Church Council is my Church Council led by Patrice. Patrice goes along with everything I say and want. In addition, the members of my church council never disagree with Patrice. All I need to do without even keeping a council meeting is to tell him that you will be in charge of the fairs and it will be a done deal."

"Darling are you sure? I still do not feel comfortable until I hear that the church council has met and selected me to be the coordinator of the plans for the fairs."

"Listen, Elizabeth I am willing to bring Patrice here for him to advise you that I always get his agreement in matters concerning the church council and he in turn gets his way with its members."

"Honey, I never like to argue with you. In fact I love to cooperate with the man I married," Elizabeth whined.

"Let us have no more discussion of these matters, Elizabeth." Aaron said, raising his voice.

Elizabeth capitulated. After all she was the old-fashioned type of wife, faithful, devoted to her husband and never keen to go against his wishes. Shortly after this there was a knock on the door of the manse.

"Who is there?" snarled Aaron.

"It is me," came the reply.

"Who is me?" snapped Aaron.

"It is me, Felicien, known to your father, mother and sister Cindy as Theresa!"

"Come in Ms. Felicien," called Elizabeth.

"Good afternoon Misses, and Reverend Aaron, how are you?" Theresa asked.

"We are fine," said Elizabeth showing no hint that she had come close to incurring the wrath of her husband. "What brings you here?"

"I've come to speak to the Reverend but you can hear,

too."

THE NEXT DAY at 10.30 a.m. at the institution known as the Cathedral of Helen Isle, many persons of all ages had come to pay their respects. An octogenarian known familiarly as Sister Sheila had died and her funeral service was in session. Father Kirk, a brilliant inspirational orator and preacher had just gone into the pulpit. He started by asking all present to observe two minutes silence for the departed. After this he said:

"Man that is born of a woman has but a short time to live… Let us reflect on this as we consider our own mortality…"

In one of the pews at the back sat Aaron listening. There were those who recognized him and could not believe that he did not go into the sanctuary. There had been the convention by which clergy visiting the Cathedral of Helen Isle were welcome to be present in the sanctuary or chancel. But Aaron opted to sit at the back of the church.

"Brothers and Sisters in Christ, our departed Sister Sheila requested that there be no eulogy. Her sense of humility no doubt caused her to make this strange request. In our country most people opt for eulogies and choose beforehand the relatives or friends to deliver them, but Sister Sheila demanded that we should not sing her praises. I have heard so many eulogies, such that on some occasions I have found it difficult to connect what was being said as praises to the persons lying in their coffins. If we had the privilege of singing Sister Sheila's praises no one would deny that she was a good woman. Much as I shall obey her request not to have a eulogy, I still must say that she served as Treasurer on our church council for twenty years and made such a contribution that today our Bank Account has in 430,795 dollars."

Aaron was now more alert than ever. He thought to himself, '$430,795!'

"Yes, brothers and sisters in Christ, Sister Sheila made an outstanding contribution as Treasurer and the extensive repairs we will undertake will bear testimony to her tireless service. But I want us here to reflect on our mortality.

We are born, we grow up, we experience many things, we each have our differences one with the other, a few flourish, many remain poor. We all have our thoughts; many grow old, we die.

My perspective on these matters is that while we are alive we must do our very best, not only to achieve for ourselves but to be of assistance to others while practising virtue and clean living.

Our religion through the Holy Bible, stresses that we should do good. We have to love our neighbours as ourselves. We have to be consistently respectful of God and our fellows. When tempted into resentment, hate, anger, greed, false pride, lust, envy and sloth, feelings of revenge and bitterness, all of us have to halt before giving in to what can often be our overpowering urges to do wrong. The practice of what some call the seven deadly sins fills us with negative feelings and separates us from God.

If I had to sum up the Mosaic law as is laid down in the Old Testament I would urge all to respect our fellow human beings so as not to want to take from them nor to hurt them. I would urge respect for our elders and devotion to the only true living God. If we all work at avoiding sin in all its forms we experience peace. The Christian hope is Life Everlasting."

By now Aaron's interest in the proceedings had ended completely and he was anxious to get out.

"If we do good, we are obeying God. If we practice total obedience to God and free ourselves of sin we can experience eternal life. But we must be determined to do that which is right. Each of us must surely want peace and everlasting life as opposed to eternal damnation. We have to earn our way to Heaven.

I can express it another way: if you don't work for something, don't expect it. I Repeat, if you don't work for something don't expect it. I believe that this deep philosophical proclamation can be turned around and be made into: if you work well enough for something, look forward to getting it.

And so, my brothers and sisters in Christ, for you to receive your Heavenly Reward, do good and love your neighbours as you love yourselves."

The service inside the church building finished with 'Rock of Ages Cleft for Me, Let me hide myself in Thee'.

As the mourners left to go outside into the churchyard, Aaron slipped away quietly after having decided not to got to the graveside. On his way home he thought about the announcement that Sister Sheila had toiled for years to raise funds for her church. He did know Reverend Kirk and his wonderment at how Kirk's church could be so rich soon converted itself in Aaron's mind into deep envy and resentment. On the way home he obsessed and obsessed first about $430,795 and then continued obsessing about money. Such obsessions were no means rare with Aaron. They were no doubt strengthened by the prospect of his having to go to the Ranch later on.

When he arrived back home his wife was once again entertaining Miss Felicien.

"My good husband," Elizabeth greeted. "Miss Felicien, a good neighbour and friend who is close to Merle, has interested me in our people's plans to promote a progressive programme to uplift our people.

"What?" Aaron was curious.

"Mr. Aaron. I am sorry, Rev. Aaron." Theresa started apologetically. "Many of our villagers and others too, are looking at starting a Cooperative and a Credit Union. We believe that these two groups can do very much to uplift and advance our people."

"I really do not know much about what you are talking

about," Aaron admitted.

"Well, let me see how I can explain." Miss Felicien had never taught but she was still prepared to offer a lesson:

"You see, right now our fishermen and fish vendors operate strictly as individuals. They are not united. If we get all of our folk whose livelihoods depend on our fishing industry to come together to unite, after paying membership fees and saving up, they would be able to buy fishing equipment and materials cheaper, put together their heads to do their work more wisely, bargain stronger for better and cheaper boats building and lumber, and work more effectively towards protecting their interests. They can share know-how and rely on each other in many ways and they would be better off than now, functioning as individuals. In the same way if we all in the communities of Castries, Dennery and Micaud and others band together practising honesty, mutual respect, cooperation and love to put together savings, our group would jointly own more money than each of us as one person will have and then we can assist each other very, very well."

The mention of money took Aaron's mind back to Kirk's reference to how Sheila had raised a lot of money. Now Aaron was all ears.

"If we can have rules by which persons' savings are protected we can build up so much money that we will be able to lend members money on easy terms. Right now here in Helen Isle many poor people have been unable to borrow from banks just because our banks turn them away for reasons which only the banks know. Sometimes banks refuse to lend, having decided not to allow loans to poor people. These banks do not give proper reasons for refusing the poor."

Elizabeth nodded in agreement since she had known many honest people whom the banks had not accommodated. Aaron himself as priest, had been approached by some of the more hardworking people in the city and its environs who had complained that banks just did not lend them money and often seemed quite suspicious of them.

"Anyway we feel that your lovely wife and you, Father Aaron, are sufficiently educated to play an important part. Many of us are not highly educated but since those of us lower down need help, guidance and direction, persons who have benefited from an education can have a definite role to play in uplifting the masses."

"Yes," agreed Elizabeth, and she continued:

"At the end of the day we are from the same island. In our case we are from the same districts. It is true that some of our residents, a minority, do hold special advantages over the majority of us who are poor. In the interest of greater community consciousness we have to set common goals. Any differences between us are not that great and may be more artificial than real. I support the position you are taking, Theresa and I will speak to my mother and father as well as my parents-in-law."

Then Theresa reminded: "You know that your father-in-law Mr. Zaccky as we all know him has been a member of my sou-sou for years. He is honest."

"And," interrupted Elizabeth, "any venture designed to help poor people must have honesty as an ideal. In my experience truth and honesty count more than anything except trust and respect for God."

Theresa liked what she was hearing from Elizabeth. Elizabeth had a reputation among those familiar with her as the typical original Helenite wife. Honest, loyal and devoted to her husband.

Aaron left the living room where they had been sitting and went off elsewhere in his house. Theresa noted mentally that he did not ask to be excused and being not too judgmental, felt that it was more a lapse than a demonstration of an absence of manners. But Elizabeth knew that her husband was both angry and impatient. Trying her utmost to appear unaffected by Aaron's departure, she sat still for a brief moment, then said to Theresa that she herself knew who she was and even though she did benefit from a sound advanced education, she would never set herself apart from her people nor manifest any notions of superiority based either on the fact of her education nor status nor the reality that as a priest's wife there were those prepared to exalt her to a lofty pedestal.

"Theresa, Ms. Felicien, I want to say that I do appreciate your visit. The plan you have should be supported. Right-thinking people should lend their support to this honourable venture."

At this point Theresa departed. As she left she hoped that Aaron would give his blessing to her proposals. In the house, Elizabeth pressed Aaron to take part.

"I am not interested in any Cooperative or Credit Union," Aaron protested.

Then Aaron shifted their conversation back to the question of raising funds for the victims of September 11th. Elizabeth mused quietly to herself that there would be no funds for the victims who were dead.

"Are we raising funds for the victims?" she queried.

Aaron said, "We are raising funds for those who need these funds."

"Are you sure that we are going to have the type of support system that will allow us to raise the maximum amount of funds. I think that our efforts to raise funds would do with some careful, careful planning," Elizabeth cautioned.

"Listen, Elizabeth, have confidence. When you married me you had confidence that your marriage to me would be good for you. I have not ever heard you complain. Most days you smile and are happy and are a good hard-working wife. I propose holding two fairs. These fairs will come off because before I came to St. Gabriel's, the Greater, there were no fairs around here. The beauty about holding fairs is that the people in these areas are looking to enjoy themselves and would come out for the fair. They will bring their children.

Then consider the cause. If we put the cause aggressively by serious mouth to mouth advertising, we are bound to succeed."

"Honey I am not objecting to your plans," Elizabeth whined wistfully.

More than a tinge of fear gripped Elizabeth. Even though on this occasion Aaron was actually paying her compliments, in part, she sensed that he was intolerant of the concern she was expressing.

"Listen Reverend Aaron," Elizabeth was being deliberately polite to hand him some stature. She knew him so well as to know that he gloried in titles and loved to be made to feel important. For this reason she used a non-familiar appellation.

"All that I want to do is to show you that very, very careful planning is necessary. One area of concern is whether you know your congregation well enough to mobilize them to work in the planning, the purchase and procurement of supplies and such like. You have to contemplate having to put people to work. For example, who will be overall chairperson of the planning committee, how much money do you need even before you hold the first fair...."

Aaron was listening, but all the while his idea was to select four or five persons whom he knew and put them in charge.

"Honey," now Elizabeth resumed the familiar and the romantic.

"You know that you can count on me for the fullest possible support for your fundraisers but can I raise another issue?" she inquired.

"Do you not want to rethink the position you have taken on the Co-op and Credit Union? I feel strongly that as a resident of this community and a national of this beautiful island, I should be an active participant in the activities and institutions that mean much to our people. I want to be of the people. As my loving husband I would like you to side with the scores and scores of people who I believe will join the Cooperative Movement. I make bold to say that you as my husband cannot in principle stop me from associating with good groups..."

Elizabeth knew she was taking liberties. After all she had an abundance of proof that her husband was frequently chauvinistic. She moved more closely towards him and made as if to pat his head. Aaron seemed to like this.

"Honey, please try to find out about cooperatives with the view to getting involved. Let the two of us as lovers and you as a leader in the community become belongers to a cause which in my heart I feel is worthwhile."

"Listen, Elizabeth, love," Aaron said sarcastically. "My mind is on the funds we have been discussing and how to raise them. Once again I must tell you that I will not enter any cooperative movement. Do not see me as a belonger but you have my permission to join if you want. You join. Things like cooperatives and credit unions are for persons like you and my parents and those other people. I am no belonger."

Elizabeth withdrew her hand and the patting ceased. She pondered to herself as to what manner of person would wish to alienate himself from the projects, plans and programs of his own people. She thought that in any tightly knit community all people should stand in solidarity with each other to achieve their aspirations and to further their common interests. Yet she would still stand by Aaron. She felt deep down inside that she, like her parents-in-law, knew loyalty and understood the need to identify and to empathize with those around her. Her own parents had inculcated strong moral values in her. She was prepared to be a belonger. She again told Aaron that he could count on her support. She assured him that her intended involvement with Theresa and others would not subtract in any way from her solid engagement in his activities and in his life.

The diplomatic manner in which she presented these

assurances to Aaron was so clear to him and so genuinely expressed, that he did smile and showed happiness. He said:

"By the way, wifey, I forgot to tell you that the elections for my church council will soon come up and I must have my own team, come what may."

Chapter 17

COUNSELLING SESSION

SHE TOOK HER SEAT a mere two and a half feet from Aaron. The two sat across the table from one another. He was careful to wear his priestly black cassock and he did not forget to wear his off-white collar. Cassock and collar contributed to the cloak of the clergyman. He summoned an aura of formality at the start of the interaction with this young lady who had come to see him. Those who had arranged this first meeting between Hester and Aaron did not know of his inexperience as a counsellor. Their belief was that every priest, especially in the high churches or in the places of Trinitarian worship, was automatically a counsellor.

Aaron had told the four ladies who had approached him to counsel Hester that before he could sit with his new client they each had to make a financial contribution to prove their seriousness and as a charge for the time it would take him to diagnose Hester's problems.

Hester went because Isabel had insisted that she needed counselling and three of Isabel's female friends, in support of Hester's grandmother had actually spoken to the youngster in the presence of Isabel and had demanded that she see Aaron if she felt that she could not relate to Father Fred.

Now the time had come for Aaron to set about helping Hester. He had carefully arranged for the four ladies who had accompanied Hester to sit outside, out of hearing. Aaron took out a large green notebook, the type Sangster's bookstore would sell for EC$50.00.

Before doing anything with this notebook he handed Hester a double page of foolscap paper and directed her to write her full name, date of birth, names of parents and guardians, the names of her five best friends and other personal data. In addition, he invited her to write three reasons why she came to see him. Hester complied. She did feel more relaxed and comfortable largely because this her new counsellor was black and did not appear too talkative.

Aaron looked at the completed questionnaire and immediately two things struck him: her age and one of the reasons why she had come to him, which she stated, was her dislike for the first counsellor. Exceedingly surprised that she was as young as she wrote, he was completely taken aback by the fact that she had actually seen another counsellor before him. He fought hard with himself to conceal his resentment that he was a counsellor of second choice, that rather than select him first, he only came into the picture after contact had actually been made with someone else.

Aaron's ego was badly affected. So impacted on was his ego that he decided to commence his questions by asking why somebody else had been chosen as Hester's first counsellor. He started with this question:

"Tell me, is it true that you went for advice and help before you came here to me?"

"Yes, Sir."

"How long ago was that?"

"About eight weeks ago," she replied.

"Did you see the other counsellor on your own?"

"What do you mean, Sir?"

"Did you make your own decision to go to your first counsellor?" Aaron asked Hester.

"If you mean whether it was me who decided to go to see that man?" Before Hester could conclude, Aaron intervened.

"Who is or was that man?"

"He is a white man called Father Fred," she responded.

"Would you have decided through friends or family to go to see him?"

"If I had a choice I was not going to see him," Hester assured.

Aaron started to feel better. Here was a brand new client who, though having seen another advisor, seemed to have preferred not to have seen the first one if she could have avoided him.

"Did someone make you go to see that man?"

"Yes, my grandmother did!" Hester indicated with a sense of emphasis.

Aaron's ego was now experiencing a positive boost.

"You write down that your name is Hester Veronica Uriel Mellowes, can I call you Hester?"

"Yes, sir, for a start you can call me Hester. Please do not bother with my long name! Later I may be able to tell you what to call me if you wish, sir," Hester declared.

"Would you admit to me that you have come to see me because you prefer to deal with me rather than with that other counsellor?"

"Most definitely yes, sir!" Hester said loudly but with the best possible pleasantness in her sweetly sonorous voice:

"Are you sure that your preference is for me to advise and help you. Do you want to admit to me once again that you would rather...."

"Sir, I do prefer to deal with you," she said nicely.

Hester had no idea what contribution she was making to Aaron's sense of self-importance and to his ego. What Hester did like about her encounter with Aaron was that she could live with the types of admissions which Aaron was requiring of her. Nor did it occur to Hester that she was actually making Aaron feel good about himself. Aaron knew though that he was really extracting words from Hester which were calculated for him to feel superior to that other counsellor whom this young lady had seen weeks earlier.

"Come closer to me," Aaron asked Hester.

She hesitated for a moment. Then she obliged although an idea hit her that if any or all of the four adults outside saw this move to be physically close to the priest, they would abandon any idea that she was been counseled. While this thought struck her a sharp odor came in her direction off Aaron's breath. Could it be a mouth freshener, she wondered secretly. Unknown to Aaron, Hester inhaled deeply in an effort to work out the true, exact nature of what she was smelling. Then she figured out that what she was smelling was some kind of strong drink. She was not sure if it was brandy or whisky.

Hester was sufficiently street wise to calculate that this man was a priest but was human enough, male enough, to be a drinker. Then Hester figured out that if he was prepared to confess that he drank alcohol that he could not judge her herself if she confided in him that she liked strong drink and other substances. Then Hester declared:

"Not so close, Sir."

"I only asked you to come close for better eye-contact," he said, slightly sheepishly.

"Now, father, I smell something...."

"The Bourbon?" He asked. He mentioned this word deliberately. He was sure that if she was born at the time she indicated on the foolscap, there could be no way that she would have known of Bourbon.

"What?"

"The Bourbon," came his response.

She did not know Bourbon but the experience and wisdom she had learnt from the streets convinced her that whatever Bourbon was, it had to be an alcoholic drink.

Aaron himself was bluffing. He had not taken any Bourbon but had been drinking a malt whisky from Scotland which one of Beejay's friends from overseas had given him. His close friendship with Beejay had exposed Aaron to the many experiences which Beejay narrated with particular reference to Beejay's accomplishments and material possessions. Beejay had been telling his friends about Bourbon and its origins in the southern parts of the United States.

Much as she worked out that Bourbon must have been an alcoholic beverage, Hester did not think that there could be a category of special drinks, if the effects of all strong drink were anything to go by. Hester also started to think that her grandmother and her friends had constantly been warning her about the dangers of drugs and drink and had gone so far as to state that she had become addicted to these substances. The fact of her alleged addiction, Hester thought, had brought her to this man who himself had obviously been drinking even though she could not say that he was drunk on this occasion.

Aaron noticed that Hester was not speaking but appeared deeply engrossed in thought.

"A penny for your thoughts, Hester."

"Oh, nothing."

Aaron decided to take charge of the interaction.

"Tell me," he queried. "Why were you made to undergo counselling?"

"Grandma felt that I needed counselling. She has been thinking that I have personal problems."

"Do you think you have problems? By the way, have that age and date of birth which you wrote down for me been correctly stated?" he asked.

"Why?" Hester asked.

"Two things. If you are as young as you have indicated and I doubt it, you will be a schoolgirl and therefore should normally go or be taken to one of the guidance counsellors who work with school children! Secondly, from all appearances you are highly intelligent, so much so that I doubt that you are experiencing difficulties. Normally if someone is as young as you describe yourself and they have problems, these problems are bound to interfere with school work and learning. At the age you state, you must be in school. Have you brought your school report?"

Aaron omitted to mention that he knew that there would have been counsellors who would have demanded that in counselling students in high school it was an imperative to have their parents or guardians present. Yet he asked:

"Did you not think, Hester, that it would have been a good idea if your grandmother had been here present?"

"No, sir."

"Why not?"

"My privacy… and I dare say your privacy." Aaron was impressed, especially since whenever he had been in trouble in high school he had begged the authorities not to involve his parents.

"Can you say why your grandmother wanted you to go to counselling?"

"I am not quire sure, sir. I do not know exactly what grandmother's problem is."

"What made her choose that white man?"

"Probably her friends?"

"Do you think that your grandmother and her friends knew of me before a decision was taken to carry you to that white Catholic?"

"I don't know," came Hester's answer.

"If you had known me and had to choose a counsellor assuming that you also knew him, whom would you have chosen, Hester?"

"Call me Hessie or Hess for short." Hester was now becoming more and more comfortable with Aaron. "Yes, call me Hessie or Hess."

"Answer the question."

"What is the question again?" She inquired, pretending forgetfulness and ignorance together.

"I have asked you if you would not have seen me as your counsellor of first choice?"

"Do you want me to answer or rather do you expect me to answer truthfully?"

"Yes, Hessie."

"When I answer I wonder what you would think of me?"

"Just answer."

"Of course I would, if I had a say, have selected you, and not only because you are black," she said with a grin.

"You really mean that?" Aaron asked.

"Oh, you seem to have a problem with my age. Now, sir, age is only a number, my experiences and wisdom are much greater and higher than the age my folks have granted me. I cannot prove the exact date of my birth. I was told about my birthdate and age in a kind of hearsay way. I cannot dream of being so young."

"Well then," Aaron continued. "You must understand why I have expressed doubts about your age!"

"I find that if I accept the age my elders have given me then I would be forced to deal and mix with little children."

Their conversation continued. Clearly if those waiting outside were under pressure for time or had sensed that no real counselling was occurring inside, they would have been angry and impatient.

"You have mentioned, Hessie, that if you restricted your interaction to those in your immediate age group, you would be turned off as you said by 'those little children' as you have described them. Tell me about your best friends."

"I have Hazeen and Tara…" Hester started.

"Are Hazeen and Tara in your own age group…?"

"No, they are older," Hester replied with a strong sense of pride in her voice.

"Do you see older people as your equals and those young enough to be in your own age group to be inferiors?"

"I love to lime and interact with people like Hazeen…"

"Tell me about some of the interests hobbies and activities

which your real friends pursue," Aaron asked curiously.

Hester hesitated. Was it, she wondered, whether this man whom she was actually coming to like was going to pry into her business with the aim of penetrating her privacy?

"Oh, my friends are normal people doing normal things. They are good girls who like good parties and good fun."

"You admire your friends, don't you?" Aaron asked.

"Yes, my friends treat me well and I do trust them."

"Now tell me Hessie, about those classes of people whom you do not trust."

"Father, I would say that if a person is just like me and behaves just like me I can accept them."

"Well then," Aaron resumed. "You are a person who is very similar to me! Should I say that you are a person after…"

"Yes, I can help you. You are a person after my own heart," she declared.

It was clear that Hester had decided to put aside any harsh judgmental idea she had held at first about priests who reek of alcohol. She had reached such a level of comfort and ease dealing with this man that the one negative which she had sensed had now been cast aside. Then Aaron asked Hester:

"Do you really know for certain why those ladies outside brought you to me?"

"For counselling."

"Why would they think you need counselling?" Aaron questioned, much tact accompanying his question.

"I feel that they do not like my friends," Hester suggested.

"Why do they not like your friends?"

"They do not like my friends because those persons such as my grandma are old fashioned. But my friends, male and female, are modern and in the groove…"

"Have your old people told you that you have come under the influence of something called peer group pressure?"

"Yes they have been saying that I have been led astray."

"Would you trust me enough to confide in me?"
"Yes."
"Then what problems do you have?"
"None."
"What things have you been doing which irk them?" he inquired.
"What do you mean?" Hester asked.
"No doubt you do things that they do not like. What have you been doing either about which your grandmother has doubts, or things to which your grandma objects?"
"Nothing really!"
"Trust me Hester. There must be something or some things or many things about you which your grandmother and her friends would rather that you do not do."
"I cannot think of anything especially since my grandmother and her friends have been acting on rumours and hearsay!"
Gently Aaron, in a rare show of patience and tolerance, asked,
"What are the worst rumours that have been spread about you and what things you and your friends do together that displease your grandma and grandma's peers?"
"Sir, you are asking too many questions at the same time!.."
"Okay, Hessie, firstly what are the worst rumours that your people and grannie have heard about you?"
"That I use a lot of strong drink especially stout!"
"Is that true, Hessie?"
"If I go to parties or am with my friends I take a couple drinks."
"How many?"
"Just a few," she lied.
"Have you every got drunk?" Aaron asked.
"No."
"Have you ever felt sick after drinking?" he inquired.

"No, sir."

"It's alright. You do not have to call me 'Sir' each time. Have you ever regretted drinking?"

"No, sir. I love to be high," she bragged.

"Do you get high so often as to want to be high over and over again?"

"Yes!"

"Don't you think that you are depending on the drink?"

"No, sir, and when I drink I do not fall down."

Then to Hester's surprise Aaron observed that when he took alcoholic drinks he never fell down but 'mauvant langues' liked to criticize drinkers.

"Have you ever taken other substances to get high?" Aaron pressed.

Hester looked him straight in the eye then held her head down. There was a silence that lasted. Then Hester asked:

"What do you mean by other substances?"

"Dope." Aaron said.

"I don't use dope. Have never used dope!"

"Do you find, Hessie, that your grandmother and her friends resent your own friends and criticize them?"

"Yes, sir."

"Why?"

"Old-fashioned people like their own way. We young ladies love liming and partying. Those old-time people feel that every young person's party is a time for drugs and drink."

"Hester, do you have a problem with drugs and drink?"

"No, sir. I can drink and function."

Hester was doing her best to throw Aaron off scent. She was sure that he himself was a drinker, but she surmised that if he was as old-fashioned as her grandmother he would be opposed to ganja and other illegal narcotics. She had no proof that Aaron consumed anything other than alcohol. The manufacture, sale, purchase and consumption of alcohol were legal as far as Hester knew. Possession of certain narcotics was banned.

"Hess, are you sure that you do not have a problem with drugs and drink?"

"Honestly, Father, Sir."

"Then why are you here for counselling?"

The reality was that Aaron was secretly enjoying Hester's company and was prepared to accept whatever she told him. If he had a problem it was more to do with what he was going to tell her grandmother and the older ladies outside. He had already resolved however that come what may, Hester definitely needed more time to interact with him even if any future interaction excluded references to drugs, to Hester's personal problems, and to counselling. He was however going to bring this first session with this precocious teenager to an end.

"Hester, I have diagnosed your problem."

Then he paused and looked her firstly in the face then his weary eyes went in the direction of her chest while his imagination took him behind her yellow blouse to what caused the blouse to bulge in front of her chest. Hester, fearing a negative diagnosis decided to wait for him to disclose his findings.

For some minutes the two looked in the direction of one another their body language summoning up a curious eagerness to know each other more. Then Hester asked:

"Will there be future sessions with you sir?"

"Definitely. But in future you can leave out 'Sir' and 'Father'."

"What has been your diagnosis?"

"You are too precocious. Precocious youngsters always confuse and baffle the older folk."

"What does precocious mean?"

Without informing her that this was a word he had learnt from Mr. Lovejoy in recent weeks, Aaron said these words to the youngster in front of him:

"Your old people feel that you are too big for your boots but I have a far more favourable impression. I am going to have to tell them that this first session has seen you make progress out of your difficulties. I must also say to them that follow-up, considerable follow-up, will be necessary in the coming days. Tell them not to become bothered. I will work out how much more money your grandmother and her friends have to pay. If they cannot pay I will still see you. Always make sure that if and when I need to see you, you will be available."

"I will be available," she promised.

Chapter 18

THE CREDIT UNION

SHE SAT IN THE FRONT ROW accompanied by the other pioneers. On her left were Zaccky and Sarah. On her right were Ipsie, Merle, Sarah and Miss Germaine. This was the moment Theresa had waited for. It was just after 5.30 and people were still coming. To her these people were serious and eager. There was a definite air of expectation accompanied by a clear happiness. Theresa was actually wearing her Sunday best and on this occasion she wore a neat hat of medium rim, pink in colour matching her lovely dress. Head bowed, the tears welled up in her eyes. These were tears of joy, for her campaign had been highly successful. She paused, as the gavel with its sharp noise struck the podium inviting silence.

"All stand, please," It was Father Fred. "Let us pray."

Everyone complied with the Priest's command.

"Almighty and everlasting Father, we your humble faithful servants, stand meekly before your Eternal Throne! Forgive all of us our debts and help us always to forgive those who have wronged us. We all confess that we have sinned."

He paused and asked: "Would you join us in repeating these last words: Forgive all of us our debts and help us always to forgive those who have wronged us. We all confess that we have sinned."

Zaccky's voice was pitched at a higher tone than anybody else's.

"Help us dear Heavenly Father to realize that all power,

all goodness and all this world's precious resources come and flow from your divine beneficence. Let us ever remember that by your Grace we are fed. By your mercy we are healed. By your will we have our being. This evening, Father, we thank you that you have brought us here safely and we ask you always to protect us not only this day but always.

Bless, Almighty Father, all the people of Helen Isle and bring all of them to an understanding of your wisdom, mercy and power. Let, Dear God, the weak be strengthened, let the old and infirm be energized. Let, Father, those few in this island who are wayward find the right path – that path of rectitude and of truth.

Father God, Great Almighty imperishable Spirit, this occasion is a special one where we assemble to bless you on guiding all of us to launch two societies which we feel will honour you while making their members more prosperous. We are glad, dear God, that we can remember you. This occasion has seen us come together to work together. In your word, Father, we have learnt that a house divided against itself cannot stand. Teach us to unite. Help us to learn and practise all the principles of cooperativism, unity, brotherhood, sisterhood, fraternity, honesty, democracy and openness.

Dear God, we have also learnt that in your word it has been said that you have come to give us life and to give it to us abundantly. May there be an abundance of obedience by us to you and may none of us be ever lawless nor ungrateful nor dishonest either with ourselves or with you. Look down on us this day and grant us all that will guide us to your perfection. We all ask these things in no other name but your Holy and Divine Name. Amen."

It was now Henri's turn. He came up to the podium. A citizen knowledgeable in Public Relations had advised that rather than have a head table the pioneers should sit in the first seats and Henri as the principal spokesperson should be at the podium all alone just as Father Fred had just been a moment ago. Clearly brimming with emotion and unfailing pride, Henri moved purposefully to the podium with its microphone. His responsibility was to speak on cooperatives and use the occasion as much as to educate as to require those present to spread the word.

Boyse from Bimshire and four others from that island had been invited to come to this first ever meeting of the cooperatives-to-be.

"Reverend Father Fred, pioneering members seated at the front," Henri thought he saw someone like Elizabeth sitting fairly close to the front.

"All our elders, grandparents and parents.... George Charles...." Henri paused deliberately and as he did, so his audience started to wonder where he was coming from. Yet many clapped their hands gleefully.

"If a history of our nation was written now, George Charles will have a place. If the history of Helen Isle is written by a historian who commences to put together the affairs of this country in 2025 or 2050, George Charles will still have a place. If you wonder why I am here paying tribute to George Charles it is because of what he stood for and what all of you stand for as you sit in your places right here and now....."

There was rapturous applause.

"For those of you who do not know George Charles, he aligned himself with a world movement that preached that 'Unity is strength', that trumpeted the motto: 'Where there is no vision the people perish'. You are here to unite. You are here because you have vision."

A youngster at the back turned to his girlfriend and said to her chuckling, that for a person to lead Grenada they must have vision thereby ruling out blind people. He told her the law was intended to deal with Gairy but would definitely have affected Brizan. The two chuckled but still were listening to Henri. The applause resumed when Henri repeated his last two statements:

"You know unity, you have vision, you, Helenites, will

never perish for want of foresight. Let us also remember Allan Bousquet."

Thunderous applause.

"We have here with us a man from Bimshire. He is a man of many parts. Mr. Boyse would you and your friends please stand?"

Five Bajans stood up led by a short and large man.

"Mr. Boyse is a man of many, many parts. He is not scheduled to speak before question and answer time but I have learnt from him that Cooperatives are in Bimshire and that J.M.G.M. Tom Adams inspired the growth of Credit Unions by Government policies that aided their development. I better say supported their growth. Mr. Boyse will tell you how Tom Adams helped build Credit Unions in our neighbouring island to the south of us. Today is for all of us historic. Today must be recorded in the hearts and minds of all progressive people. Poor people can be progressive people. People who help themselves increase their self-esteem."

Henri was both reflecting the ideology of Father Fred while simultaneously coming over as a kind of political platform perorator. His audience was paying the closest possible attention. The strategy of having one person all alone speaking from the podium was working, for all looked in Henri's direction.

Mavis and Stella were sitting next to each other admiring this simple young man from lowly origins who was largely self-taught, providing inspiration to those present.

"You know fraternity is the key to all this. The Rochedale pioneers preached fraternity. Thrift is essential. Am I speaking to the converted? Yes, thrift is essential but all of you are thrifty because you try to save. You, my friends, are not wasteful."

There was more cacophonous applause, more noisy than ever.

"The institutions that have motivated you to come here today are both indigenous and perceived to be informal. I speak of the sou-sou movement which is present all over Helen Isle. Believe me, those who have organized and supervised sous-sous would have set the stage for us to proceed to move our thrift to a higher level. You know who runs the sous-sous nearest to you. You know how our children have benefited from sous-sous. Also never to be forgotten are those who keep livestock of different kinds."

Leonard was all ears and Easyboy who had been persuaded to abandon his selfish parsimony was present savouring the fresh and sweet words of Henri. At the front Merle reached over and squeezed Theresa's hands. To them Henri was frankly in finest form.

"I come now to speak of another principle by which the Cooperative Movement is informed. I speak of equality of rank among members. Our Fisher's Cooperative also has four committees comprising twenty-four members. Both organizations' committees are equally made up. The Credit Union has twelve men and twelve good ladies and the same is true for the fishing cooperative. Equality. Women have always been equal to men. You doubt me? Ask Ismay."

More loud cheers went up.

"Away with the old chauvinist view that women must follow men…"

A few of the older folk and fewer very young ones appeared a little taken aback.

"For too long women have been exploited and made to feel inferior. We have to emancipate and empower all persons. Away, away with discrimination against women. Let the world rejoice that all women—oh pardon me—all ladies, do deserve to stand up equal to men and this must be the practice not only in institutions but in society as a whole…. As we bend our minds to stop the discrimination among women let us love and support them."

A young girl no more than seventeen whispered a question to the adult next to her.

"Do female teachers who are spinsters still get fired for bearing children out of wedlock?"

A shrug of shoulders met the question followed by: "Be quiet and listen, garçon."

Henri then explained.

"I speak as a male but I also speak as a human being. Our fine ladies are humans, our males are human, so on that score all persons are equal. Simply because down through time from the Stone Ages the male appeared to be breadwinner should not mean that because history has shown that women were forced to depend on men, that they should still be placed in a more lowly position than men. Right, Ismay?"

The message was certainly beginning to impact. Even those who believed that men were the true leaders in the home and in society were appreciating what Henri was saying.

"If equality is to be one of the pillars on which we build our two institutions, each person must be able to have the guarantee of all the benefits, and if burdens are to be borne, we, each one of us, should bear such equally. There must be no imbalances based on gender. For the information of those persons who still do not know how the systems within a cooperative or credit union work, there will be here this evening a serious question and answer session and in future weeks we will be staging a number of workshops by which the masses will be educated. For the time being I want each of us to set our minds on savings."

At this point six persons entered.

"Oh I see some more of our friends from Anse-la-Reye who work as fishers. Some of our soulmates from Dennery are here already," Henri observed.

"In the case of the Fishers' Cooperatives which has to be a separate organization, the idea is for members to save money and pool their other resources with the aim of achieving proper economies. Remember, unity is strength, if we stand united we cannot fall. One fisherman might find that on his own the costs of building a boat or even repairing one might be out of his reach. By now being able to call on the resources of colleagues, his goals can be satisfied. The society of Fishers will have open membership, democratic control, thriftiness in operation and transparent payment of dividends from surpluses. It will have to be registered. In the medium and long term, insurance has to be one of the objectives. Yes, insurance, which individuals find out of their reach can be had by operating and functioning together united in common solidarity.

For the first twenty-four months, the Credit Union will be no more than a savings society. You have to creep before you can gallop. Bear with us. A pool of savings built up to certain level will be necessary before there can be any borrowings. Am I clear? For a while all of us in the credit union will defer our desires to borrow. It is good discipline to postpone the desire to be gratified. Yes defer gratification for a while….."

Father Fred's eyes light up. What a philosophy, he thought.

"Now I want to thank all those who have worked hard to interest persons in our efforts. There will now come a question and answer period followed by the vote of thanks to be delivered by Zaccky. After the vote of thanks, Theresa will do the closing prayer. I thank you all. May God bless us as he blesses our efforts."

"I have a question." A middle aged gentleman who was actually wearing a suit asked, "Why do you say that the Fishers Cooperatives must be separate from the Credit Union?"

"Is there anybody who wants to help the brother?" Henri asked.

Trevor stood up and explained.

"There are to be two different bodies. The reason is that the Fishers' Cooperatives will be a Producers' Cooperative which though intended to enfranchise members in the same way as the Credit Union, is different. The way it is to be set up, will see it with its own President and leaders, and its own committees and its resources must be kept separate and apart from those of the Credit Union.

If you ask whether the same person can be a member of both the answer is yes, but Government has insisted that no persons should be an executive member of both organizations at the same time. The Fishers' Cooperative must be different and have its own government. In fact the Government did say that whenever we have doubts it will help us.

My sister sells fish on weekends, you may know that she fries and sells fish. She is to be an ordinary member of the Fisher's Cooperative, but she has also joined our savings club after the Government said that this could be done provided she did not hold executive office in both. The Credit Union is strictly a Financial Cooperative. A financial cooperative is somewhat different in role and function from a Producer's Cooperative although both are moved by the same underlying philosophy…"

A youngster jumped to her feet. "It makes good sense to keep the two separate…"

Just then Matthias arrived having got a ride straight from a rum shop in the city. In the manner that marked his condition, tripping over six people, he made it to the last available seat smelling of his favourite substance. Those who saw him pretended to ignore him for fear of triggering an outburst.

"Yes it makes good sense to keep the two apart," continued the young lady. "If the affairs of one gets mixed up with the business of the other, irregularities and conflicts will happen and transparency and accountability will be compromised…"

As foreign as Father Fred was, he was moved with an overpowering feeling that these people in this gathering were intelligent and focussed. There was something special about them.

Just then Matthias, who had been beneficiary of six drinks

paid for by tourists in the place when he had been before his arrival, blurted out:

"Are you here to tell us how we can get around globalization? Our bananas are in trouble!"

Matthias was like a parrot repeating what the generous tourists who had been his benefactors had been discussing in the rumshop in Castries. As was his wont after he had imbibed any kind of Bounty Rum, indeed any other brand of liquor, Matthias was off to sleep in a jiffy and the question and answer session continued uninterrupted.

"As I was saying," the youth continued, "prudence requires that there be no intermixing of the resources of the two. It makes good sense to run the two as distinct, business clubs."

'Business Clubs', registered in Henri's mind. The concept of business club did sound most profound. Another question was coming, this time from a lady who clearly was either in her late thirties or early forties.

"Why is it necessary to have us save up regularly for such a long time before we can borrow. I have my children to feed and educate?"

Henri invited any willing person to answer this question. Merle stood.

"My sister, firstly never let us think of using a credit union to borrow for food. This basic need should always be met from outside of credit. Secondly. I must tell you that to be in a position to lend, a credit union must have fairly substantial funds."

The questioner interrupted. "But suppose before the credit union can lend, I wanted any of my savings back, is that possible?"

Merle wondered if such a person would really make a wise credit union member.

"Let me help you, my dear sister." Merle was allowed to continue. "The short answer is yes, you can get back your savings but each member is encouraged to save, to save, and to save; and above all to be so thrifty as not to want to touch their savings. Do not, my dear sister, be so present-time oriented as to want always to consume now. I read that an anthropologist called Lewis who studied the ways of poor people accused the poor of being so present time oriented as never to take part in institutions like savings clubs. Did you not hear a short while ago that deferring... postponing the desire to be gratified makes sense?"

"But I have my four children. They have to eat," protested the lady questioner.

With a tinge of wickedness and sarcasm Merle told the lady.

"I feel that if you did not defer gratification, you might have had many more children."

A raucous laughter went up.

"Forgive me, sister but our foreparents who must have been worse off than us, had to cut and contrive... had to find alternatives. When they did not have a pig they made a goat do." Merle said.

"It is alright for you to talk but if I want a chicken I will not take a fish," the questioner declared.

"Okay let me continue," Merle pleaded, as she spotted Matthias and noted that not even he was giving trouble.

"My sister, I have heard stories about people who borrowed for the wrong reasons or of people who borrowed when they did not have to do so. Fortunately we are going to press on with a positive education programme. By the time the Credit Union gets going, one of the committees will teach people thrift and wise money management."

Merle concluded:

"We save for months before borrowing is permitted, so as to build up a proper pool or store of money. It cannot be otherwise. If we start lending too early we would regret it. We might end up with more money outstanding than is sustainable. My sister, do not feel that you must withdraw funds regularly, and then later on borrow willy-nilly. Sound, sensible management of money will allow our business club to survive and in time when we lend for providential purposes our members will benefit. It is our intention never to have delinquent members, but instead wise people, from the working class, who will work to contribute to the welfare of all of us and generations to come."

Permission was granted for Sarah to do the vote of thanks. Zaccky had thought that consistent with role of the females in all of this and the total contribution they made to communities, that this was an evening for the women to shine.

Sarah put in an excellent vote of thanks, then came Theresa's turn to say,

"Eternal Father, Maker of all Humankind, Maker of us all, we lift our praises up to you..." she paused, overcome by emotion.

"My brothers and sisters..." The tears were not being held back.

"My brothers and sisters join me in rendering thanks to you for granting us your favours. Help us to be the best possible cooperators we can be. Bless the cooperative movement wherever it exists. Grant us, guide us and protect us. May we and those to follow ever be grateful for how you have always helped us. Inspire us, Lord and let no one divide us. Help us to glorify your name while we trust and treat all our brothers and sisters lovingly. Help each of us always to respect ourselves as your children. Inspire us to respect each other..."

Refreshments were voluntarily provided by a majority of those who attended, and for hours the new cooperators mingled and chatted.

The Rev. Aaron Isaac Zacariah Ezekeil Fromgence was noticeably absent.

Chapter 19

THE FAIR

IT WAS 2.30 IN THE AFTERNOON. Already scores of persons from all over the island were present. Patrice had so mobilized support for this venture that many adults accompanied by their young children had already come. Aaron had set up a type of private office on the premises. Only Patrice was going to be permitted to be in it when Aaron allowed.

The little children were dressed in their finest. Although in Helen Isle it was a tradition that people wore their best clothes to church, on some special occasions they would dress up in the same way as they did for church. Stalls and Tents were established and there were the usual games like lucky dip, toss the ball, the Chinese auction and thombola. Hotdogs and soft drinks were on sale and anxious children were pressing their parents – in most cases mothers, aunts and grandmothers to purchase goodies for them. In all there were some twelve tents and seven stalls, but the bar was in the open air close to Aaron's office. The weather was fine. Not a rainy cloud was in sight and the soft, cool breezes lent a special life to this event.

By 4.00 p.m. there were close to three hundred people and carefully chosen music was enhancing the activities. Calypso, mild reggae, some old rock steady and some spouge by the Draytons Two of Bimshire were being played. Off and on recordings of some Negro Spirituals were played to add variety to the selections.

At half past four, five members of St. Gabriel's arrived and set up what they called a food bar, al fresco. No doubt driven by their sense of culinary culture, they came armed with a huge iron pot and an array of ingredients. By special leave granted by Patrice, they came to prepare and sell Bouillon soup. At the other bar which had been opened around 3.30 p.m. somebody had put up a sign "Adults Only" and bottles of Chairman Reserve, Bounty Rum, Heineken beer and Mt. Gay were on display along with other strong drinks.

A grand time awaited all. In his little office, more like a make-shift hut, Aaron was observing proceedings. The excitement outside was clearly affecting him. At this point Patrice was moving around ensuring that all was going well.

There was an absence of security. No policemen. No security guards. This allowed Aaron to find further justification for having his special booth, for he had instructed Patrice to ensure that every forty-five minutes the cash from each stall and tent was to come to him with only a basic float left back at each one. To Aaron, however much Patrice could be trusted, in all matters affecting this money, he as priest in charge intended to exercise such dominion that he was going to offer answers to no one if he was questioned. Congregations, their females, friends and well wishers must know that they have to trust their priests completely. He alone would know the total profit, and the decision as to how the proceeds were to be distributed was exclusively his.

Close to a stall when a game by which players tried from some distance to throw a large football through the hole of a display board, Charlotte and Maylene were having a conversation, each one with a coke in her hand. Charlotte was saying:

"I am here because my aunt Ismay encouraged me to attend because this fair is a fund-raiser."

"I was persuaded to come because many of my villagers told me that there was to be a grand event designed to bring us all out in support of a worthy cause," Maylene advised her sixteen year old peer Charlotte.

"It is really to raise funds for the victims of that fateful day Tuesday, 11th September, 2001 and has been organized by one of our nation's churches, St. Gabriel's," Charlotte advised.

Then Maylene inquired of Charlotte,

"Do you not see a good few whites here some of whom must be American tourists. Some whites who reside on our lovely island are also here!"

The two who were seniors in their high school, continued talking for some time as they slowly moved around, viewing all kinds of items in the various stalls and tents. They were attracted to a tent which had for sale all types of books. They stopped outside and Maylene observed:

"Charlotte you did say that the proceeds or profits from this fair are going to provide support to the loved ones of those who perished or suffered on account of what happened in the United States of America in September 2001.... Do you feel that there are those who think that America should be defeated in a big war in the future?" Maylene asked.

"I am not sure but my opinion is that America has her enemies!"

"But why?" Maylene asked appearing unsure.

"I can say that they could be those who are jealous of America, then there are those who hate America," Charlotte declared.

"What are the reasons?"

"Our teacher was saying last week that many countries and hundreds of individuals feel strongly that the foreign policy of America for the last hundred years is responsible for the way many think of her," Charlotte indicated.

"What do you think is the problem with the foreign policy of the Americans?"

"The teacher said that by 1783 America had been independent of Britain and by 1900 was becoming quite rich and powerful!...." Maylene's interest was heightened. "Let me finish. The teacher was saying that after the year 1900 America had been saying that it was supreme in many parts of the world."

"Would some countries then feel that they have been treated unfairly by the United States of America?"

"Definitely," Charlotte appeared adamant.

"In fact within America itself, there were and have been many Americans who have felt that they were treated unjustly in their own country," Charlotte continued.

"What?" Maylene appeared to be disturbed.

"Yes, definitely, despite what we might have heard, the blacks and minorities living in the United States of America have for years felt exploited and abused by many mighty Americans!" Charlotte sounded defiant.

"I have also been hearing that America has not had the very best record in promoting world peace." Maylene was inviting a response.

Charlotte said: "There are many blacks even those who did not belong to the Black Panthers or the Black Power Movement who have for years been saying that the status quo within America has been doing violence to their rights."

"What was the Black Power Movement?" Maylene asked.

"It was a Movement that sprung up in America in the 1960's and 1970's. It was a response to how Blacks were forced to sit in the back seats of buses. Many were refused proper jobs. Many white landlords were unwilling to rent their houses to blacks. The school system had been promoting white values while forcing the blacks into the ghettos and slums. On occasions whites attacked blacks and beat them and the law did nothing to bring justice for black people. The movement towards improving things for blacks started when a black, named Rosa Parks, refused to give up her seat on a bus to a white person. The law was that blacks had to give their bus seats to whites.

The establishment within America, according to our

teacher, had been promoting a kind of white supremacy. In fact in the southern part of the United States there were those who promoted doctrines of white superiority over other races. Rosa Parks went to jail under a wicked law for not allowing a white her place in a bus."

"Are you saying that the superiority to which you are referring has been a big factor in the attitudes of American governments towards the rest of the world for more than one hundred years? Is it that the same way supremacist white America treated blacks, they have been treating the rest of human-kind?"

"A study of world history since 1783 written by non-Americans or by fair Americans would teach a lot about America's behaviour." Charlotte was emphatic.

"What do you mean by fair Americans?" Maylene's curiosity continued.

"By 'fair' I certainly do not mean fair-skinned nor white. I mean historians who are unbiased and present a balanced picture of the American attitude to others," Charlotte emphasized.

"Anyway, the two of us need to read some more about American foreign policy." It was clear that though Maylene had just learnt much from Charlotte, she felt that the two should do more probing.

"The point right now is that we have a function which I understand is to raise funds for persons who are suffering since the attacks on Americans some months ago," Charlotte observed.

"Do some in America suffer hunger and low standards of living?" Maylene inquired.

"Of course. Many poor people live in America even though overall the country is rich. America does have a society split up into social classes, racial groups and minorities. Although many blacks through their natural talent and ability have made it, there are those who will still argue that there are still strong racial undercurrents. There have in recent years been stories on videotapes of blacks being beaten by policemen in America with injustice apparently following after. And I heard that years ago matters were so hostile for blacks that special suspicions exist where the deaths of Malcolm X and Martin Luther King are concerned."

"Do you feel that there are many nations and peoples who feel that America is very hostile to them?" Maylene was inquisitive.

"Of course," Charlotte responded.

"Somehow though I have been raised in a family, community and society where love and peace are so encouraged and practised that after September 11th I felt very strong feelings for Americans, whatever the record of their leaders has been for a hundred years." Maylene said.

Maylene's sense of empathy was clearly visible. "I understand what you are saying. I am sure that the events of September 11th wounded Americans' pride and made that country feel exposed and vulnerable."

"It was a matter that reminded me in a way of how Goliath was brought down." Invoking a Biblical story, Charlotte described how the mighty could be brought down.

"Are there any lessons for Americans from the events of September 11th, 2001?" Maylene's curiosity continued.

"Yes, many. I make bold to say that those events will continue to raise some very serious questions, but in view of everything the biggest lesson is that America has to look at itself closely. It has to take stock."

Charlotte did not intend to sound triumphant but her point was quite strong.

"Yes I agree. It seems that many people are suspicious of the Americans. I heard some banana workers arguing that the Americans are greatly responsible for globalization and that globalization is a big threat to our economy, especially our bananas and that America has special friends whose bananas are to be preferred to ours." Maylene observed.

Maylene was showing a clear appreciation of aspects of U.S. foreign policy.

"There are those who are cock-sure that globalization is going to be rigged to suit American exports and American investors while our weak economies will be thrown into economic dependence and even economic and financial despair and weakness." Charlotte appeared to be on the attack.

"But suppose in a few years some very smart country begins to prosper more from this globalized world? America had better watch China. A radio programme recently was suggesting that in the very, very near future China may get more out of globalization than America at this time," Charlotte started to sound a little prophetic.

"You know," Charlotte, "we can agree two things. Firstly America has been badly wounded. Their suffering will not go away easily and of course the United States of America must take careful stock. I feel it (America) must check itself. Yes, powerful America has to do some serious soul searching. If the leaders of America do no soul searching, they will continue to discover that they have many enemies."

At the precise moment when this conversation of these two precocious teenagers ended, there was an exchange between Patrice and Aaron. It was now 5.15 p.m. and Aaron had not yet left the booth he designated as the Fair's Office to go out among the people. This bothered Patrice.

"Father, there are now quite a few hundred patrons outside supporting this venture. It is my opinion that you should go out among them and mingle. You have been in here alone for the most part. I have been coming back to you at intervals to bring in the cash."

"Why should I go out mingling among those out there? I prefer to be alone."

"Father, your wife is out there and others attached to our

church have been conveying their appreciation to those who are spending their money. Would you go out there please? You know that you can trust me to protect the funds."

"I have not been able to count all this money accurately." Aaron snapped.

"Do not bother about the money. The money will be safe. Think about how wonderfully the people have been supporting your cause."

"They are not supporting my cause. You must know that my intention is to send all the money to the United States and you know for what too!" Aaron declared.

Patrice's patience was dissipating.

"Sir, would you please go among the people, shake their hands, lift up some little ones and show appreciation. I have not checked with your wife but I know many people must have been asking her if you are here and why they have not been seeing you."

Just then there were cheers and noises of celebration. A young child, not a toddler, but certainly not a teenager either, had managed to toss the football through that hole in the cardboard which had up to now been missed by scores of players. It had cost one dollar for three throws and for some hours this game was so popular that a considerable number of persons had tried to penetrate the relatively small hole. The hole was barely big enough to accommodate the football. Adults had thrown the ball. Some children had tried but it was only this nine year old, Jake, who had succeeded. This particular tent had been the location where a great amount of cash was being made. Elsewhere on the compound sales were exceptionally high and there was no doubt that even though closing time had not yet come, the Fair was destined to be a success.

Just then Elizabeth entered Aaron's booth. Immediately she sensed that there was some tension between her husband and Patrice.

"Excuse me, Patrice, I need to speak to our Rector."

Elizabeth's formality did not go unnoticed. At least Patrice did recognize that she referred to Aaron as Rector imparting a particular formality to the word. Patrice started to leave.

"Oh, Patrice do not go so far, I would not be long."

Sure that Patrice was no longer in earshot, Elizabeth in soft tones said:

"Honey, follow my advice, go out there by yourself and spend about half an hour moving around talking and interacting with the patrons. You will not find time for all of them but you will be seen. I will call back in Patrice and he and I will stand guard over the cash."

Reluctantly, Aaron left the booth, but managed to put on enough face and grace when he started to walk around that no one could sense that he had to be coaxed into going out among the people. Aaron was surprised to see so many people. In a business-like manner he shook hands. Few detained him, for their view was that he intended showing his appreciation by meeting as many people as he could. Someone noticed that he had been smiling delightedly with the whites and tourists who were there. He was seen speaking to one lady who, though apparently white, had been behaving as though she was not a true tourist. In fact this young lady had walked some distance with Aaron to the stall where the strong drink was being sold and the two had had a conversation before he walked in north eastern direction to speak to some more people.

The lights were now on and even though Aaron did long to return to this booth, his office; he hesitated for a while especially after a young man said to him:

"Congratulations, Father, this fair or rather this grand bazaar is the best I have ever been to. God bless you and your work. I trust that you will be able to dispatch a huge sum of money to America. This fair, Father, shows how popular and loved you are."

The youngster's flattery clearly had its effect and shortly

after Aaron returned to the booth in euphoric mood. Patrice and Elizabeth could not help but realize how happy he had come back to them.

"Thanks for going out there, my husband."

"Thanks for showing your appreciation to the large crowd outside," Patrice obliged.

"We are doing better than I thought, Patrice. A young boy just a minute ago told me that this is the very best fair ever held in this country."

"I told you there was justification in mingling with the people."

"But, Patrice, do you not think that we should have called it a Bazaar rather than a fair?"

"Call it what you like, Father. Our people have been motivated to come out in support. Where a people are properly mobilized for positive action, amazing, even revolutionary results are possible. I have a deep faith in our people and theirs is a most secure destiny under the will of the Divine Master...."

Aaron was amazed at the poetic philosophy here postulated by a man who had always been his chief lieutenant and in his church the principal mover in the young priest's support system. They continued talking. Night had fallen but most adults remained after ensuring that proper arrangements had been made for the safe return of children. Each adult who had left, did so accompanied not just by their own children from their nuclear family, but they took along neighbours' children as well.

Back in Aaron's booth he and Patrice counted the hundreds of dollars. At the end Aaron told Patrice that it was his wish that arrangements for delivery to America be left entirely up to him.

"Yes, Father, and if any doubting Thomases ask any questions I will ensure they get appropriate answers."

"Do let them know Patrice, that in all matters in my church

they must trust me fully and never doubt my integrity."

Chapter 20

COUNSELLING TWIST

HE STROLLED BRISKLY AND PURPOSEFULLY from the place where they had left the borrowed car. His quick pace was not to avoid being identified as the man who had left the car at the bottom of the hill, but to do as he had planned, on this, an occasion he had looked forward to.

As she held his hand and followed Aaron, Hester's two feet accelerated at a speed that permitted her to keep up with him, concealing the fact that in the last ninety-six hours she had slept only for five difficult hours. During the fifteen minute mini-sprint up-hill much of her troubled life flashed before her.

How at age nine she had proved such an incorrigible pupil in her London primary school that on the strong advice of the principal, her parents Dora and Daniel had been urged to withdraw her from school. Deeply disturbed by her conduct which by no means differed at home from how it unfolded at the Pembroke Girls School, Dora and Daniel had decided to dispatch this strapping strong-willed child back to Helen Isle to be raised by her paternal grandmother, Isabel. Their belief, based more on optimism than a realistic evaluation of Hester, was that Isabel would so discipline Hester as to bring her to Christian feelings.

In Hester's thoughts were her own way of consorting with tourists, heavy drinkers and 'pusher-men', selling drugs. She recalled the age at which she had met her first pusher-man, Harry, whose sole purpose was to hire her services as a mule, a carrier, who would be both retailer and sales agent earning a commission on the amount of drugs she would sell for him. She thought that after earning substantial amounts of East Caribbean dollars, pound sterling and U.S. dollars for her work for about thirteen months without being a heavy drug user, she had really started by experimenting with marijuana, the great weed, before graduating to cocaine. She still remained unsure if she was fully addicted either to the ganja or the coke, or even to alcohol which she consumed in liberal amounts if her narcotics of choice were unavailable.

She reflected too on how she also served - and not infrequently – as a call girl selling her body to tourists. And yet she both could not understand either how much she had earned, not even a rough figure, nor why she seldom had money. Now she had met a counsellor whom she really fancied and who was certainly her kind of man, whatever his marital or other status.

Not yet fifteen, Hester stood at six feet, almost as tall as the man who was on the verge of being her very next lover and her sturdy figure combined with her height would have designated her a 'spartan' in earlier times. Indeed her physique, which stood in contrast to her conduct, bestowed a special elegance on her which was not yet diminished by her wanton use of narcotics and spirits, nor her multifarious nocturnal activities.

"Hey, you are rather quiet, honey," Aaron whispered.

"I am like this for a first," she lied.

"Tell me, what is on your mind," Aaron demanded.

"Not much," Hester returned.

"I hope you are not scared," the priest queried.

"Dear Heart, very few things make me frightened," Hester appeared to boast.

After but two counselling sessions, Aaron could not seriously admit to himself either that he had diagnosed any fears in Hester nor even that he could recall in detail the experiences that she had narrated to him during the two half-hour sessions which they had had. What Rev. Aaron knew was that after a modest amount of interaction with this individual a curious type of compatibility had rapidly evolved between them. Keenly observant, Hester, too, through sheer intuition, realized what her counsellor wanted from her.

"Honey I do feel a little under but in a funny kind of way. I do not want you to misunderstand me. But can I play a prank on you?"

"Play your prank then you will know how I'll take it," Aaron urged.

"Father Aaron, it is my pleasure to be at your service, tonight," she declared.

Accepting her words at face value as a prank only as far as the words went, Aaron took what she said, exactly as they were intended and was wise enough to know what form she intended the service to take and would figure out in detail all the constituent elements of the same. And of course how Aaron adored being called 'Father', especially since he had started to realize that fewer and fewer persons were using this word when they addressed him. His mind, though, quickly refocussed on Hester's figure, in his mind the perfect figure and he hoped that nothing would destroy it or cause its fine size to change.

He was now holding her left hand more firmly than ever as their climb uphill continued. It did strike Hester that he launched forward up the incline in the dark so fluently that he must have been exceptionally familiar with all of the area.

By now a sleepy sun had descended below an indulgent horizon. The sea below aquamarine and angry with high billows some four or five hours earlier, had settled down in the dark, on relinquishing its blue hue and had assumed a sedate calm. Except for a few inquisitive whistling frogs, all was silent and all the waves the sea brought to the shore seemed more to kiss the small cliff below, than to lash it.

The month was November. The time was eight o' clock, but it was dark enough all around, and sufficiently secluded, that miscreants could use this ambience to embark on carefully crafted conspiracies.

Considering her way of life—what it was that would have brought her here—she cleverly calculated that this was one place where anyone could both trade in weed and crack without being easily detected or simply use it to light up and have a smoke or hit a rock. Immediately at hand though was a new prospect, a new client even, who could offer her many possibilities. At this stage she trusted him and continued to allow him to lead her. She was by no means impatient and interestingly his brisk pace slackened as he too appeared to be taken in by the atmosphere and the whistling frogs.

Then Hester felt she saw two recognizable pieces of silver metal, each one moving with Aaron and clipped to his hips.

"I see something shining," Hester told Aaron. "And they seem to be on your hips," she insisted.

"Never mind, darling, I wear these things in case I may need them."

"Have you ever had cause to use them?" Hester was curious.

"I am only bringing them here with me in case of emergency," the priest responded.

"Do you think that you may need them tonight?" she quizzed.

Aaron thought that Hester was sensible enough to work out that notwithstanding the changing times in Helen Isle with violent crimes on the increase, guns were not the tools that he had intended to put into use on this occasion.

"No, Hess, I doubt. Out here is so far that I feel only other persons of like mind to ourselves would want to come here. In any case, the weather forecast is for rain in this area any time soon."

"What? Rain?" Hester asked.

Then her mind seized the idea that when the two got into full flow some water on their bodies at the right time, could in a 'kinky' but splendid way, lend ecstasy to the proceedings of the night.

"You know, Father, this is a most romantic setting. I can see the stars high above, dozens of them, still the night is dark. But few clouds are above. Right now no sign of rain. I feel I have heard a few birds chirping." Hester was almost poetic.

Not to be outdone, Aaron guilty of not making the best use of his days either at school or in Seminary, and a firm believer that no female should outdo a male, made bold to utter:

"Behind us, lovers in the dark, a slender lowly path smart, and winding its way in crooked style from bottom to top, awaits the sweet dew of the night. Dark sky above looks down on us with its secret blessings. Still sea is at rest as moon hangs suspended in the company of silent, small stars smiling sweetly...."

Aaron paused. Never before did he realize that he had it in him to put together such language although he loved words. He held her tightly around her waist and squeezed her. A cackle of delight met this embrace as the two sat together on the large root of an almond tree.

For a while she, thrilled by the warmth of his body, just sat awaiting his next move. He stretched her across his body, his left hand now placed across her shoulder as his right hand moved in the direction of her navel. To her he was already demonstrating the type of expertise she hoped he had. Her breathing soon became heavy.

"I think I am in love," Hester gasped.

"With me?" he asked.

"Yes, darling," Hester replied.

"Well, then...."

Before Aaron could say anything more Hester was busy taking off his grey short sleeve shirt. She leaned over and put her lips to his. He pushed his face entirely in line with hers and could not help but notice that together their two faces were almost of equal size. He wondered... and wondered. How could a girl so young be so big, tall and strong?

By now the yellow moon had moved virtually fully and directly over the tree beneath which Aaron and Hester were busy fondling each other. Hester, prideful and arrogant as always, teased Aaron and inquired.

"Do you not feel that I can teach you a thing or too?"

He paused and said nothing. Male chauvinist that Aaron always had been, the idea came to him that no woman could teach a man anything. Yet, fully infatuated with this specimen of feminine humanity, he grunted under a deep breath.

"Carry on."

As the moon moved reluctantly, slowly, over two large dark clouds it felt as though some kind of eclipse had suddenly occurred. The two, fearless, proceeded to engage each other in ways they both approved, orally and congenitally, for some time, each one glorying in their physical endowments. They exhaled... they gasped. Lascivious lust gripped them down to their very bones. At the end, they both fell asleep by which time the sea's tide had changed, and waves, now bigger and stronger, had started to lash the cliff below.

Oblivious to the time of the night, both dozed off into sleep, unmindful of the lonely lovers' lane and any likelihood of being rudely aroused from their slumber.

Hester woke up first, partly because a wave larger than any other that night furiously struck the cliff below. Were the two of them not some distance up from the ground level, the waters would certainly have doused them. Feeling both fulfilled and eager to repeat what they had done but on another occasion, probably tomorrow night, Hester started to dress the limp body beside her, beginning by putting on all garments below the waist including his socks. She did not think it was yet time to shake him out of his sleep. Her next move was to have him fully clothed, then to move over him solely to admire his marvelous body. Then it was as though Aaron had started to snore when she thought she heard a noise other than one caused by the sea or the wind. She moved rapidly, almost simultaneously putting on his left shoe and shirt when suddenly....

Yes, she had heard a noise, then saw two beams of light. She shook him up. The lights were coming closer to them. Rapidly coming awake and dressed in all but his right shoe, Aaron wondered whether he should shoot in the direction of the light, or wait.

Remembering that he was a priest set to sing mass and preach at a friend's church within hours and entirely insensitive to the safety of his companion, Aaron decided to run and to do so fast. Within seconds he had fled skillfully and rapidly down the winding track.

"Police, Police" two noises came. Immobilized, Hester too unfamiliar with the setting, did not move but stood, then sat back down under the tree.

"Police, Police."

"Goodnight," Hester greeted the two gentlemen diplomatically. "How can I help you gentlemen?" Hester continued.

"We are policemen."

Ignorant of the fact that they were talking to a minor, the two men took out I.D. cards.

"So you are policemen?"

Bowled over by her pleasant manner and of course the courage displayed in the circumstances, the two policemen took out more lights and marvelled at the lady standing before them.

"We are searching for an escaped robber and came here," the first policeman whose dark uniform carried three stripes proclaimed.

"Who is that man who just ran away?"

"Sir, he is my lover and companion. He is not from here.

He is a visiting tourist, born in Senegal but lives in France and has an interest in Caribbean affairs. I am in love with him. He comes from the top of French society and ran because he does not want to see his picture in all of Europe's newspapers. He told me when I first met him last year that in Europe they call him, His High Mightiness, the CSAR...."

Then the second policeman whose two torch lights were surveying the area, spotted a shoe. Hester made no attempt to resist his taking it, for she worked out that if she cooperated things would be pleasant for her.

"Please accompany us to our vehicle." By the way my name is Sargeant Demille.

"Yes, Sir."

The police officers did not touch her and she made her way down hill, Sergeant Demille on her right and the constable whose name had not yet been revealed to her, trotting on her left. Then when they were half-way down the hill on the steepest slope of the incline, all three heard the dark bushes ruffling.

"Police," the two men shouted.

A greasy, half-naked man fell heavily as he tried to escape. His fall made it easy for both officers to pounce on him, searchlamps blazing in his eyes. Shocked, Sargeant Demille and the constable lay hold of the dirty greasy, character and swiftly put on handcuffs on him.

Just as they were contemplating taking this young lady to the station to question her concerning an individual who had ran away from the area earlier and with some evidence of an abandoned shoe, Sargeant Demille asked her loudly.

"Is he the man who was your companion?"

"No, Sir." Hester excused herself.

Then, without question, the arrested man shouted.

"I will tell you the truth if you do not beat me. First I do not know the woman who is with you. Secondly, I have been living in these bushes in the night and in the day with my gang who was responsible for my entry into Helen Isle."

"I am Sargeant Demille," one officer told the nasty, greasy man.

"I am coming, Sargeant."

Both wondered if their subject was really telling the truth, but it was clear to them that no one in such a dishevelled state could possibly have any kind of rendezvous with a lady of that type. And so when the four came to the bottom of the hill close to where Aaron had hours before parked his car, Officer Randal, the constable, sat behind the wheel after inviting Hester to join him for a ride to her destination. Sargeant Demille sat with the handcuffed man in the back. Before putting this wanted man in the car, Sargeant Demille had put shackles on his feet to ensure no escape. The policemen agreed to put Hester off just outside the La Toc Hotel. They made their way with their captive to the Castries Police Station.

Hester faced one difficulty. How would she explain her very late night out to her grandmother? Then a workable idea struck her. She would tell Isabel about being kidnapped before being rescued by the Police. She would go back to Sargeant Demille and ask him a favour. From what she had calculated, Sargeant Demille was an understanding person. Then idea after idea occurred to Hester. In circumstances where Isabel had grown increasingly suspicious of her, she would cook up a story for Isabel and such a story would be one which Isabel would swallow.

Hester walked back to the police station and asked to see Sargeant Demille. The officer at reception, without asking questions, called out Sargeant Demille.

"Sargeant, I need to speak with you." Sargeant Demille followed Hester as she made her way outside of the police station.

"Sir, I am going three miles from here and it is getting dark, I am scared of walking alone."

"Okay, I'll take you home in one of our vehicles."

Without realizing it, Sargeant Demille played right into Hester's hands.

The two hardly said a word to each other as Sargeant Demille drove Hester home. Her mind, taking into account its true nature, marvelled that the relatively young Sargeant asked her no questions nor made any proposals to her.

On reaching Isabel's house, Hester invited the Sargeant in.

An anxious grandmother, waiting hours for Hester's return home, thanked Sargeant Demille for bringing home her ward. Then Sargeant Demille left and said that he had to go back to work. Without being asked for an explanation detailing the reasons for her lateness, Hester recounted the below story to her grandmother.

"I had just left the house of a very good friend and was standing alone in the road opposite her house. The sky was dark and it was after 5.30 p.m. A car drove up and a man pointed something at me. When next I knew myself after coming to, I heard something like gun shots and heard a police car. I was very, very confused. I found myself in the back of the car rather giddy. It was as if I had been sprayed with a drug. The police looked into the car and told me not to move. Then I noticed that there was another police car nearby and the police were running three men and firing shots. I believe those three men were in the car in which I was driven away. I tell you, Grandma I am lucky to be here.

It seems as if those three men were criminals wanted by the police. They must be criminals to have kidnapped me. Oh how lucky I am. Anyway, the police rescued me and took me to the doctor. All that the woman doctor found that I was drugged. She called the drug some name which I never heard and cannot now remember. The police then took a statement from me and brought me home to you. The police were nice to me and told me that I was lucky not to have been raped nor killed."

"Thank God, thank God," exclaimed Isabel. "You are here safe."

Not one to put people in her business easily, Isabel told Hester that she would discuss the matter with no one. Then the two went to their separate bedrooms and were soon off to sleep.

Chapter 21

OCCULT RITUAL

THE THIRTEEN LEOPARDS INCLUDING Beejay and Aaron reached the graveyard. Beejay, a Leopard for years, claiming to have first joined the secret society while in Tortola, had arranged everything. In fact, in Tortola the society actually went by a different name, but Beejay decided to introduce the name 'Leopard' to Helen Isle to bring something new but also to prevent any Helenites from going to Tortola to research and verify the truth.

Each of them who had volunteered to come to the graveyard to take part in the ritual had a piece of grass or bush in his mouth. Members of a society which admitted no women, this was the night when their leader was going to introduce them to new novel mysteries. These mysteries would follow special occult incantations.

However, as he had explained to the other twelve, Beejay had to bring certain precious items in his quiver. In a type of knapsack covered with what passed for a Leopard's skin, Beejay had one phial of very greasy oil, one small tin of corn and seven sticks of incense. He did meet something of a challenge in persuading his followers to accompany him on the basis that to be an accomplished leopard a man had to, in the company of his brethren, go to a graveyard in the middle of the night. Fifteen members refused to show up and were told in stern tones that after the ritual they would face disciplinary action for disobeying their leader, who as head of the group was in the same role as Melchisedec.

Aaron's fear had to do with being found out by his congregation and so he persuaded Beejay to have all participants wear jet black masks. Intrigued by this proposal, the leader agreed that all including himself should wear these masks. Any uninvited person or stranger would be bound to feel awe in case they trespassed in the graveyard during what was to be a unique ritual. Lasting for half and hour after which the inner 'few' would repair to the Ranch, Aaron was a member of that small group. Beejay, not nearly as large and sturdy as Aaron, next prepared his following.

"Is everyone calm?"

"Yeah," they replied trembling.

"Not so loud. We do not want to arouse the suspicion of any stranger who may come into these portals."

"Okay, boss, go on," some urged him.

"Does anyone have a bad heart?"

"No," they chorused together quietly.

"Does anyone suffer from high-blood pressure?"

"No," they whispered.

"You are right to speak in a whisper. Our society is not open to the public and the last thing I, as your leader for life would want, is for some busybody, some metaphysical neophyte either to barge in on us or to eavesdrop. Shortly you will observe some mysteries. The passive but brave observance of what will shortly transpire, will take all of you to the ninth degree of our lodge and will imbue each and everyone of you with the highest possible courage and fraternal fortitude.

Now is everybody ready?" Beejay inquired.

It was a dark, lonely night. All was still. Even the whistling frogs and their larger minions, the crapauds, were asleep. Beejay went outside the graveyard to ensure that no busybodies were around.

"Now brethren, what you will witness has never been the fortune of women, cowards nor the undeserving. Those too talkative and worldly to take part are always excluded. The faint-hearted exclude themselves."

Beejay was being so animated that he was no longer speaking in a whisper.

"Now, say after me softly and slowly."

"Yeah, though I walk through the valley of the shadow of death I shall fear no evil...."

Aaron grew most alert. The other eleven were expectant. The words which were to be recited registered with Aaron more than with his brethren. They murmured softly.

"Yeah though I walk through the valley of the shadow of death, I shall fear no evil."

Aaron had heard these words time and again before

"Now next, say together: 'Nam, yo-show, show, eime meleneck'."

They got those strange words out when suddenly the graveyard lit up with flashing incandescent lighting. Growler, a coward who was more or less coerced by Aaron and Beejay to come, took three steps backwards.

It was now midnight. Suddenly the lights went off. Other lights came on in an array of seven different colours.

"Yeah, nam yo-show, show, eime meleneck," Beejay said fairly loudly.

The lights of seven colours quickly flashed on and off and after a few seconds the whole graveyard lighted up brighter than before. A white sheet appeared from behind a large stone tomb, flapping and flapping, bowing, going down and elevating itself over and over. Fitz and Growler were sore afraid. Aaron was lost in wonderment.

Soon another white sheet encasing some large body rose up, then dropped heavily in an open grave with a loud bang, only to raise itself up groggily, performing some backward flops in front of another white sheet. Off went all the lights again. Seconds passed.

To Fitz, Growler and Easyboy these seconds were like an eternity since the fear in them was beyond measure, and description. But despite their fear the three trusted Beejay who was no criminal nor trickster, they thought. Surely as far as they were concerned, there were mysteries occurring, putting another side to the reality of their existence. Prior to this experience, Beejay had been careful both to explain that their society – their order - was mystical and secretive and also that every experience through which they would be put would make them stronger in character.

As all members, including Fitz, Growler and Easy-boy had previously been through various initiations and had survived, they were comforted in the feeling, although summoned with difficulty, that all would be well. In addition, Beejay had carefully instilled in them the view that fortitude, manliness and courage would be theirs in addition to occult knowledge. And so like the other ten, Fitz, Growler and Easy-boy stood expectantly and did their utmost to conceal the tremor in their hearts and knees.

Then suddenly once again lights illuminated the graveyard, but this time it was clear that a larger object moved slowly under the lights and then disappeared. Once again Beejay howled

"Repeat after me brothers, Nam, Yo-show, show, eime, meleneck."

All complied. The lights grew very, very dim. So dim, they were close to going out. Now a noise like shrieks punctuated by weird hisses filled the air. It was uncanny. The lights came on again. What seemed to be large purple monsters moved towards them.

"Do not move. Fear not, my brethren seeing is believing. Now raise your voices and say nam, yo show, eime meleneck."

He knew no busybody or outsider could stomach or stand this.

"Let me hear you say 'Nam, yo show, show, eime mele, mele, meleeneck'," Beejay demanded.

The responses came. At first just about eight of them did the incantation, but all joined in at the second 'mele' since by now the monsters retreated into the dark. The lights were all out now. An inquisitive moon at the half stage part concealed by enormous dark clouds, started to peep out. Tall dark trees were somewhat visible in the graveyard. Bright lights close to three dark trees appeared; this time some forty or so fell from where the first light had been spotted. What appeared to be a black and white pig appeared followed by what was clearly a grey horse.

Then Beejay directed.

"Say after me 'Yeah though I walk through the valley of death'."

Then it seemed as though the horse made a somersault and disappeared from view.

"Brethren, you have withstood all. Our short ceremony is now almost over. You now must repeat 'I shall fear no evil'. And you finish with the magical words, 'Nam, yo-show, show eime meleneck'."

Relieved, the less courageous were delighted to repeat these funny words.

Once again there was darkness. The moon had retreated behind the clouds and Beejay told them they could go but that he needed Pierre, Aaron, Easyboy and the Secretary who refused all names but Mr. Lovejoy, and whose nickname was Elijah.

Some five minutes after the others departed in Growler's van, these three made their way with Aaron and Beejay back to the Ranch.

Back at the Ranch: "Have you taken the names of those fifteen persons, note I am not saying brothers, who did not show up, Brother Secretary?" Beejay inquired of Mr. Lovejoy.

"Worthy Leader and Master, I did not take down the names of the fainthearted but their identities are not beyond ascertainment."

"Brother Secretary, how soon can you procure the list of the rebellious?"

"Verily, I can reflect for a short while and my brain, fecundated by my genius, will readily supply me with their identities under the influence of my marvelous memory!" the Secretary proclaimed.

"Brethren," said Beejay, "I seriously feel that strong action should be taken against those who backed down."

"With regard to every strand of your majestic authority, worthy master, the first step is to ensure that not one of those fifteen persons tell anyone that we repaired or invited them to repair to the cemetery," the Secretary advised.

Then Pierre made a recommendation,

"Let us get all of them here tomorrow for an extraordinary meeting and so I am moving the adjournment of this meeting until 5.00 p.m. tomorrow to warn them not to talk before confronting them."

Beejay was minded to agree with Pierre, especially since he had borrowed $3,000 from him, but before he could say a word, Easyboy, who had undergone a personal change in the last few weeks, a change that was miraculous, spoke up and urged:

"Look these men are still brethren. We have degrees in our fraternity. They have failed the degree which we did tonight. For their cowardice, rather than being harsh with them, we should let failing the degree be the sole punishment."

"I have to think about that." snorted Beejay.

"They did not only fail the degree, they disobeyed me, their earthly most worthy master," Beejay appeared uncompromising.

"Let us not resolve this troubling matter now. Let us meet them first. Let us try to convince them to attend the meeting proposed for tomorrow." Pierre urged.

"Okay we will persuade them to come tomorrow." agreed Beejay.

"May I advise that you let Mr. Lovejoy, as Secretary and as a man of words conduct proceedings," Aaron suggested.

"I agree." said Pierre.

"Alright. The chairman for tomorrow's meeting will be Mr. Lovejoy."

The next day, just as he was leaving his house about 3.30 p.m., Tallboy and Lester stopped to see Beejay.

"The eighty dollars you gave is not enough. Smallie missed his pig and horse and when we took them back he caught us after he had missed his animals and told us that we borrowed his animals to serve others and for him not to call the Police we would have to give him $50. Then the electrician who rented us the lights said that when he checked them so many were blown that we would have to give him $40.00 more," said Lester.

Beejay did not like this at all, but did fear that these two men, who were in the habit of spending long hours in rumshops, might spill the secret and the brothers in the fraternity would think ill of him. He stopped and scratched his head. Then to his relief he noted that they were asking for less than a hundred dollars. Fearing that if he did not pay they may follow him around, he pulled his right pocket and out dropped $100.00.

"Take, this. You have been very good allies. Take this and never say anything to anybody at all. Would you swear?"

"We swear," Tallboy promised and Lester assured Beejay that the secret between the three of them would never be revealed.

As fate would have it, Beejay never saw these two characters again. He was to learn that the two were chosen to go to sea working on an ocean-liner that took them to the remotest parts of the world.

Beejay was still concerned that those members of his fraternity who did not make it to the last night's event may go around spilling the word if they were dealt with harshly. In the months preceding this evening he had always got all the fraternalists to cooperate with him, but he felt he was losing his hold on the group. He both wanted total control and if he could be guaranteed such, he could recruit new members. He also wanted to ensure that his society, 'The Leopards', would never be held up to ridicule nor be seen as persons who practiced black arts. How could he be sure that these brothers would turn up this evening and if by chance any dropped out of the group, would remain faithful to their pledge of secrecy.

Another cause for worry was if the fifteen decided together to try to replace him as leader. Apart from his small clique of gamblers, Beejay had only led this cohort of twenty-seven members by a mixture of appeal to special knowledge he claimed he had, and to outstanding personal achievements, none of which had been objectively verified. Beejay felt lonely and feared that this evening's meeting would not come off. He started to become confused and to compound matters he had not been in contact with the inner circle, so that he did not know how they were thinking. He wanted some revenge against those fifteen, but figured out that stern action would not only cause them to leave, but that the secrets he had passed on to them could be rudely divulged.

It was now 4.50 p.m. Beejay was sitting alone downstairs the Ranch. Then he remembered the many drinks he kept upstairs and ascended the stairs to take a double brandy to quiet his nerves and to imbue him with courage.

Minutes after, the meeting was underway, now under the chairmanship of Mr. Lovejoy.

"This grave convocation has been assembled to avert the compromise of our august organization. The tenets of loyalty and fidelity stand paramount. But few who adhere to our basic fundamentals are above our constitution."

He was clearly referring to himself, Beejay and Pierre though not that sure if Aaron was also so privileged.

"My responsibility here is to ensure the sanctity and unity of our fraternity."

Beejay was falling asleep.

"Before arriving at the true corpus of proceedings I require that each one reminisce on what courage stands for. A precept not to be lightly regarded, courage is not many removes from loyalty and fidelity. I hesitate to charge those who did not attend last night's initiation with disloyalty or infidelity."

He was careful not to use the word 'refuse'.

"However, I must essay this view. To be contumacious borders on being irreverent. My mood, however, does not brook hatred or revenge. As I invoke my authority I must say that of all the possible sanctions, fines, suspensions, flogging, confiscation of earlier degrees or life ban, life ban is the most serious because it represents exclusion and ostracism."

The fifteen who had been properly mobilized were very attentive.

"But what would it profit our fraternity to lose fifteen members who merely experienced a lapse in their courage? Nonetheless our majestic master does feel as though his authority has been undermined by the contumacy of a dozen and a quarter brethren."

Those of the inner circle seated at the head table were as impressed as the fifteen with the quality language oozing sweetly and smoothly from a worthy initiate. In addition, all who were awake felt that the matter of discipline had been left to the right man who was always known for his sense of diplomacy.

"Let this matter be considered quite serious. Forgiveness for non-attendance may be easy, but there cannot be any condonation of the deep disrespect meted out to our leader."

At this point Beaver stood up: "May I interrupt?"

"Yes, what sayest thou?" Mr. Lovejoy inquired.

"If all of us apologize to our leader in writing and assure him of his greatness, will this be good enough to have this matter closed?"

Beaver, a building contractor, had helped Mr. Lovejoy build his apartments both by not charging the full labour costs and supplying materials without asking him for more than half the price and Mr. Lovejoy was still grateful.

By this time Beejay had awakened groggily and he interjected:

"What do you mean?"

"The motion before us," replied Mr. Lovejoy, "is that those who did not attend should assure our revered leader of his greatness and in the same written missive, apologize unconditionally."

"Alright, I agree," grunted the leader.

The meeting ended.

Chapter 22

A PROPOSAL

HE HAD MET FRANCINE at the fair staged to raise funds for the victims of September 11th. She, a very attractive twenty-five year old, had come from a privileged background. Rumour had it that her parents had emigrated to Helen Isle thirty years earlier from England. Her father was a white businessman who built two hotels in Helen Isle. Her mother, a mulatto, called in Spanish-speaking places a Morena, was as rich as Lisle, father of Francine.

On meeting her at the fair, Aaron was immediately drawn to Francine. She, a lively, extroverted young woman with a flair for adventure and even dangerous games and pastimes, easily picked up the strong desire that Aaron experienced for her. The two quickly exchanged telephone numbers and agreed to establish contact between them. Both understood that the occasion of the fair—with so many persons present and with his wife not far away—Aaron would be as discreet and cautious as possible.

Strongly-built and possessed of the structure of a powerful six foot Olympian athlete, to Francine, Aaron was a man among men. She sensed that he was virulent and instantly believed that he would not allow his calling as a priest to stand in their way. To Francine, Aaron's wife definitely possessed a physically well-ordered husband and her immediate desire was to take this man.

Their first meeting after the fair came one night at a restaurant called 'The Hen and Eggs'. She had arranged dinner for the two of them. Before they reached 'The Hen and Eggs', Francine had fantasized, even obsessed at the prospect of a fling with this reverend and even if not a relationship, certainly a sizzly affair.

Seated at Table No. 7 under velvet lights, Aaron, fearless, especially since there were yet no other patrons in the restaurant, started by thanking Francine for inviting him out.

"I did have a very special meeting tonight, but I called it off so that I could be with you," he whispered.

Francine, so overjoyed that he accepted her proposal to dine never asked about the details of his meeting, its participants nor purpose of the meeting.

"Thanks for coming," she said.

"Let us make tonight the first of many."

As she was saying so, Aaron remembered how Beejay, Grainger and his other friends had earlier arranged to play poker at the Ranch where they assembled no fewer than five nights a week to practise their craft.

"What's on your mind, dear?" asked Francine who caught out Aaron in his engrossed frame of mind.

"Nothing," Aaron volunteered. "At least nothing is troubling me, especially since I am in such fine company."

"I am flattered," Francine offered, as she looked across the table at him. "What are you having for your first drink, Mr. Charming?"

"At this early stage I'll have a coke." Aaron replied.

Francine remarked, "You are going very soft, why?"

"I'll have something stronger after the first course."

All the while Aaron was thanking his lucky stars that this very beautiful woman had invited him out.

"Are you so quiet all the time?" Francine asked.

"No, not really," Aaron muttered.

All of a sudden the thought struck him that if he remained so preoccupied and quiet, Francine would either feel that he was not interested, or that he was far too quiet for her in that he was foolishly pretending to be overawed by the occasion.

"I was merely casting my thoughts at what could be happening at the meeting which I have missed to be with you!" he told her, haltingly.

"Come on, you have me here. I object to your placing me after a meeting. After all here you are and your meeting must be far away," she said firmly, almost rudely.

Aaron, recognizing that so far he was coming over as a bad actor, reached over to her and held her right hand firmly in his. She made a pretentious soft gasp, then started to giggle.

"Why?" Aaron questioned impatiently.

"I am left-handed," whispered Francine rather romantically.

Sensing that there was little point in switching his grasp to the other hand, Aaron pulled her towards him and as her indulgent face came close to his, paused, obviously teasing her. She, adept at all types of romantically driven play, stopped her face from touching his, evidently both having time to wait for more and equal to this type of exchange, which the two waiters in the restaurant chose to ignore. Then Francine decided to drop what in her mind she considered to be a little bombshell.

"You know, Father..." she was choosing her words deliberately, intent on teasing so as to heighten the tension. "We had a choice...."

Aaron started to wonder what she was talking about.

"Yes I had a choice," she dared to say.

"I did not have to invite you here, you know," she declared boldly. Now Aaron surmised that he had either spoilt things or Francine was going to chastise him for being too slow.

"I could have had my staff prepare dinner to be served in my apartment, but since this is our first time out together I decided to bring you out under these beautiful lights, lights which are not present in my apartment, and enjoy a kind of outing. In the future I shall have you come to my apartment, after the most careful planning so that no one would easily find us. You know people talk a lot. If you came to my apartment and loquacious people saw you, there would be a lot of talk and the inevitable gossip."

"What are loquacious people?"

"Father?" Again Francine decided to impart some formality to the evening.

"Look, Francine, you do not have to be so formal with me."

Somehow Aaron now started to look and act in a more relaxed fashion. In fact, he was becoming more and more aware of Francine's overwhelming charm and was coming fully under its influence.

"Do not act so formally with me Francine," Aaron insisted.

"By the way, my dear," Aaron asked. "What are loquacious people?"

"I feel," she answered, "that the word loquacious is a very old word. I learnt it from my mother. It means talkative. In olden days poets used it a lot. It can be used to mean 'babbling' or 'garrulous'."

"What?"

"Darling, I am not going to allow you the opportunity of requiring me to define this word. You must have heard the word garrulous used to mean talking and talking non-stop."

The idea struck Aaron that Francine was both naturally intelligent and educated. He started to think that here was an individual with astonishing beauty blended with brilliance of mind. He believed instinctively that she was wealthy, probably from the moment she was born.

"Francine, I must tell you that I am really enjoying your company. I feel that you are definitely my type of woman."

Now Francine hesitated. The drinks came. Should she simply thank him or should she try to calculate both why he had just uttered these words and the reason why within the last few seconds he had started to lighten up, even though he had had nothing to drink?

"Are you folks ready for your first course?" the young foreign waitress enquired.

"Are you ready for your first course?" Francine asked Aaron.

"Did you notice that the menu was already on our table when we first sat down?"

"To change the topic a bit, Francine, I want you to tell me some more about your apartment," Aaron requested.

"Oh, that?" pretending that her apartment was the last thing on her mind, while bringing the menu right up to her eyes. The waitress intervened:

"Ma'am I can tell you what is on the menu. It is divided into four parts. I can also say that in case you wish to order things which are not on the menu, I can tell you what we have tonight."

"Do find out what this gentleman is having," Francine indicated to the waitress.

"Oh, I will wait for you," Aaron said. Aaron's mind was not yet focussed on eating. He was savouring other things which he was experiencing. Coming to a restaurant which offered privacy. The fact that there were no busy bodies around. The soft inviting lights above his head. Francine's warmth.

Instinctively Francine discerned that there in front of her was a person whose concentration, at the level she desired, was firmly set on her.

"You know, darling, tonight promises much."

She uttered these words after noting that the waitress had moved away to offer the two of them more time to decide what they were going to select for their first course. Shifting her mind back to dinner, fully aware that Aaron was providing her with the opportunity to decide what she was going to have before his thoughts came upon his choice, she said to him:

"I think I will have onion soup with garlic bread as my first course." She then paused deliberately.

He seemed to be pondering his selection.

"Does my choice of first course meet your approval?"

"Go ahead and order," he urged. "Since you have such a fine sense of judgment, I think that I should follow your lead."

Aaron awaited her response. He delighted in the fact that she had just said that she wanted her decision about her first course to be upheld and endorsed by him. She in turn was impressed by his gesture to choose what she was going to have. Then Aaron remarked:

"I like this place. I like the privacy and the setting."

She moved her face closer to his and, enjoying this gesture, Aaron obliged by allowing their noses to touch.

"I was about to ask you about your apartment." Aaron said.

"I have lived in it alone. Right around the apartment itself there is an aura of quiet. You may feel that I like excitement and adventure. Yes, I do when I go out, but while I am in the confines of my house I love to be quiet. Have you ever considered that there is a class of person who to all outward appearances delights in thrills but privately prefers quietness and even solitude?"

The mention of this word solitude reminded Aaron of the lecturer in seminary who would always say that there do come moments when the human spirit craves solitude.

"Do you think, Francine, that it is possible for anyone to draw on sentiments of solitude when in company? I do not mean to sound as though I am setting up a contradiction, but I think that your superior intellect would guide you to an understanding of what I am getting at."

Then came Francine's swift reply:

"If you mean that the two of us can jointly experience solitude as we twin later on in my apartment, I am fully with you."

A mild sensation of masculine arousal started to interact with Aaron's undergarment. He sniggered.

"What is on your mind? A penny for your thoughts?" she pressed him.

Now Aaron grinned expressively.

"Francine, I must say to you. I am now your captive."

The waitress was approaching their table once again. Before she could reach them, Francine called out to her.

"We are both going to have onion soup and garlic bread."

She then gently pulled her face away from his and sat erect in her chair. The waitress turned in their direction and smiled.

"My apartment is some distance from here. Not too near nor is it that far. I have lived in it alone for about eight years. Later this evening I will start by showing you around it. I think that you not only understand, but appreciate that you have to accompany me to it as soon as our dinner is completed."

"Oh, I am definitely going there with you, Francine."

"Yes, you should be coming."

With such a direct invitation Aaron was now sure that the expected dinner should be put out of the way as soon as possible. He longed to be alone with Francine in what he considered to be the right setting. As good a place as this restaurant was, it would be no match for Francine's apartment. His belief was that there could be no waitresses nor servers in this apartment if he was getting his facts right.

"I must say that you are in a remarkably appropriate mood. I think that you are right to feel relaxed. In your field of work there must be times when the people get after you and inflict their issues, concerns and problems on you. My advice to you is to find time to relax. Whenever you feel stress and tension, please appoint me to bring you tranquility and solace." Francine sounded emphatic and sure of herself.

Aaron started to chew on the word solace. His mind went

back to his days in seminary. The word solace with its soft sound and comforting impact, was another of the words he had learnt during this training for the priesthood. Then he remarked to himself, that this woman in front of him had her way with words. She was different and not just because of her colour. At this moment if he was going to be honest with himself he had no regrets at being away from his friends in the Ranch. There was definitely something different, distinctive and special about Francine.

By silent consent the two moved swiftly through the first course. It was only their sense of tact and diplomacy which permitted the second course after which they left the 'Hen and Eggs'. The speed with which they consumed their dinner, abandoning the third course and dessert and their swift departure would have led any onlooker to speculate that the two had to go to face an emergency. Certainly, this was the opinion of the waitress, whose gratitude for the hefty tip did not obstruct the thought that this odd couple had to do something and it was urgent.

They arrived at Francine's place, entered and just as Francine was about to turn on the lights she heard Aaron say:

"There are two important things before you do anything else. Firstly do show me around this lovely place. I have seen nothing like this posh place before."

She hesitated, surprised both that he had remembered her promise to take him through the apartment and that he was actually deferring—however temporarily—the big event of the night. Then she fancied that he must have more time than she had felt he would, which would be a very good thing. He did say that there were two important things, but only made mention of one. Her mind simply could not make out what the second request was about. Since it was clear that Aaron had time, she too could be patient. She therefore took her time as she explained the various features of the showpiece of a living room.

"I am impressed. To say that this is a good apartment would be to elect to use the wrong word. Its carpet, the chairs elegantly upholstered, the computer room not to mention its screen and monitor, the style and layout of the bathroom, the beautifully varnished cupboards. I could go on and on. Congratulations on having acquired such a fine residence," Aaron declared happily.

"Now my second request is not a difficult one. The location of your main cupboard is so strategic that the moment I arrived here my eyes caught hold of that Napoleon brandy, there in the green bottle. In view of my choice to take no alcohol when I was with you in the restaurant earlier, I think I have done well enough to attempt a Napoleon now or rather a couple shots of Napoleons."

"Are you going to have your drinks with so much light on?" she pressed him invitingly.

"Leave them on," he insisted.

After some drinks the lights did go off. Aaron left the apartment five hours later with an envelope of bank notes and a promise from Francine to take him to England. He arrived home at about the same time he would on any night when he left the Ranch.

Chapter 23

OLD TALK

THEY WOULD ASSEMBLE THERE AS OFTEN AS five times a week. Their primary purpose was to gamble, but they frequently consumed copious quantities of alcohol while discussing all types of topics. They regularly told stories. Beejay, whose place and authority at these sessions was kind of hallowed, would tell most of the stories. He had licence to do so primarily on the basis of the fact that he had travelled to many places outside of Helen Isle and had made many overseas contacts.

On this occasion, just about half an hour after they all arrived, the topic was about the decline in status of males. The topic had not been introduced before in this forum, but among the hot topics over the past week were cricket, boxing, history, politics and sailing. Beejay would hold the attention of the group with his graphic description of the passage-ways of sea that linked the several islands from Helen Isle to Puerto Rico and beyond. He frequently fuelled their imaginations with tall tales of life in all the Virgin Islands and the way of life of the inhabitants of those places. He had in the past spoken of the tensions between the Soviet Union and the United States of the 1960s and 1970s, and one of his favourite topics was the philosophy and style of persons in the Black Power Movement like H. Rap Brown, Angela Davis, Stokeley Carmichael and Dick Gregory.

The discussions were 'enriched' by his lectures to the group about the Black American heavyweight boxer, Muhammad

Ali. Beejay had watched many of Muhammad Ali's fights on film and had read articles about this icon. More than once Beejay educated his followers about Ali's refusal to be conscripted to go to war in Vietnam, and how he lost his crown as undisputed heavyweight champion of the world as a result. The issues of racism and the radical movements of the 1960s and 1970s were raised.

In Beejay's mind the occasion to play poker and tonk should always be enlightened by moments when his group should delight in intellectual discussion and in all the sessions there was always debate and drinks, and banter and laughter as well. But on this particular night the matter of girls forging ahead of boys along with grown men being made to look inferior to women, were the topics of discussion.

Beejay made the observation that many women were making important strides and that there was an independence of spirit becoming evident among some females, especially the ones who had the good jobs and careers. In all this, Aaron alternated between listening and obsessing about when fortune would favour him with a big win. He was unhappy that most nights he would draw hands of bad cards and of all of these companions, Aaron was the one who would regularly have to borrow money most frequently from his peers because he lost more than 94% of the time. He was tempted to think that a few of his fellow players had marked the cards or otherwise manipulated the draws. He was not willing to admit that he was a bad player. Aaron remained preoccupied, but became more alert and more involved when Beejay poured him additional shots of whisky or when Beejay himself spoke.

Beejay went on to make the point that overall in Helen Isle more women appeared to be pursuing higher roles than before and many of them appeared to be goal-setters and trend setters. Pierre, who always gave the impression that he was never short of money, turned and asked Aaron if he had noticed that many young boys in the community were doing worse than the girls in school. Aaron did not answer and so Pierre then put the question open-endedly to the whole gathering.

Beejay said:

"I have been hearing that in both our primary schools and the secondary ones in the past two or three years girls have been definitely doing much better than boys. At the University of the West Indies female students now outnumber the male ones too! If this is so.... if it is a fact that boys are underachieving while girls are proving to be superior students, then somebody in authority had better act, else males would end up being completely inferior."

Pierre, a male chauvinist, lamented: "I think my brothers, that we would be doing guesswork on this matter. We do not know for certain."

Then Beejay intervened:

"Until proper research is done we cannot be a hundred percent sure."

MEANWHILE, NIGHT AFTER NIGHT Elizabeth would remain awake for hours on end. She had been married to Aaron for just over three years and as patient and long-suffering as she was, she was beginning to experience deep frustration. She wondered to herself if her marriage was really working. Her husband would return home between 2.00 a.m. and 4.00 a.m. and more often than not he would smell of alcohol and would take his bed and be off to sleep in no time. Here she was married to a priest. She was living a good life. She did not know what kept her husband out so late at night. They hardly talked, and in her judgment, Aaron was never home with her enough. Yet she neither asked him why he was regularly out so late nor was she tempted to think that he was seeing another woman.

A woman of deep faith, Elizabeth believed that some day some event would occur which would explain her husband's conduct.

There were other things about Aaron that Elizabeth took note of. People came to their house to see Aaron privately but she felt that their numbers did not suggest that Aaron was the busiest of priests. No clergy came to visit her husband. She was sure too, that he did not visit fellow clergy regularly.

On the occasions when Aaron was home he did not read the Bible nor religious literature to any significant extent. Frequently he seemed preoccupied and distant. It was as if he always had something on his mind. He seemed lonely. She did see her husband, but usually anytime after 2.00 a.m. and he would still be asleep when she left for work. This was the position nearly every single night and day. Was he a lonely man? She wondered.

Elizabeth was exceptionally aware that she was capable of child-bearing. Never once had her husband discussed their having children. Then she thought she should look at matters fairly. She decided to try to see if there were positives in her husband. He was tall and physically very strong. It would have been wrong for her to judge him as coming home after 2.00 a.m. every morning. Once or twice per week he would come home fairly early. He did do some reading, though she was not quite sure what he read. He was often quiet and quietness could be taken as a virtue. He did some physical exercises four times a week. Many times he would cook rather than wait for her to cook. But she wondered if these positives exceeded the negatives. He never seemed to have enough money and regularly borrowed from her and at his instance he would convert what she had loaned to grants, she thought. The fact that he never repaid her meant that she was subsidizing him heavily!

BACK IN THE RANCH, Sollie who had years earlier preceded Aaron's attendances there, was speaking:

"I have not travelled as much as you, Beejay, but in the five Caribbean islands which I have visited, there are concerns that today's boys are not matching up to the girls in school. There is even talk in the neighbouring islands that many boys seem afraid to play outdoor sports, simply because they want to come over as clean and tidy. There are islands where many schools were not mixed schools. Bimshire and Trinidad had had all boys' schools and the debate there is that before coeducation, boys were aggressive, strong and robust."

Beejay interrupted:

"Oh I have a special word. Based on all you have said you are suggesting that many boys, especially the ones in coeducational institutions have been inhibited." Aaron did appear to be listening and looked in Pierre's direction when Pierre began:

"Boys ought to be boys. They should never be made to tremble when faced by girls. What is your opinion, Brother Aaron?"

"Let me listen after our boss Beejay pours me a drink," Aaron insisted. Pierre continued:

"I am having difficulty," he was now shuffling the cards "with certain things. When I went to school nearly every school was a mixed school at the primary stage. In the same single sex schools, years ago, there was still some feeling that since males and females would be living in the same communities, they should not be separated at school. They should have been allowed to interact with members of the opposite sex at every stage of their experience and careers."

"Good point," Beejay was now intervening. "But how could an educational system allow mixing of the sexes at primary stage but separation at the secondary level?"

"I cannot say for certain," Sollie resumed. "But has it been the case that the colonial masters had fears that adolescents mixing in the same school with teenaged boys and girls together was a dangerous thing? Was it that the colonial masters were suspicious of having coeducational institutions or was it that they simply transported their own practices to us here in the Caribbean?"

Aaron was now sipping his scotch and ginger and did appear interested. Then he stood up and told the others that he was going to the washroom.

"Is he alright?"

Sollie interpreted Aaron's behaviour as a curious mixture of disinterest and indisposition.

"Oh, yes." Beejay proclaimed. As leader of this group, Beejay would often in the most imperious manner imaginable, speak with such authority that that very special ring—the distinctive tone he imparted to his words—left no doubt that in his own subjective estimation he was a person who wielded all the power. He had a way of being loyal to his friends, but hated when anyone challenged him or refused to comply with his wishes. Above all, he had a lot of time for Aaron and to him the young priest could do no wrong. Significantly, Sollie and Pierre never saw Aaron as a threat since both of them felt they stood secure in Beejay's esteem.

"Can I say something, Boss?" Sollie inquired. "I find that Aaron does not seem to listen nor to take careful note of all we do and say. Like the two of you I like him but he keeps me guessing and I would feel better if he could really play cards better. Then he would be a better competitor and the standard of our games could be raised higher."

"Don't you worry about the young man," Pierre cautioned. "The fact that Beejay has included him means that he has something in him."

"Do you think though…" asked Sollie, "That he really enjoys our highly intellectual and thought provoking discussions?"

"I know he fires a good drink," Pierre observed. "Oh we were talking about young boys and the fact that today's young boys are different from us, but you know that I am tempted to look at male achievement in a broader sense. This world has had males who have succeeded against the odds. There have been black males in the Caribbean who achieved greatly as far back as the 1930s. I have no doubt that with facilities for good health and education many of our forefathers could even have achieved in the 19th century, even during the days of slavery."

Pierre then assured the small gathering that he knew what he meant when he spoke of the 19th century. He then brought this dimension to the discussion.

"Now let us look at the life of Dr. Martin Luther King. I doubt that it can be said that the blacks of his era, he included, were born with silver spoons in their mouths. On his ability King became an achiever. Highly educated, brilliant, and orator of orators. Now we have here before spoken of persons involved in the struggle to advance the cause of blacks. At Beejay's urging we in here adore Muhammad Ali. The message that persons like Muhammad Ali and Dr. Martin Luther King would have given to young black males would no doubt be to strive hard for excellence and to let their ability work for them. You know there are black role models whose record are there for all to see. Persons like George Washington Carver and Booker T. Washington so achieved and are such beacons in the lighthouse of history that their lives are worth emulating."

Beejay did not let Pierre continue. "My deputy, your words are very, very eloquent. Your message clear."

At this moment Aaron resumed his seat at the table.

"My friend and brother," Beejay looking at Aaron, said: "You just missed a message delivered so brilliantly and with such fine words that I now hereby demand that Pierre repeat the last things he said about Muhammad Ali, Dr. Martin Luther King, George Washington Carver and the famous Booker T. Washington."

Pleased that Beejay was admiring how he was speaking, Pierre who had not been drinking too much, poured a fairly large rum, sat up straight, raised a toast without requiring the others to join him and was able to repeat all that he had said a short time ago. Conscious of what had transpired behind Aaron's back, Beejay said to Aaron.

"It would be very good if you get information on outstanding black people."

"I will," Aaron promised and lied simultaneously.

"Now," Pierre resumed, "Every boy who lives among us in this island should have strong, positive role models. Too many mothers do not let their children's fathers see them. I believe that many of our boys are so dominated by their mothers that they cannot act or do anything when their mothers are not physically there for them. Somebody should do research on the extent to which mothers could be a factor in stifling their sons."

"Then," Sollie joined in, "Somebody should do a study on whether our mothers are insisting on higher standards from the girls and the girls respond by excelling, while boys are not encouraged to excel."

"Well, then," Pierre put in. "There should be research on if mothers spoil their boys which causes them not to want to work hard."

It was clear to Aaron that the other three were throwing around ideas and looking at possible causes for male underachievement. But he sat and said nothing. Aaron was feeling lonely despite the drink he had taken.

"Now," Sollie started again, "Is there also a problem of men, yes grown men not doing well? I have heard about something called male marginalization, which certainly must include adult males."

"Pause there, Sollie!" Beejay requested firmly. "We have to play another game before this debate and conversation continue."

Beejay now shuffled the cards. As he did so, he winked at Aaron. Aaron knew that particular look. It both meant that

Beejay was up to something and that Aaron would benefit. Unlike the other two, Beejay was not at all troubled by Aaron's failure to add to the discussion. As though agreed beforehand to rush this game in order to get back to their conversation, three of them took their hands and made their bids almost thoughtlessly. Aaron won this game and was in theory entitled to $4,000. He understood, however, that he could keep only $1,000 since he had come to the table on this night in debt to the other three present with him. He wanted to leave and take his net winnings with him. He sensed, though, that for the others it was still fairly early and more rounds of games were to be played.

"It is now for me" Sollie started. "To raise this very serious matter of women outdoing men in recent years. Already tonight we have heard of how girls are beating boys in our schools, not only in this nation but also in other Caribbean islands as well."

Sollie stopped momentarily to think. He was unsure of how he ought to continue, because despite grave difficulty in assessing and understanding Aaron, he was positively certain that there were no larger male chauvinists anywhere in Christendom than Pierre and Beejay. He wanted to make honest observations, but was reluctant either to trespass on the sensitivities of these two men or, in the process of assessing the situation, to come over as being excessively inclined to be on the side of women.

"Make your point," Pierre demanded.

"Come, say all you want to say," Beejay insisted.

"I was only introducing the topic for discussion. I will come back after all three of you have made some early pointers and I will comment after hearing you." Secretly, Sollie hoped that Beejay and Pierre would make whatever points they wanted to without bashing women.

"Let us pause for liquid refreshment," came the command from Beejay.

They drank. Of note Beejay, as formally as anyone could be, proposed a toast to Aaron for winning the recently concluded game.

"The topic of relations between men and women stir up in me," Beejay commenced, "Memories of my having learnt of some individuals who agitated in England years ago. I speak of the suffragettes, militant women, who argued that women had been the victims of oppression. They clamoured for rights, more rights for women and they have succeeded. I challenge you my closest colleagues, to do your homework and do not only find out what 'suffragettes' means, but also aim to discover what they stood for. Check to see if certain persons in the Caribbean without labeling themselves have adopted many of the policies of these women. Much of what these so-called liberators trumpeted has been passed into law in the Caribbean, although I cannot say with truth that there have been serious suffragette societies in the Caribbean."

Sensing that Beejay was exercising considerable restraint, Sollie raise his right hand and the former stopped. Keen to encourage Beejay to refrain from attacking women, Sollie said

"I regret that I cannot get hold of information on suffragettes right here and now. It is clearly your wish, most excellent leader that we three learn from you."

Sollie knew Beejay so well that he could get his way with him by simply appealing to Beejay's sense of self-importance.

"Would I be out of order if I suggested that we men have been cocky and complacent for years?" Sollie continued.

Rather than interrupt Sollie, Beejay wanted to see what philosophical points or facts this speaker would raise.

"My opinion is that women are seizing opportunities which men have been ignoring."

"Yes," Pierre intervened: "Women have also been setting goals and working to achieve them. Many of them are excellent managers of money."

Sollie was astonished. Two male chauvinists to the one had spoken. It was now Aaron's turn. Sollie looked in Aaron's direction. Aaron had fallen asleep. The game ended. In fact the discussion also ended.

The other three drank while waiting on Aaron. Sollie, who had given Aaron a ride five and a half hours earlier, gave him a lift back home after he came awake.

Chapter 24

RECOVERY

"MY NAME IS ANTOINE AND I AM A POLY-ADDICT. I returned to my homeland here four years ago and through this wonderful fellowship and the help of my higher power whom I call God Almighty, today I continue to be free of all my many addictions. Today is my anniversary. I first got this invaluable programme while I lived abroad in Akron, Ohio, when I was a patient in the famous St. Thomas hospital there. During my days of using and boozing, at first I thought that food, sex, gambling, drugs and alcohol provided the good life but things reached a head and I realized while hospitalized that my life had become completely unmanageable."

Outside of the meeting room rented twice a week from the church council of St. Gabriel's the Greater, Aaron could clearly hear Antoine's words. He stood close to a wall just outside his church hall under a very large saaman tree. Something encouraged him to listen. After all, when he first came to the church, this group was already meeting there and though he had never visited it nor spoken to any of its members, he had succeeded in persuading Patrice to raise its rent seven times in the last eighteen months. That Patrice neither required him to account for the increases nor even to deposit all rent monies collected into the church's bank account gave licence to Aaron to see this strange group as nothing less nor more than a curious appendage to his church, providing personal income for him as leader of St. Gabriel's the Greater.

Something inside gripped Aaron's attention. He noticed

at least thirty persons listening intently to Antoine, and this speaker's manner of delivery of his personal testimony was proving most interesting. Sure that no one inside could see him, Aaron continued to listen to Antoine.

"I started using and abusing at age fifteen. I tried marijuana. Often I used marijuana with wine. I ate voraciously, often waking up in the middle of the night either to heat food which was in the fridge or even to cook a fresh meal. By the time I was seventeen I had grown to hate school and was weighing two hundred and ten pounds while carrying a height of five feet, two inches. Oh, how I loved to frequent the red light districts wherever I went while I was in the U.S.A. Oh how the gin and scotch whisky chased away my inhibitions and how I made the red light districts my regular haunts. I dropped out of college and I did odd jobs like working as a Porter or Messenger or Labourer. I could not keep a job more than three months since I would be fired for being too drunk or too high or too weak and tired to work. I had turned my back on religion...."

Now Aaron was all ears.

"I regret to share with you that before I left home to live in the wild, my parents had ensured during my boyhood that I attend church and Sunday school. But addiction got the better part of me and life became wine, food, gambling, songs, drugs and women. I hate to inform that there were men in my life too, on occasions, especially when I was short of money. I lived a horrible and nasty life and my way of life stood in stark contradiction to the values which my parents had passed on to me before I left this island."

Outside Aaron listened, even more but by now he started to become agitated with bitterness and anger.

"When I gambled I did so to excess too. The reason: I am poly-addicted. My addiction is a compound addiction with its constituent parts, each very, very grave and complicated. It has been easy for me to become hooked on bad things. For four years I did quit drugs, alcohol, sex and gambling to train as a psychologist and I was fortunate to qualify. I remained bone dry while training as a psychologist, but as soon as I graduated I started to use and abuse again. Four times I came to in jails and was hospitalized in New York, Philly and Pennsylvania. Yes, I did travel within the U.S.A. or better still my addictions drove me all over the States. I got married to a girl when I was twenty-four years old...."

Shivering with bitterness at this fool's confession, Aaron wondered why Antoine did not put proper structure and sequence to his story.

"It was whilst I was dry that I married an American called Susan. Even before I resumed using and abusing drugs, sex, alcohol, food and gaming again, the marriage was not a happy one especially since my wife kept telling me how selfish, bigoted and resentful I was. She even dared to tell me, the world's finest psychologist, how bitter and egocentric I was. Well, whenever she told me so, which was at least three times daily before meals—when I was at home—I became so enraged that more than ten times in our sorry marriage I struck her. On the last occasion she called the police and I awoke in jail in Akron where I had returned. Let me say though, that this last episode in jail just before my drying out at St. Thomas hospital was described to me from its cause right down to the event by the police who told me that I was both violent and very sick and that I was in need of help!

Immediately after leaving jail I went on a terrific bender. I ate large amounts of hamburgers, French fries and other fast foods and in three weeks I was weighing 270 pounds. In those three weeks I gobbled down many, many beers, gambled, smoked marijuana, drank very, very cheap wine and came to regularly in what I would call disorderly houses, often waking up next to some person I did not recognize. I remember that while I was on that, my last bender, I was once in an old dingy bar in a ghetto drugged and drunk and almost penniless. I strayed into a room barely able to walk and some persons, themselves high or half-drunk, were gaming. I barely recall being in a betting game and I was bluffing when some poor soul passed me $500 and told me I had won. My memory about what I did to win is still unclear but I do clearly remember drinking some gin and whisky before being taken to the St. Thomas hospital.

At hospital they kept me for six long weeks. I remember at first being told by a nurse that I was dehydrated and had come into the place hyperventilating. They did their best for me and administered sedatives and vitamins, and in my last two weeks they made me attend meetings at which, I was told, I would hear similar stories to mine, find real new friends and be shown a programme and way of life that, as they said, would get me out of the gutter. They assured me that I would find fellowship, but had to commence by admitting personal powerlessness over all my many addictions.

On my last day in hospital, a fellow from Texas came to see me. He told me what using and boozing had done to him and after sharing some pretty scary experiences he had gone through, he asked me: 'Do you want me to be your padrino?' I was so desperate that without knowing what a padrino was, I said, 'okay'. Carlos, as he told me his name was, gave me too different big books, each from two different fellowships and showed me around town so that I would know where meetings were. He encouraged me to make new friends in both fellowships and kept telling me to go to meetings and not to use any mind-altering chemical substance in any form. In time I came across a fellowship that assisted over-eaters and one that assisted gamblers and all the four fellowships I attended were based on each member practising a twelve step programme."

Uneasy, Aaron was listening and no one inside the meeting was aware that the parish Priest was on the outside eavesdropping. Aaron did not know most of the people inside, but was sure that someone sitting at the back was Father Fred. Inside, Antoine continued.

"Today I have back my sanity and my life. I make myself available to all who would listen. Today I am the sponsor of five pigeons. I do not lecture to them, I simply share my experiences. I have become their padrino. I believe the steps started to work for me when I admitted and accepted personal powerlessness over many addictions and I certainly came to believe that a power greater than me could and would restore me to sanity.

Everyday I turn my will and life over to the care of my creator. When I get up in the morning I ask the Almighty to take control of my will, to govern my thoughts and actions and to bring protection over my life one day at a time. Even before returning to this lovely island where I was born I spent five days with Father Francis of Akron reviewing and taking stock of my life."

Now Aaron was all ears.

"I spoke to Father Francis about my behaviours and actions—my excesses. I told him about my greed, my lust, my excuses, my envy, my mistakes, my resentful thoughts and after about six two-hour sessions with Father Francis, I felt as though a great burden had been lifted off my shoulders. Just before going to Father Francis, I had listed all my personality flaws, including self-righteousness and self-justification alongside anger, avarice, lust, ruthlessness, wild fears, arrogance, sex, greed, brutish selfishness and many more shortcomings...."

As Aaron continued to eavesdrop, he could not help but wonder how many people in the world would provide a detailed account of their weaknesses, carrying confession to absurd lengths and how captivated Antoine's audience was. Then Antoine continued:

"Yes, I had to discuss my faults with another human being."

This galled Aaron, for if he had to do a confession, he would limit it to a general confession, not letting anyone see into any dark practices he might have done. Aaron recalled that at seminary, confession before a priest was optional, the idea being that in a close intimate relationship with a supreme being, one could confide in that being in the absence of any other.

"....After those sessions with Father Francis, I learnt that I had to identify all persons I had hurt with the aim of willingly approaching them to make restitution. Yes, I spent several hours in close, careful reflection resolving to try to remember each person I had harmed, whether someone from whom I stole or someone I cheated on, somebody I used and abused or someone to whom I showed resentment.

Top of the list was my American wife Susan, but through conscious effort, I recall short-changing store owners by swearing that my bills were miscalculated. I went to a few shopkeepers and businesses, apologized and paid what I had owed, sometimes going back years. In instances when I had exploited girls by playing on their emotions and using them, I went back to them and asked their forgiveness."

For Aaron this clearly was the limit, and he had had enough. He looked around quickly and as the sun set he quickly sneaked out of the southern gate of the churchyard, wondering which cult of crazy characters had been using his church hall and what was their ultimate purpose.

"I know that this is an open meeting and a few of you may find my speech and action here this evening to be strange. But among us is a man of God, Father Fred who though not a member of our fellowship can use fifteen of my minutes to speak about the value of a twelve step spiritual programme and its therapeutic effects....

Friends, it has been my pleasure sharing my experience, strength and hope. When I was in the deep abyss of active addiction in many ways I was useless, but today my gratitude and selflessness place me to be of service not only to all of you but also to the still suffering addict. Thank you very, very much. I am still Antoine and I am a clean, sober poly-addict.

I now call on Father Fred to speak of the spiritual angle of twelve-step programmes."

Suddenly a man put up his hand craving attention.

"This is my first meeting." He was interrupted by very loud applause. "My name is Matthias and I too have a problem with drugs and alcohol."

"You are in the right place," an elderly woman shouted. "But sit and listen, when the meeting is over someone will talk to you and you will be shown how to keep in contact with the fellowship. Let's hear Father Fred," stressed the elderly woman.

Then Father Fred came up to the head table:

"Before I actually start to talk about the real value of the twelve steps, since there is a new person here I want to urge him to avoid the first unit of every mood altering substance, one day at a time. Many people find that when they have problems living one day at a time represents a useful start. In my religion I often take comfort from the words of Matthew 6:34. '*Take therefore no thought for the morrow: for the morrow shall take thought for the things of itself. Sufficient unto the day is the even thereof.*'"

Father Fred thought that if given a chance again he would explain Matthew 6:34. All were listening closely to Father Fred. Father Fred himself noted that more than half of those present were white and were clearly expatriates.

"For anyone seeking to get rid of a problem it is necessary to disregard the future completely. The burden of living one's life in the future is unbearable. I recommend day-tight compartments. I recommend the now. Someday I will talk to you more closely on the future. But today is our current account. So, to Matthias my advice is to quit your habits today. I call them habits, but they are really behaviours that are puzzling to most people.

Why do some people—a majority—take one or two drinks and quit, allowing many days, even weeks, to pass before drinking again in moderation? Yet there are those who drink everyday and who are led by drink, whose actions under the influence of drink are unpredictable. Then there are those who, if they take one drink of alcohol in any form have to take other drinks.

There are those who drink first thing in the morning and more often than not these are the ones who cannot take one drink and stop. They are alcoholics. Many definitions of who is an alcoholic have been advanced but let me briefly tell how I understand the programme of recovery that works under all conditions.

Accepting, after admitting personal powerlessness over alcohol is necessary before putting one's life completely under the control of a higher power. Admitting and accepting that one's life is unmanageable and that one accepts that a higher power could restore one's soundness of mind is the start of recovery. There is power in accepting one's personal addiction to alcohol. In fact there is power in admitting and accepting any personal problem because it means that one is prepared to reach out for help. Further, when one accepts one's problem, one is demonstrating a maturity which means that one is owning up to the problem and not blaming others. This is the first stage in honest confession and can set the stage for a personal spiritual cleaning.

After owning up to the problem there must be readiness to do something such as surrendering and submitting to available spiritual help. No higher power will work readily with a sufferer unless there is nearness, closeness to the higher power. For anyone including the most brilliant and active.... to gain access to the support of a higher power is necessary.

Next, if any person truly wants to change, there must be thorough personal stock-taking—housecleaning if you wish—backed up by a desire to confess in the presence of a trustworthy person, every wrong and harm done. If this is omitted, guilt, fear, procrastination and negative feelings will assert themselves to tempt the person to resume the old behaviours and compulsions of the pasts. Additionally, restitution, amends and reparation have to be diligently practiced to cleanse and ready the changing person to receive the sunlight of the spirit. These things having been done, considerable prayer and ongoing personal housekeeping must be regularly practised. Thereafter it remains for the changed person to work to help others, rendering to all a life of selfless service.

What lessons can be learnt from Antoine's story shared so honestly here this afternoon? There must be willingness to want help and if a person is seeking help he or she must want help for themselves. There must be no reservation of any kind over whether or not one has a problem and one must want to separate one's self from the problem."

Clearly Father Fred knew what he was talking about.

"The recovering person must be so unselfish as to want to share—share everything. Putting aside false pride, the recovering person has to find and practice genuine humility, else there could be trouble. A sponsor called by our friend in South America a 'padrino', can offer invaluable assistance. Note that Antoine had a sponsor.

Matthias, please find a sponsor, if possible, today. Remember today is all we have and none of us should put it off. Working with others and trying to help anyone in need are also necessary. But I better pause here and if anyone has any questions I will answer and Antoine as a psychologist can assist me, if he will."

"Can a person who having been a slave to negative habits who fails to practice the principles you have outlined, really back off from his or her bad habits?"

"Yes, if this person has will-power made of iron," Father Fred observed."

"But practical experience has shown that what people call negative habits are really illnesses! In fact many so-called bad habits lead to compulsive obsessive disorders,"

Antoine interjected, "and such disorders are psycho-spiritual illnesses."

"Can a person who is a full-blown alcoholic, compulsive gambler or addict ever control their habits?"

"Yes, if control means overcoming their so-called habits by quitting completely," Father Fred admonished.

"Can an alcoholic make up his mind firmly that he would go to a party and take two drinks and quit after these two drinks?" Someone asked.

"No, if an alcoholic takes a drink, he or she will continue to take more until his or her life becomes unmanageable," Father Fred was clearly on top of his topic.

Now Matthias the newcomer had a question.

"If an alcoholic drinker stops drinking for two or three years, can he return to safe drinking?"

At this Antoine replied:

"Once a person is an alcoholic, even very long periods of abstinence will not qualify them to recover enough to drink with any degree of control. Experience has shown that if a gambler quits gaming for many years and returns to gamble, he would probably end up gambling like in days of old even after trying to practice controlled gambling. The same is true for a heroin addict, an alcoholic; any addict. The best way to deal with compulsive obsessive disorders and behaviour is to quit those that you obsess about or have a compulsion for!"

Then another question came,

"Which people are best qualified to help an addict to stay away from their addiction?"

The meeting ended after this last question. Then cake, sandwiches, soft drinks, tea and coffee were served. Members of this group, clearly happy and satisfied, proposed a toast to Antoine, who was celebrating an anniversary and to Matthias, the new member, who was described as the most important person at the meeting.

Three members along with Father Fred offered Matthias

some cake and sandwiches and took him aside for counselling.

"You know," said the priest, "today is the first day of the rest of your life. In the world of alcoholism, a man takes a drink, and the drink takes more drink. Then the drink takes the man.... Avoid the first drink one day at a time."

"Does everybody who comes here quit entirely and change their ways?" was the question Matthias decided to ask.

"Unfortunately, no," said Annette, a middle-aged Canadian who had quit drinking and smoking cigarettes for fifteen years. "Alcoholism and other addictions are funny sicknesses and every alcoholic and addict must first overcome the problem of denial. We know that victims of diseases marked by compulsive disorders often feel that they do not have a problem. They feel that even when they overdo drinking, drugging, gambling and the like, that they will come a point when they could limit their intake or amount and practise moderation in the future. Some go on and on and never quit. So, my son, bear in mind that if you do have a problem with alcohol, the disease of alcoholism is a disease of denial. In my case alcoholism made me a liar and a cheat!"

"How best can I really avoid dangerous substances?" Matthias was very interested and raised the question.

To this Annette said, "Pledge to live one day at a time avoiding the first unit of any mind-altering substance. Avoid resentments, fears, tensions, anxieties. Make no major decisions for a while. Do not go around bars or joints where the substances are available. Take a lot of rest. Do not get too tired, angry, lonely or hungry. Try to make many, many meetings. Choose a sponsor and a co-sponsor."

"What is a sponsor?" the new comer asked.

"A sponsor is someone in the programme who understands and practises the programme who can guide you," Annette advised.

"Can you be my sponsor, Miss?"

"No I prefer a man to be your sponsor. You might have "male issues," concerns or experiences that affect men and manhood," she suggested.

Matthias was convinced that this woman was sent from above because he knew that his drinking and drugging in recent weeks had badly affected his manhood where it mattered most. He hesitated for a moment, then he asked sheepishly,

"Can Father Fred sponsor me?"

"No, he understands us and is of great help, but he has not had the experience of an alcoholic addict nor gambler."

"Okay, I'll ask Antoine to be my sponsor."

Then Annette told him"

"Alright if Antoine takes you on as his pigeon or sponsee I can work with you as your co-sponsor, but tell him everything that has affected you before you call on me and remember put your sobriety and abstinence as your number one priority. I have to go now, the others have left. Remember, first things first. One day at a time."

By now all of the others had left. It was just Annette and Matthias and after some more words of encouragement from Annette the two parted company.

Matthias left for his home feeling upbeat. He had made up his mind. He would avoid people, places and things that would tempt him to drink all day. He would attend the meetings.

Matthias never got high nor drunk after having attended his first meeting.

Chapter 25

LECTURE IN ENGLAND

TO SAY THAT RODERICK HAD BEEN CLOSE TO FRANCINE would have been the understatement of any century. A personable, loquacious speech-writer who loved to mingle with society's upper classes, Roderick was born in England, but had spent some years in France and Switzerland. He had met Francine when she was seventeen and he, nineteen. They took to each other and cavorted and caroused together whenever opportunities presented themselves. On occasions, the two would create opportunities. After all, they both delighted to take risks.

Normally adoring tall big men, Francine found that what Roderick lacked in stature and size, he made up for with his mouth. Garrulous, ostentatious and given to exhibiting his considerable learning, notwithstanding his strict adherence to the many social activities of the night, the tiny five-footer was such a reader that in his and Francine's words 'he dreamed books'.

Roderick, popular both in France and the United Kingdom made a comfortable living by writing speeches for politicians, parsons and even publicans. Possessed of an excellent command of the Queen's English, Roderick supplemented his handsome income by delivering lectures in France, Switzerland, Germany and England. His literary style as a writer was by no means superior to his manner of delivering fine lectures, though to some critics if he was sufficiently carried away he would depart from the context of his speeches from time to time to utter some banter and on occasions salacious jokes totally unrelated to the themes at hand. Roderick was due to deliver a lecture in England and Francine had heard about it. Not having seen or heard from Roderick for a full six months, Francine was determined to return to Europe and whatever her schedule or circumstances, she was going to pay for her attendance at the lecture.

Having chosen as his theme, "The Binding Nature of Morality – Yes, Morality Binds," Roderick had wished secretly that he could speak to a packed Royal Albert Hall. This desire accorded to its last shred with the size of Roderick's ego and he was disappointed that seven days before the lecture, only seventy persons, mainly first year law students had paid their fees to hear him. This figure did not change until just one day before lecture time, Roderick learnt that three additional tickets were bought. Instead of the Royal Albert Hall, Roderick had to settle for a school hall near to a place called Christ Church Avenue fairly close to the Kilburn station in London.

In planning his speech he decided to keep himself out of it and intended using 'I' only where necessary. After all, based on his own personal moral practices and in particular his continuing adulterous adventures, Roderick was going to be careful not to expose himself to any embarrassment or harangue during question time. Undergraduates were known to be aggressive, candid and probing. Instead he was going to look at custom, norms and morals first in an intellectually abstract manner. Then he would consider 'Norms and Morality in so-called Primitive Societies'. He would also explore any link he could find between morality and law and seek too to establish that laws tabooing discrimination based on gender, age or disability did have some moral foundation. Unsure if his audience hailed mainly from boarding schools or the upper class, Roderick had decided to avoid the controversial issue of morality and sexuality.

Though disappointed that on this occasion he was not going to address a packed Royal Albert Hall he was going to give this lecture his best shot and he would try as far as possible to avoid explicit reference to sex and avoid evoking laughter from his audience in ways which he had attempted, with varying degrees of success, in the past. Alert to the fact that most of his audience was made up of University undergraduate students, he would set out to raise his standards. As he brooded on the topic he wondered if females were going to be amply represented in the audience and in a philosophical way, pondered on who could be the last three persons to be booked for attendance to hear him.

On the night of the lecture, The Reverend Aaron Isaac Zacariah Ezekiel Fromgence sat between two ladies in the back of the audience. On his right and very close to him was Francine, while on his left Christine was nervously seated as though she expected some trouble, if not during the lecture itself in the period after it. Christine, friend and confidante of Francine, was brought along by her friend to camouflage matters. Aaron did not know this, while Roderick the lecturer more saw Christine, whom he did not know, than Francine whose make-up and broad hat disguised her for two-hours. Roderick started by defining morality, custom, norms and folkways and was making sense. He made liberal use of a chalkboard which was attached to a wall at the front of the room.

Aaron sat disinterested more hearing what was being said than listening closely. His thoughts drifted to what this night would offer on his return to his hotel. He had come to this lecture not only to accommodate the wishes of Francine who had urged him to attend, but also on account of the fact that she had made it possible for him to be in Europe by bearing every expense so far incurred. In his own lustful way he wondered what Christine would be like as a lover when suddenly he felt Francine's firm grip which commanded him to stop day-dreaming and listen!

By this time Roderick was raising the issue of how before economic opportunities were made available to women, men in so-called primitive societies felt bound to provide food, clothing, shelter and support for their women. Aaron did hear this and without becoming interested, proceeded to wonder again about how adorable Christine was. Pink and white dress with beads around her neck and the most stylish of pink shoes, Christine was as attractive as Francine.

"Yes early men in simple societies in Africa, the Caribbean, Asia and Europe saw themselves as breadwinners not only for the sake of their children but for their spouses as well."

This emphatic declaration registered pointedly in Aaron's mind and brought him back to the reality that it was men not women who were the early breadwinners. Roderick then spoke of what he called micro-morality vs. macro-morality.

"At the level of the individual within the household, children were taught and socialized into supporting their parents when the latter became too old or sick to properly provide for themselves. Within individual families too, there were mores that required youngsters to obey and carry out the instructions of their parents. The commands of parents in their own private households have always in non-European individual households carried a bindingness about them."

Clearly Roderick was talking about morality at the micro-level. The students in the audience understood every word. What they could not understand was that there were three full adults at the back who, though being present, each seemed preoccupied.

"In traditional African and Caribbean societies, norms first learnt in the households often transcended the ways of the household to assume a 'macro-nature'. Why do I make this pronouncement?" Roderick asked rhetorically at first, then paused for a good few seconds. As no one in the audience took him up, he said that many forms of respect for elders in particular were strong values in early societies in Africa and the West Indies in the households originally but spread and entrenched themselves to become important norms at the level of tribe, community and society elsewhere. He went on to make reference to the fact that in early societies theft, sacrilege and murder were moral wrongs before becoming crimes; that moral precepts of a sufficiently strong and binding nature almost always preceded the enactment of the more serious customs and laws. His words on the obligations which entrenched customs had decreed, were found to be quite sound by all his audience including the three at the back of the room. For those three had somehow started to pay close attention.

Satisfied that he had reached his audience, though still unsure of the heavily made up lady in the back, Roderick however noticed that she sat beside a man having the build of Lennox Lewis and the demeanor of Mike Tyson. He did make mental notes of the three in the audience but made no effort to treat them any differently from the young members in it who were paying rapt attention to all he had to say. Most of the undergraduates were making notes, probably with their eyes on question time.

Roderick then informed that he was next going to define and describe bindingness.

"To appreciate bindingness one must be certain what obligation entails," Roderick declared with a sense of enthusiasm.

"Even in the realm of the civil law an argument can be tendered that moral duty—moral obligation is cleverly intertwined with solid legal precept. After all morality is often merged into the law, though some persons cynically argue that there could be immoral laws such as laws legalizing forms of gambling and homosexuality. But more to the point, it is clear that each citizen—indeed each person present in a given jurisdiction—is bound to obey the laws governing rape...."

At this stage Aaron was not paying attention since his mind was wandering on what delights the night could present him later on. Roderick continued:

"Yes, people are bound to—must obey laws banning rape,

robbery, buggery, theft and murder. In the laws relating to equity and trusts where conscience matters greatly, persons are bound by such high principles of morality—of conscience—that they are bound to behave in particular ways. In the law of contract, parties to an agreement are bound for in such matters "bindingness" arises where there is offer, acceptance, consideration, performance and satisfaction."

Having been nodding, Aaron came awake when there was mention of performance. Without elaborating on the full extent to which this bindingness to which he referred applied, Roderick continued:

"Yes, in contracts there is performance, satisfaction and discharge." Aaron suddenly became wide, wide awake and his mind was wondering how performance, satisfaction and discharge related to the lecture and could bear potential and hope for him to fully realize at least some satisfaction, both later in the night and for the rest of his stay in England.

No longer succinct and not carefully spelling out the nexus between morality, performance and discharge, Roderick had now aroused all present to listen. Having drifted off somewhat by being very diligent in outlining the principles pertinent to concepts in contract on which he spent some twelve minutes attempting to prove binding morality, Roderick went on to establish some instances where matters and issues which were initially moral matters did ultimately find themselves elevated to a legal status. He presented a few anecdotes in support of his arguments. He concluded by showing that some immoral behaviours are tabooed even when there is no written law prohibiting these behaviours, showing how some societies, through a strong attachment to custom turned their faces against proscribed behaviour. The undergraduates applauded loudly at the end of the delivery.

During question time one blonde undergraduate exclaimed that she did not quite understand the link between pure morality and concepts like performance, satisfaction and discharge. The way she confessed her ignorance and sought clarification brought laughter from the audience and considerable interest from Aaron. Roderick now knew that he had to be cautious.

"Morality concerns itself with rectitude and correctness of behaviour. I do not mean being merely politically correct. Where there is a moral issue the question always is, is it binding on a people?"

In a contractual situation the agreement ought to be binding. I say 'ought' rather than 'is' because though most contracting parties will obey and abide by the terms which they have agreed, there are those who either refuse to be bound or find ways of not living up to their agreements. A contracting party should really place himself under an obligation that makes it unconscionable for him to reject the very conditions to which he has consented. What ought to be is what should be without more, but there are cases in which a party should perform his part in line with his agreement and does not. He ought to have performed but has failed to do so."

Then Roderick conceded that he should have focused on the fact that a morally binding agreement should be enforceable. He did say too that there were instances where what morality required was also required by law. Roderick concluded:

"Yes, I did get carried away somewhat by involving performance, satisfaction and discharge when I ought to have stuck to the fact that contracting parties are bound to render their performance and to that extent their consciences should have so worked that morally speaking they should have viewed performance as resulting from moral-rectitude and non-performance as being morally inappropriate and wrong."

The questioner had from the outset recognized that Roderick had been speaking to contractual concepts that were salacious, but did not properly demonstrate the relevance between these concepts and morals. For after all the questioner thought there were instances in real life when satisfaction and discharge result more from immorality than right behaviour.

The undergraduate was satisfied that Roderick had shown

a weakness, probably because he uttered terminology intended to excite the imagination of the audience. She accepted Roderick's attempt at clarification and allowed others in the audience to put questions.

After the questions, refreshments were served during which Francine left Aaron and others inside and went outside. At first Aaron put nothing to the fact that Francine had gone outside. However, after realizing that she was outside for more than half an hour he grew angrily impatient. What was she up to? He wondered.

The persons who had comprised the audience were taking part in the refreshments and some of them were a little disappointed that they were unable to interview Roderick for a proper length of time. Meanwhile outside the building, almost totally oblivious to the fact that she had brought Aaron into the country and to the night's lecture, Francine was busily checking Roderick's schedule to see if she could have a date with him before leaving England. However, almost each time she proposed a date and time, he was already booked. It soon became clear to her that the only time Roderick had was this very night and so she had to think fast. She would dispatch Christine and Aaron back to the hotel. She went back inside and saw Christine chatting with some of the undergraduates, a good distance away from Aaron who stood to the far east of the room pouring a drink from a bottle marked "Famous Grouse." Aaron did not see the two and Francine ushered Christine outside.

"Christine, I shall be ordering a taxi to take you and Aaron back to the hotel. When I return I shall call you from my room, however late I return. Do make a careful explanation to Aaron that I do have an emergency."

Not unfamiliar with inventing stories so as to master situations, Christine, sensing the real nature of the 'emergency', knew exactly what she would say to Aaron in an attempt to throw him off scent. The taxi arrived and Christine ushered Aaron into the back seat while she sat in the front. She eyed

Aaron to pick up his body language. At first he appeared a little dazed and gradually Christine discerned that he was both suspicious and angry.

"Francine was talking to an old friend when her cell-phone rang with news that something radically wrong had occurred to her investments and cash flow in this country and her main accountant will be taking her to an emergency meeting of her fellow investors to examine the real nature of their financial situation and what probable losses they may incur." Christine lied.

At first Aaron did not quite understand what she was saying.

"I do not follow, could you say it again?" he asked rather pleasantly.

Christine repeated what she had said and added that in the event that Francine's losses were severe, their trip to England could be ruined since Francine had confided in her that the greater part of the funding of the hotel and other expenses would be drawn from her funds in England. Aaron did believe this story up to a point, but was intelligent enough to calculate that Francine could have handled things better by taking him into her confidence directly.

His mind turned to Christine, but he did not say anything to her. The taxi-driver pulled into the car park at the front of the hotel. After they reached there, Christine paid the driver and these two guests of the hotel went to their separate rooms.

In his room, No. 312, Aaron sat restlessly looking at the Independent newspaper. Francine had brought him here. He had no money of his own, knew no one and so he was very much her captive. He felt very lonely, partly because ever since their first rendezvous she had always been close to him whenever he wanted. Up until now she was very, very reliable. Wherever she was, he hoped she would soon return for he really needed her close to him. Then his mind ran over the evening's events, lecture, question and answer session. She went outside after the lecture and never called him out to be with her. What if she was playing a trick on him? He did not know Christine well enough to accept what she had said. But, then, what if Christine was telling the truth and Francine's finances were in jeopardy? He sat up, the Independent on the desk in front of him. He could not concentrate well enough to read.

Then, having not taken off his clothes, the rather curious idea struck him to get to see if Christine would take him into her room. He knew that Christine was staying on a different floor but did not know her room number. What if Christine was a player? From time to time after his affair with Francine started, the things she would say and do, did convince him that Francine was a player. Aaron knew enough about life, about peer group pressure and that birds of a feather flocked together.

In no time he was out of his chair and raced down the long corridor. He took the elevator down to the reception desk and asked the receptionist.

"Did you take note of the lady who came in here with me? She is my friend but the whisky I took tonight has caused me to forget her room number."

"Oh, she is staying with us in Room 515," the receptionist informed him without knowing his motive.

Just then three merry Englishmen came into the reception area and asked for the location of the hotel's bar. On hearing that it was on the ground floor two suites away from the receptionist's station, they said to Aaron,

"Come on with us, we will offer you a couple of drinks."

Aaron followed them into the bar. Without asking him for his name and his purpose in the hotel, the happy English ordered a double scotch whisky for him.

"Oh we are from Leeds," one fellow said.

"We do like it here in London which is an active city. Glasses up, friends 'cheers'," he said excitedly.

Aaron, accustomed to such pleasantries in the Ranch permitted his glass to touch those of the recently arrived trio. The four proceeded to a table. Then another fellow asked,

"Do you like it here? What brings you here?"

"I have come on a vacation!" Aaron whispered.

"All alone?" the third fellow asked.

"No, I have come with a lady," Aaron remarked.

"Go, bring her let us offer her some wine."

"She went out. She had an emergency and I do not know where she is right now."

They spent three hours drinking there when he remembered 515. He told the three gentlemen that he felt like retiring.

Aaron took the elevator to Room 515. When he reached the room he knocked and waited. There was no response. He waited for a full seven minutes. No response. He knocked louder than the first time. No response. Then it was as if somebody was approaching him.

"Aaron," the person called out. "Aaron, what on earth are you doing here?"

Thinking quickly, Aaron in a loud voice said, "I have come to our room."

"This is not our room," Francine declared.

Aaron reeked of alcohol.

"Come follow me," Francine demanded, "You have had too much to drink and I am sure that you do not know where you are or what you are doing."

With Francine in the lead, Aaron stumbled down the stairs, wobbled across the corridor of the third floor and collapsed in the bed. Francine noticed that Aaron's key had been left behind in the room. He had locked himself out, she thought. Was he really that drunk or having locked himself out was he going to Christine's room until she came. Francine was speculating.

She telephoned Christine who answered the phone

narrated the story she had provided Aaron to throw him off scent and declared that since she returned to Room 515 she was unaware of anyone knocking on the door of her room. Francine decided that with her luck having run so well, she was putting this evening behind her and when she awoke next day all she would say to Aaron would be that her finances in the United Kingdom had not really diminished to any notable degree.

Chapter 26

A MOTIVATIONAL SESSION

THEY ARRIVED IN THEIR NUMBERS at the extended church hall of St. Ignatius. The news had spread through the villages by word of mouth. Father Fred, who was rapidly getting a reputation as a selfless, tireless worker for all types of people had himself gone on foot uphill and downhill to indicate that he was putting on a class on how to adjust and allow "attitude to achieve altitude." Men, women and teenagers packed the hall, neatly renovated and made larger in the recent weeks. Father Fred had found and used funds raised from benefactors and the church's bank account to enlarge the church hall and to effect repairs to the church itself. He had intended, after all, using the facilities not only for narrow religious purposes but also to bring upliftment to local communities.

Quietly this Priest, whose popularity was soaring, was feeling that more persons were going to attend than he had bargained for. He retreated quickly to the bathroom, now repainted in a pleasant mauve, not for any of the purposes to which such a facility is used, but to offer a quick prayer thanking God for such a large turn-out and asking him for inspiration to have a good three hours with those whom he had come to regard and love as his 'people'. All of the regular village folks and characters were present. He had spotted dozens whom he had never seen before.

"Heavenly Father, I come humbly to you. Forgive my every debt. Bless this beautiful island. Forgive all those who have erred. May the whole population of this island flourish in every way while glorifying your Holy Name. I thank you for the opportunity to serve. I thank you to be alive. I thank you for providing me with the resources to assist those I have helped so far. May I do your will and guide me as I set out to inspire those who are assembling here this evening."

He had gone into the room to pray undisturbed, knowing that if he had remained in the main hall there would be those, who, in seeking his attention, could have got into the way of the prayer. Father Fred hated being distracted or disturbed when praying. He returned to the main hall, checked his wrist watch and realized that the lecture and interactive session were three minutes away. Quickly, before anyone could come up to him he again asked God's guidance and thanked him as well.

Henri came up to him more to prevent anyone trying to approach the priest than to seek to capture the good Priest's attention. Instinctively the Parson sensed that Henri was protecting him from those who could not wait until after the session had closed to speak to him. Father Fred commenced his 'talk'.

"Phillipians 4:13: *'I can do all things through Christ which strengtheneth me'*." Then he paused.

"My aim today is to make each one feel good about themselves, to prepare all of you to be achievers. And before I speak to you—I do not intend to lecture to you—I am prepared to take two questions."

Up went just one hand. It was the left hand of Peter Marcus, known to all as The Artist, especially because of his exceptional ability to draw, paint and even do sculpture. Peter Marcus was perceived to be a genius and a natural. He had no formal training in Art but was possessed of rare skills. But he was often seen and indeed saw himself as being strange; called 'weird' by most folk. It was widely known that for the most part he sold his Art in Anse-la-Reye.

"How does a person control his thoughts? I experience mood swings, highs and lows. Don't laugh at me. I do not mind raising my issues in here since somebody told me that you, dear Father, have always preached the need to be honest. I also find that I think so fast that I can experience many thoughts in an instant. Often these thoughts converge even when they are not linked to each other. There are times too when I feel so low that nothing works but sleep. When I am down and feeling depressed my thoughts and ideas are abnormal.

I also find difficulty in concentrating and I easily become bored. I like people, but when I sell my art, I get laughed at. Some tourists on hearing my prices, give me heavy tips. Some locals laugh at me and tell me I am giving away my talent. On occasions I do wish that something outside of me can help me. Don't laugh, but I also get very, very bored even at parties and dances. In addition I find it hard to understand or cope with routines. If people ask my help outside of my Art, they are amazed at how quickly I get through. I come from a family that live long and if I live as long as them I do not want these feelings to continue. But then there are times when I fear that I cannot live long or better, still there are occasions when I wish severely that it can be ended, but I do not wish to let my mood swings destroy me. Be patient with me.... Look I better shut up..."

There was an uncanny hush, a pause that lasted. Some bowed prayerfully. Then Father Fred responded.

"If I am to be of any help I can only speak from a spiritual angle. Search your heart carefully to see if and how you have been selfish. Try to remember if your selfishness caused hurt and pain. Even when seeking pleasure try to ascertain if you used any person selfishly to achieve happiness for you and not for them. Even if you are right now not actively conscious of any feelings of guilt and remorse, search your heart. Go deep and deeper and deeper still, to see if you have or are experiencing the pain of guilt from having caused others harm..."

Right away Peter Marcus turned around and asked Susie, the Vincie, for pen and paper. Noticing what had just happened the Priest asked him if he was sure he was ready but Peter Marcus was not listening he was writing frantically.

"Hey, Sir," Father Fred said in a loud voice. "Do listen some more before you continue writing. Choked up feelings of guilt often caused by selfishness, and on occasions dishonesty, lead to deep-rooted fears, inner conflicts and believe it or not stress, tension and frightful fatigue. In moments of stress not just fatigue, but real fears trouble the mind and interfere with the spirit...."

"I understand," Peter Marcus yielded.

"If you choose to listen you would probably learn a lot tonight. I am prepared to meet you privately within three days so that we can talk. You did mention rapid, conflicting thoughts and a type of psychological dizziness. If such is very severe you may have to talk to a psychiatrist or clinical psychologist but you should start by locating the names and means of contact of all with whom you have had bad relations... with all that you may have embarrassed, insulted, beaten or exploited and be prepared to make positive reparations for the harm you have caused. You seem to be in a mental mess, but if you follow my advice you ought to get results unless there are serious problems that tell on the brain and mind..."

The audience was impressed and Peter Marcus seemed to appreciate the words of counsel offered so genuinely and lovingly and in a non judgmental manner.

Moments passed. No one else volunteered a question and so this question was put by the Parson.

"Can I speak now for ten straight minutes before taking further questions? Nearly eighty percent of the world's population go about their business from day to day busily earning a living or pursuing the things they want to do, never mindful of the fact that they are living below their true potential. The other twenty percent of the world attain true inner happiness as a result of having achieved and continuing to achieve. The high achievers may not even be highly brilliant or possessed of great intellect, but their lives are properly anchored largely by having healthy attitudes."

There was a murmur and some were clearly set upon in that they seemed to have been jarred by what they just heard. All were listening and most had not heard anyone speak like this before.

"Dale Carnegie, Napoleon Hill, William James, Norman Vincent Peale and others have repeatedly emphasized that attitude determines altitude. The wrong attitude, feelings of self-pity and fatalism can consign us to curious corners. A negative thinker would probably construct a small world and dwell in it wishing for better fortune, feeling that the world, wisdom and wealth favour the few without knowing that an altered attitude can turn around their lives. Most of them lack faith. They lack faith in the Divine Master and nearly all of them lack faith in themselves. Their outlook on life is pessimistic. When they are challenged and told to shake off their pessimism, they stubbornly argue that to be pessimistic is to be realistic. They justify their stance by pointing to the disasters and so called miseries that occur. They simply do not see the brighter side of life. Their lives are often full of anxiety and stress. But there are those who argue that if we believe we can achieve, we will succeed.

A deep-rooted faith can, as the Master has said, move mountains. Cassius Clay believed deep down that he could beat Sonny Liston and he did. Muhammad Ali believed he could take on the fierce George Foreman and Foreman surrendered his title to Muhammad Ali. Cathy Freeman the Aboriginal Australian, believed deeply that she could beat the odds and be a champion. Using the very words of Phillipians 4:13, Evander Holyfield put 'licks' on Iron Mike Tyson."

It was obvious that Father Fred loved sports, but as had become evident in a few moments, he was selecting icons who, Helenites considering their ethnicity, should have been able to relate to.

"Recently we launched a Cooperative and a separate Credit Union and it will be a success, thanks to the pioneers like Theresa, Merle, Henri, Isalene, Zaccky and Sarah."

The gathering erupted in loud applause.

"School teachers will tell you that when children are constantly unsure of themselves and are brimful of doubt they fall into a category of losers who come in below their true potential. Imagine what would have happened if Jesus was struck by doubt as he strolled across the sea. What could have happened?"

"He would have sunk" they shouted. "He may have drowned," someone surmised loudly.

"Stroll out there with confidence." Father Fred was in good form.

"Do not sink or go under because of doubt and fear," he upbraided. "You have to emancipate yourselves from mental slavery." He was clearly familiar with Bob Marley and aspects of black culture.

The teenagers in the audience had never, notwithstanding the respect they held for their parents, been able to relate so well to an older person. They loved what they were hearing.

"Now this business of faith. There are some who are able to summon and practise faith effortlessly. There are those who believe in a loving all-powerful creator and who testify to that effect with their mouths but cannot find faith in a crisis. There are those who have witnessed marvels and who on seeing these modern-day wonders, believe, based on things that they see and experience outside of themselves. The guarantee to a strong lasting faith lies not just in submitting to God by way of a ritual or a message in words, it is attained when the sunlight of God's spirit is the constant companion of the seeker after truth and the practitioner of right action. Clean house and receive the sunlight of the Spirit."

Peter Marcus was more attentive than ever.

"Constant confession of a sincere, fearless type can be the lasting guarantee and the sure path to a faith that will not desert the sincere, persistent one. Many stories exist about persons who had no faith but took corrective steps and lo and behold they then received the sunlight of the Spirit and then wonderful things happened in their lives on a daily basis and faith came. When faith does come, barriers are broken down, peace and happiness become available to the tireless practitioner, energy levels increase and pure love for others also comes into being, even among persons who had been wicked prior to taking stock and cleaning house. Yes, with faith all things are possible but love of one's fellow man, love and respect for one's brothers and sisters are necessary for the type of growth for which we exist.

Let me mention something now which to me is important. Self, one's ego, can be a burden without one even recognizing it and things, negative things happen, which are often caused by ego. Experts believe that ego gone wild is a large factor in many psychological and psychiatric cases. Get the ego properly deflated and problems cease! Often our ego forbids proper action and stands in the way of wise decision-making.

It is widely known that many people seek pleasure—sometimes as an escape. As you grow up and aim for true maturity, never put pleasure first. Do not misunderstand me. Pleasure in its proper context is justified. But if the pursuit of pleasure is a mere escape or cop-out, one's maturity and spiritual growth can be held back badly. The famous black psychologist Scott Peek, writing in *The Road Less Travelled*, was adamant that the seeker after growth had to learn to do the hardest things first—undergo pain first before going after pleasure."

Now his audience, which had grown even larger, was totally silent and their attention to his words did not waver. They were understanding the language he was delivering and found his message clear and convincing.

"Temptation always encourages all of us to seek the simple way if the harder way seems awesome. Defer the pleasurable. Never procrastinate. Do your utmost to seize the day. The ancient Romans said *'carpe diem'*. In dealing with your issues now you will be surprised what comfort can come later. Procrastination is a severe form of laziness. When we procrastinate we are not only lazy, we may even be fearful to take action now, timid that the immediate challenge may be too great for us. Never procrastinate. I once heard a young lady say 'Do not do today what you can do tomorrow'. Clearly that young lady was not living in the now and she was wrong to be a procrastinator.

Believe that the Almighty wants you to lead a stress free life by your knowing that you can achieve if you believe, but it is often necessary to take action to ready yourselves for the coming of very strong feelings of faith and trust. When any person through faith believes that all is and will be well, such a person does not become complacent nor drift away from life's responsibilities while saying to themselves that all things must work in their favour. The believer still has to rise each day and face the day determined to do the best they can. Focusing on helping others and being of service to serious institutions is a necessity. Identifying ways of glorifying God and his Son Jesus Christ, not only by prayer, and worship but also by positive action is an imperative. A thankful heart is an absolute necessity.

Those who seek to glorify God must allow their faith to be surrounded by Christian love, unselfish service, gratitude to God and respect for all humanity. Considerable tolerance too is a prerequisite. Tolerance is needed to help all of us live well with those with whom we have our differences.

I believe the intention of our Triune Majesty, Father, Son and Holy Spirit has always been that we live on earth to work with each other in harmony. Recently, after some years of fine examples set by some pioneers among you, with God's help you established two very, very important institutions that will make a difference."

Many in the audience jumped to their feet.

"If each of us lives selflessly in solidarity with each other, constantly practising tolerance in the midst of divergent opinions and attitudes, we are well on the way to doing the will of our Heavenly Father. Only believe that all is well and will be well and happiness will be yours. I pause now for some other questions."

A teenager put up her hand. "What do you do with fellow students who cheat and disobey teachers? "

"Speak lovingly to them in private and tell them that being honest is a very, very good thing. Tell them that those who obey persons in charge of them are on the way to learning discipline."

"Thank you," said the teenager.

"Father, I have a fifteen year old son who is getting very, very wayward. He is not like anybody I know."

Isabel, like the others, waited for the answer.

"The Lebanese poet Kahlil Gibran said words to the effect that parents might give their children bodies but not thoughts. You have to sit down with him and tell him all your concerns about his behaviour, after you pray that he would change. Let him know that adolescence is a period of change and many youngsters experience strange emotions and temptations in adolescence. Find out who his peers are and if he is on drugs. Ensure that he comes home at proper times. Put a strong father-figure in his life as a priority. Watch his moods. Let him know you are his parent and you have the benefit of experience. Do not be afraid of him. Believe deep down that you can discipline him. Find quality time for him and never stop talking to him. If after these words from me you still are not satisfied let him come and see me with you for a private session."

Father Fred was more demonstrating his willingness to help than putting forward a definite position that he could solve the problem.

"Any further questions?"

"I have a cousin who is vulgar in personal conduct and who is a suspected male prostitute." One woman lamented.

"If this person is an adult, then that is his problem and he must be willing to do something about it. Much as you feel very bad about his conduct, if he wants help he must seek help. He must really want to change. Yes, I know you feel bad but you personally have to learn to accept the things you cannot change. It might seem hard, but all of us have to learn to accept the things we cannot change."

Another hand went up.

"I have a young daughter who clearly wastes her money, wastes mine and I suspect borrows other people's money and may not be able to pay back!"

"Again, assuming that she is an adult, and is working for her own money she does have a personal problem. Your part in it has been providing her with cash even when you know she is a spendthrift. Yet she does not seem to be the typical Helenite.

Permit me now to make some observations on what I have learnt about this island. Before 1838, like other Caribbean islands owned by the British, this country would have seen serious oppression coming out of slavery. For years after emancipation there was widespread poverty. Yet the spirit of your great grandparents and their successors was never broken. Through improvisation, thrift and very hard work backed up by an enduring community spirit your ancestors and you have survived. You have had values based on industry, cooperation and respect for and belief in God and you have come this far.

What you can do—at the risk of being mocked as being old fashioned—is to sit your daughter down and explain the way of life of the exemplars of this wonderful island. Tell her about thrift and the need to save. Warn her against being overly materialistic. Let her know that pretty clothes and fine shoes owned by one person in abundance, are not true investments. No doubt you love her, but if you continue to give her you will continue to spoil her and she would not to change. Stop giving her. Practise tough love.

As far as borrowing and not repaying is concerned, teach her that failing to pay back borrowed property is dishonest. Teach her about honesty. If I can be of any help, never fail to call on me......"

"I have a problem," a young man interrupted, "I cannot help being a litter bug. I just litter and litter. I feel that I am a litter bug."

"It may be, there is a very strong possibility that you litter because of a compulsion, a driving force. Every time you feel like dropping a piece of garbage, postpone dropping it until you come to a place where it can properly be put away. When the feeling comes to dump it, defer dropping it. Be alert to the fact that you have a powerful urge and do not give in to the urge. Put off littering until later you find somewhere where the litter can be safely put away. What I find remarkable is that you have owned up to your problem. You have admitted that you have a problem. Now having admitted your problem, know and believe that there are ways to deal with the problem." The priest encouraged.

"I do not really have a problem, but I want to say something," a young lady intervened.

"I have a friend who is also Henri's friend. Six months before applying to go to teacher's college, he told a group of us that deep down in his heart he believed he would succeed in getting into teacher's college after applying. He kept talking about his deep belief that his application would have been approved. You know something? He is in teacher's college today. I just wanted to share that." she concluded.

"Faith! Your friend had a faith that worked. Believe me, Faith works. If there are any persons who need to see me I will be available soon."

He took out a small notebook and entered the names, contact addresses and where necessary a few telephone numbers. The session ended and they all went away energized.

Chapter 27

A TRULY SICK MAN

"I AM SCARED. Yes I am very, very scared," whispered Linda.

"Why?" Aaron asked as softly as she spoke.

"For thirteen years I kept my marriage vows. The older folk of Helen Isle have been adamant that women walk straight."

"What are you saying?" asked Aaron.

"Here in Helen Isle there are several wayward men who have many women and get children all over the place, but I have been trained to believe that a woman's virtue is paramount." Linda said.

"Look," gasped Aaron, "you're using big words and even sounding religious."

"I am sorry," lamented Linda, "but all like now I feel both scared and guilty."

"My belief is that if you do the things that cause you fear and guilt over and over, you will overcome such lousy feelings." Aaron interjected.

"Father, are you sure we are doing the right thing?"

"Look, Patrice has gone to Martinique and he cannot see us."

"But suppose someone finds out and tells him? Suppose my mother hears of this?"

By now the two were in the centre of the Ranch, for these past few days not in its normal use, because Pierre, Veejay and others had gone to Bimshire for nine days to gamble. Aaron's desire to bed Linda along with his ongoing fling with others had kept him back in Helen Isle.

"Have you been here before and have you brought anybody else here?" Linda was curious.

"No," snapped Aaron.

"And how did you manage to have keys to open it up?"

Suddenly she tripped. Unfamiliar with this place and walking two quickly in the dark, her feet struck an empty Mt. Gay bottle and Aaron had to grab her to prevent her falling.

"Will you please turn on the lights?" Linda requested.

Pretending that he did not know where the electric switches were, Aaron, who spent nights on end in the Ranch, drinking and gambling, continued to hold Linda's hand firmly and took quite some time locating the switch. In his mind what the two of them came to do did not require lights, but since this was their first night out together he was going to heed her advice.

Still though, Aaron, male chauvinist through and through, decided to test Linda and to make her wait while giving the clear impression that he was very unfamiliar with this setting. He continued to grip her right hand with his left hand and did a fine job groping in the dark in a way that made the room larger than it really was. Again Linda tripped, or rather collided with an empty Heineken case her right foot knocking it over. A little superstitious, she started to wonder what traps had been set for her.

"I am searching desperately hard for an electric switch," Aaron assured, while skillfully pretending to be impatient.

Linda allowed her left hand to move away from his body when she felt something that appeared like a flat piece of hard plastic with a shaft sticking out. She pressed the shaft and on came a light, mildly yellow in colour. She spotted an untidy room with a couple of tables, benches and lots of empty bottles. To her far right was a partition looking to be made from a Guyanese hardwood and in the middle of this partition was a closed door.

"Let us sit down," invited Linda.

"Okay, it looks as though you are very tired from the walk up the stairs," Aaron suggested. The hard fact was that although agreeing to accompany him on this night, Linda had doubts.

"No, I am not really tired, just concerned that things may go wrong," Linda observed.

"What do you mean by go wrong?" Aaron asked.

"Go wrong if we are found out. I am married and you are married," she appeared to be having second thoughts.

"I am such a careful planner that with your cooperation I can so manage matters that you need not fear," Aaron said, with a touch of confident arrogance.

"So you say," Linda said, the diffidence revealing itself in her tone of voice.

"Listen, I must tell you that I know how to protect you with the best secrecy."

"Are you naturally secretive," she inquired.

"In my career I have to hold many secrets. People come and tell me things which I hold close to my chest. Wives tell me things that show me they have gone astray. Business people tell me about their dealings both to confess and to confide in somebody they trust. I am like a fridge. I can keep."

"Tell me, Father, have you ever been in this position before?" Linda was pressing for an answer.

"What position?" Aaron demanded, clearly resenting being questioned in this manner.

"Well, forget it," Linda repeated, correctly sensing Aaron's mind.

"Hey, why do we sit outside here?" Aaron was suggesting that the two of them should go elsewhere. A little naïve and certainly inexperienced in these matters, Linda did not realize that Aaron had intended taking her elsewhere on the premises.

Able to see all of his surroundings, Aaron got up and

pushed the door in the centre of the partition.

"Come in here with me, dear," Aaron did not only sound inviting, a definite tenderness was in his voice.

Nervously, Linda stood up both prepared to do as he wished while fearing that in the next few minutes she would do something he wanted but which her instincts and training rebelled against. As she walked slowly behind the partition Linda could feel tiny droplets forcing their way against her eyelids. The light in the adjoining room allowed her to see a bed well made up presenting itself with a clear freshness that did come as a surprise to her. She did not intend to come over as a complete novice and so with some expertise she removed the top cover which was on the bed. This cover was of a light blue and it was clear that it was clean and probably recently put on.

"Does a place like this have a maid and cook?" This question entered her thoughts but she did not have the courage to ask Aaron.

They sat on the bed in silence for a short time. Then Aaron excused himself, went back out into the main hall of the room and quietly went behind the bar where the light permitted him to see a bottle of Johnnie Walker whisky. He gulped down a sizeable portion straight from the bottle and returned to where Linda was sitting.

"What did you go out there to do?" she asked.

Already, as far as Aaron was concerned, this woman had been asking many questions. How could he tell her that he gulped down whisky both for courage and as a possible aphrodisiac? All of a sudden Aaron felt cowardly although he could also feel the sensation of the whisky rising up in his brain.

"Again I ask you what did you go out there to do?" Linda queried.

Always a bit on the superstitious side, she had always had a fear of strange places. She also sensed a weird kind of aroma coming from a place nearby, probably under the room where they were. In a moment of unusual honesty Aaron told her:

"I went outside for a good shot of whisky."

If Linda had been aware of the old folkloric beliefs that potable alcohol bore potential to destroy negative emotions, she probably would have requested Aaron to bring her a drink.

"Tell me, why do you like the strong drink?" she inquired.

His mood already definitely altered by the substance which he had imbibed, he replied:

"To tell the truth I am in the habit of taking strong drink at this hour every night."

"Are you sure that that is not a very, very, bad habit?" she asked.

Having heard vaguely about how there is such a thing as alcohol dependence she pressed for more.

"Do you find that the drink does do something for you?"

Aaron now started to feel that his companion was trespassing dangerously on forbidden territory. In his mind he wondered if she was beginning to believe that he needed drink to be more of a man.

They continued talking for several moments, she asking about his hobbies, his view of life and such, he responding with half-truths and vague short sentences, half-drunk, but sensible enough not to provide her with too many intimate, private details. Then Linda noticed that Aaron started to tug violently at the belt across his waist, while still lying on the right side of the bed. To this, a kind of chill enveloped Linda from the top of her head down to each of her ankles. She started to perspire. Surprisingly, Aaron pulled himself with considerable effort from the bed and wobbled groggily to the adjoining room.

This offered Linda temporary respite. She needed this break to execute a struggle with her conscience that she had to undertake. Just as she convinced herself that she was proceeding to something she desired, Aaron, rocking from side to side barely able to keep his equilibrium, re-entered the room and somehow made it onto the bed.

Minutes passed.

If ever Linda had seen a drunk, certainly here was the drunk of drunkards. Then a harsh snoring started. It was so loud that she, unfamiliar with the location where the Ranch stood, feared that someone outside might pass and hear what to her were like explosive sounds. He certainly had passed out. How long would he lie there? Certainly not until next morning, she hoped. Yet she dare not wake him since this poor man did need to sleep.

Ninety minutes passed and she did drift into a light sleep. Then he came awake. Somehow he was aware that he had company. She, not now as inclined to follow through with his obvious wishes, asked him:

"Are you alright?"

"I am high on the whisky."

"Why not just let us talk for a while?" she suggested.

"About what?" came the abrupt question.

"We can speak about your life. The things you like doing. Any special interests you have."

"Alright." Came the meek 'compromise' of a man made the worse for drink.

"Before I get too personal with you, Father Aaron." The words 'Father Aaron' struck Aaron like a ton of bricks. For he thought his own over-indulgence did not bar him from himself wondering if in his current state he deserved to be called 'Father'. The probability was that if he were sober he would not only have loved the title but would have demanded any amount of important epithets and even adulation. Such was the size of Aaron's ego. Now drunkenness did evoke some feeling of confused humility. His mind drenched with drink, he grunted.

"Why call me Father on an occasion like this?"

A little surprised that Aaron appeared to reject being addressed as 'Father' Linda did hear words unclearly muttered by her companion that sounded like "I have no children" come from Aaron's mouth. What was the state of mind of this fellow outside of drunkenness Linda asked herself.

"Is his physical handsomeness and apparent stamina a veneer, camouflaging a weakling, a coward and a drunk?" She speculated to herself.

"You said we should talk." He said this so slowly that it was obvious that he was making a strong effort to speak.

"Yes," she said. "Before I get to finding out about your personal likes and dislikes, have you heard that there is a strong interest in introducing Black Studies in this Island?"

"Black Studies?" he queried.

"Yes, Black Studies," she advised.

Some relief had by now come to Linda and she was more relaxed. She now knew that she could temporize, for the man next to her was rendered impotent by alcohol.

"Well, let me put it another way. It is known that we come from West Africa. At least our ancestors did. So we are Africans. Africans were sent packing in different parts of the world called Colonies. You get Africans in America. Africans were seen in England certainly in the 18th century. I know that we are from West Africa."

Then Aaron muttered slowly and sheepishly: "Garçon, the only thing I know about West Africa is that it gives us hurricanes."

Shocked, Linda now knew that strong drink 'doth make mankind into mad maniacs'. She was speechless while he dozed off again.

IT WAS NOW PAST ONE in the morning. She desperately wanted to get out of this place and back to where she was going before daybreak. She needed to get out of there without being found out. She stood up. The light from next door permitted her to find the switch for this room. She tried the switch.

On came three lovely white florescent lights. Her feeling was that in a short time the brilliance of the lights should act to awaken Aaron. But the other issue was: was he in good enough condition to drive or would she have to put her unlicensed skills to the test and drive him? Then clearly if she did so she could not drop him off and walk home at the hour in the dark. If she drove to her destination, then he would have to take over.

She had to make a choice. She elected in her mind to drive to her sister's place in good time before her sibling arrived from her holiday overseas. Her sister was scheduled to arrive at 4.30 in the morning and Linda had always had a key for her sister's house. Even if it caused an argument, he could not drive her if he was still so drunk. She sat looking at him. Clearly well-endowed in physical terms, he must be the type of man pursued by women. She herself found the strong feeling of desire for him undiminished by the fact of her marriage. The only complication was that her standards and morals up to now were adequate enough to prevent her from being led into temptation.

She felt though that she had worked on her mind well enough on this very night, to dismiss qualms of conscience. It did take effort, but just as she was on the tiptoe of expectation, having convinced herself that she was ready, he got himself lost in an alcoholic coma. The coma was bound to end. In the near future expectancy would become reality but the doubt now was whether he was sober enough to function—at least to drive! Another doubt was that did he not appreciate his identity as a descendant of proud African people?

Some minutes passed before he came awake. He did so without any drunken look in his eye.

"I want some water," he demanded.

"I do not know here," she pleaded.

"In here is so bright the light will take you next door and you have to see empty glasses and a tap. Bring me some water, please, please."

She jumped up and went next door. Clearly Aaron was experiencing an emergency. She brought the water using a pint glass. Somehow he drank it more slowly than she thought he would. He tugged and pulled at his pants once again, this time to be sure it could be on and buckled to his waist. The idea of undressing had evaporated from his head. He sat up. Some clarity had come back, though his mouth and breath reeked of the substance he had devoured. He went next door and brought the half-filled bottle of scotch to the room.

"I am not drinking anymore here. I shall be taking it with me," he declared.

"So long as you drink no more tonight. Do you really think you can drive, dear?" The word 'dear' so registered that it seemed to inject new life in him.

"Let us go. I am available to you tomorrow night, darling," Linda promised.

He did drive her to her sister's place. He left her without even looking to see if she got into the house properly. He continued to drive and picked up the bottle of scotch again.

No one was on the road at this point. He gulped down more than two gills of whisky. The moment he did so the desire for an affair returned. He drove another three miles feeling the full effects of the liquor. He now became the storehouse of a being, activated by liquor and lust.

Another half mile down the road he thought he saw somebody looking like a woman. He decelerated and pulled up beside an elegant figure. He made out the make-up on the person's face. Before he could stop properly the figure in the dark with the most enchanting voice Aaron had ever heard said:

"Good night. Can I come with you?"

Aaron's condition, part inebriation, part lascivious, allowed for no hesitation. He stopped and in entered this attractive looking person.

"Do you want me?" Came the inviting question. "If you really want me I will show you where to drive me."

By now Aaron's lower being was feeling arousal.

"Do we have to go far?" Aaron asked.

"Not really. Drive up the hill some more and I will tell you how to park."

Soon Aaron was following the figure down a corridor in a very, very dark place. The place smelt both of tobacco and ganja. At last Aaron was accompanied into a room as his party led him with the softest of hands.

"Listen, I normally charge between $50 and $100 for my services. But before we get to it, let us have a drink," came the invitation to Aaron.

Aaron was craving more strong drink. A glass was poured and offered to him. He gulped it down and reached for the other person.

"You are going to be surprised but I will make it pleasant for you. I am not what you think I am. I am called Muscle Martha. Look at my lovely arms."

Too drunk to understand the caution as to identity, and now completely overpowered by drink mingled with desire so potent to deny self-control, and having come too far with this stranger, the two bodies joined, Muscle Martha playing the inferior role while Aaron performed the role of superior. The relative tightness he had to penetrate produced no real suspicion certainly not for the first four or five minutes. Their bodies conjoined now in non-heterosexual union. To Muscle Martha, this man was a worthy suitor.

Around 3.45 a.m. Aaron came to, outside in the street in the car, remembering only that he had gone into a house with a woman. Muscle Martha was the name of a notorious male homosexual who was a prostitute and transvestite. On reaching home his wife Elizabeth, who once again had remained awake, now being fed up (she was past mere concern) at the hours kept by her husband, clearly realized that he was drunk and reeking of alcohol. She could smell the alcohol. There was another odour. The odour presented no pleasantness. Before she could utter a word her husband fell off the bed as he tried to lie down. She turned on the lights in the bedroom. Both Aaron's shirt and pants were on the wrong side. He also came home without underpants.

Elizabeth further realized that but one shoe was on her husband's right foot. Somehow his left laceless shoe was on his right foot. She was deeply bothered. However he smelled both from the mouth and elsewhere troubled her. Surely he would have to clean up unaided.

She retreated to another bedroom as Aaron lay sprawled across the floor of the matrimonial bedroom. Elizabeth went to sleep, her last waking thought was that however much a person may drink, drunkenness never absolves anyone. Sober or drunk, each person should bear responsibility for their actions. No one should, she thought, be able in any situation or forum, to blame a self-induced condition for wrong doing. Ultimately, each person must own up to their actions. This was her last thought.

Somehow she still managed a good sleep.

Chapter 28

A PECULIAR SERMON

"WOULD ALL OPEN THEIR BIBLES to Leviticus 20:13. Please go into your Old Testament to find this portion of scripture."

There was a mixed sense of shock and surprise in the church that Sunday morning. It was over the fact that Aaron actually commenced his sermon by quoting a Biblical passage. For months Aaron had entered the pulpit and preached without quoting from the Bible, but on this day he decided to quote it:

"*If a man lies with a man as one lies with a woman both of them have done what is detestable.... their blood will be on their heads.*"

Then an even greater surprise.

"Would the church repeat the words of Leviticus 20:13 not silently but aloud?"

Most marvelled that the wording of the verse in their Bibles differed somewhat from what Aaron had read, but the message was by no means unclear.

"My brothers and sisters in Christ, from earliest times there has been holy law. This holy law must be obeyed since its rules and principles apply for all time. There does exist a high form of law, some thinkers call it the original law of nature. God made nature to operate in perfect order.

For weeks now our blessed island has been a place in which there has been debate, very serious debate, about a moral aberration known as homosexuality. But let me commence by looking at some aspects of the laws of nature. All of us know that if we plant and rear a banana shoot the end result will be banana plants, not mangoes nor coconuts. If you plant the seed of a lime you will get limes as a result. Within nature, according to the natural law, we get morning, noon, afternoon and night. The wind blows. The seas and rivers ebb and flow according to certain fundamental laws. The egg of a chicken, if subjected to certain conditions, will produce a chicken. If a male cat mates with a female, there will be a kitten born as a result.

We were created in such a way that our bodies are subject to the laws of nature. Laws govern thirst and hunger and by particular means thirst and hunger can be made to subside. The small passage of scripture on which we are reflecting both creates a ban and suggests that in human affairs the laws governing intimacy, romance and ultimately marriage are so set that just as the woman Eve was created for the man Adam, the laws of nature governing sexual relations encourage heterosexual unions.

Our beautiful little island is seeing a debate on homosexuality. Most people when they first hear of homosexuality think of relations between a male and another male, but when a woman lies with a woman that too is homosexuality. Implied in the message of today's Bible passage is that it is not right for women to be lovers of women. At first, Leviticus 20:13 does appear to address in a direct way the question of male homosexuality. But there is more to it.

Right now here in Helen Isle we are confronting homosexuality. There is a considerable discussion. We are aware of the controversy surrounding abortion which too is a moral issue. But do not think that homosexuality is merely a male activity. There is female homosexuality as well. There are those of you who would have been hearing of Gay Marriages. Up to a few years ago the word "gay" meant happy or merry. Today it means something else. I remember reading of two women who years ago called themselves gay. They wanted something they called marriage. Like any bad thing it did not last. One sued the other for something called palimony. Gay marriages must be seen for what they are. Mock non-authentic affairs."

It was true that in a largely homophobic society most persons opposed gay marriages, but many in the congregation had never heard Aaron speak with such force. Few doubted that in every respect he was a real 'he-man' and if physical attributes were the sole contributory factor to a marriage, then Elizabeth should have been happy.

"As a theologian I first had to go to Theological School and I attended one of the oldest in the Caribbean. I attended the one known in Bimshire to have been set up by a Christopher Codrington who owned property there and in Antigua. In my studies in theological school—at which I excelled I may add—I learnt that the original and best definition of marriage was: the union of one man and one woman for life excluding all others."

Some of them in the church today were more impressed with their priest than ever. He did usually preach with fluency and a good command of language and if his new delivery was all then he was the consummate reverend. Yet a few were wondering why he was preaching today with so much blood in him and persons were wondering if he was deliberately seeking to take over the leadership of the moral debate on prostitution, homosexuality and abortion.

Ismay, normally a member of St. Ignatius, had dropped in to the service to see how the son of her friend Sarah was doing. Having never seen Aaron conduct a mass before she was unaware that he often tried to chant the ritual from memory only to lapse and make errors. So Ismay had been content with what she had heard up until then but in any event the sermon in St. Gabriel's the Greater always preceded the main and more important parts of the recitals for the Eucharist.

Continuing his sermon Aaron challenged his flock to avoid

homosexuality, debauchery, midnight-rambling and related wrongs.

There were some persons who were absent on this occasion. Patrice was reportedly overseas. Others missing from this service were Yvonne, Trevor, Agnes and Faroud. Then just as Ismay was thinking that she really needed to see how Zaccky's son was conducting mass, Aaron shifted gear.

"Now I have not been at this church very long but it is my intention to rule in a strict manner."

One young lady turned to the person sitting next to her and asked: "Is something wrong that Father has to get so strict?"

"Yes, I have to be very strict. Small communities are known to generate talk and gossip."

The young lady now asked her neighbour, "Are there rumours going around about people practising homosexuality?"

"I have not heard any rumours about our church members being involved in that business," came the reply. Aaron continued:

"Our main purpose here is to attend church for worship. The organs of the church must never be abused."

"But I have heard the organ. It sounds alright," the persistent young lady turned around and said to four people seated behind her. "And the church only has one organ."

"Will you listen, please?" An elderly lady upbraided this overzealous young lady.

"You, listen!"

"We do have organs in the church, the main one being our church council." Aaron now had flames in both of his eyes. "Members of our church council should not spread rumours. Rumours result from gossip. Gossip is bad. I do not want 'mauvant langues' in my church."

Ismay, who had for the most part been paying close attention to Aaron's attack on homosexuality, noted the sudden change in the tone of the sermon. Now she listened for the details and content.

"It is very, very bad when ordinary members bad talk each other. Evil talk is corrosive. Wickedness can be the consequence of gossip. No member should set out to assassinate the character of another member. I will soon get to the point. I am not the type that would wink at evil, nor can I ignore injustice."

All present were listening carefully. It was not a packed congregation, but most persons hearing this sermon from its start were remarking to themselves that there was something strange from Aaron's mood. The idea of Aaron inviting persons to open their Bibles while he preached was entirely new. He started by denouncing homosexuality. Everyone sympathized with the position he had originally taken, for like most members of society those who worshipped at St. Gabriel's were homophobic.

"I want to make it very clear; 'mauvant langues' have no place in this church. If little children tell lies, we as adults chastise them. If people go to court and lie we call them perjurers. Now I am your shepherd. The role of the shepherd is to feed, care and protect the flock. Those who come to church here are sheep. I, as shepherd, hold the staff which is a rod. Call it Aaron's rod if you wish. Now to tear down or sully the good name of your shepherd is worse than perjury. I will tolerate no attacks on my name. I will deal harshly at all times with those who undermine my authority. I am your leader."

Then he shouted: "Righteousness exalts a nation but sin is a reproach to the people!"

He stopped for breath. If he had been preaching in a sectarian or fundamentalist church there would have been those who would have shouted back "Amen" or "Alleluia"

Aaron picked up his bible. Frantically he turned the pages. He was very angry and it showed.

"Now I have opened my Bible. In seconds I will read from it. It contains truths. Ladies and gentlemen, I have opened my Bible to Isaiah."

He stopped. His finger ran rapidly over the pages of the Bible. Sometimes two pages stuck together and were flipped.

"Now there are sixty-six books in the Bible. You know something, there are sixty-six chapters in Isaiah. No coincidence. Truth is truth."

All were amazed and wondered what Aaron would do next.

"I go back now to the fifty-fourth chapter of Isaiah. I am now at its seventeenth verse which says: '*No weapon that is formed against thee shall prosper; and every tongue that shall rise against thee in judgment thou shalt condemn.*' I say unto you all, no weapon or evil aimed at your shepherd shall hit its target.

In case you are wondering what I am talking about, without going through the right channels and determined to spread lies on an innocent man, some persons who are members of this church have strayed. But to imagine that the main organ of my church was implicated in wrong doing. Even if not all who have been members were involved, I want to say to you that believe it or not, at the level of church council your devoted leader has not only been vilified, his character was slaughtered in the worst way. Imagine someone at a recent church council meeting alleged that I own a car on which there is no debt but that I have been forcing the church to pay monthly installments to my bank. Imagine that. If I did not owe on my car the church would not have to pay for it. Then there are those who have put it out that I like my own way."

All eyes were now steadfastly glued on Aaron.

"I have my sources. Even before I could settle down to my Ministry in this church within weeks some ill-informed and I am sure wicked persons put out the evil word that I love too much money and that I treat the church's money as my own. I am not rich. If I were a thief I believe I would have been rich...."

"I know poor thieves," someone said fairly loudly. It was that insistent young lady in the light blue dress with matching high-heeled shoes. All who heard her ignored her. Aaron pretended that he did not hear her.

"I feel so grieved and hurt at what has been said about me. Who said that words do not hurt? The wicked words wildly said about me hurt to the same degree as sticks and stones. What choice would I have as the shepherd supervising sheep? You know something, ladies and gentlemen? Those persons who put out bad things about me plotted and planned. I would be surprised if any of you had heard these bad rumours. I would really be surprised. The people who have been bad talking me have been rather careful. They have managed the business of making sure that some people know while most people are not supposed to know. The rumour-mongers have controlled their gossip."

The young lady in the light blue dress sat up straight and before she could say or do anything the person next to her put a hand over her mouth. Now the young lady understood that she should really sit still.

"You know, ladies and gentlemen that so clever are the devious that they are not easily found out. If all of you who are hearing my voice were put into my position, you would easily conclude that you would have no choice but to act. And so, I have acted. I am the ultimate leader of this church and therefore with immediate effect the following persons will forfeit their positions on the church council. I am also considering banning them for life from my church. You want their names? They are: Stella, Yvonne, Trevor, Agnes.

There is no need for me to identify them in any more detail. They will not sit on my church council. Patrice who is loyal and whom I trust will continue to lead the church council when I am absent. In the near future I will announce the reconstituted church council. I now end with words of Psalm 37: *'Fret not thyself because of evil-doers neither be thou envious against the workers of iniquity. For they shall soon be cut down like the grass....'* "

Chapter 29

DEATH

HE KNEW THAT HE HAD TO DO SOMETHING. It might mean acting through an agent or hireling. In the last five months he had tried many, many things. He had taken two trips overseas. They did not work, for the problem still haunted his mind. He had consulted with three psychologists and he was sure that he had wasted his time. He went to a psychiatrist and in his judgment the pills he was given did not remove his problem. He was not sleeping well. Embarrassed and deeply hurt, he had now stopped going to church. He lost faith. His performance in his job was so badly impaired that his supervisor had spoken to him about his declining productivity. He had virtually lost his appetite. He would go on long walks, yet could not relax. He knew he was losing weight rapidly.

Nothing was working for him. Six months ago a happy man, Patrice recognized that his world was shrinking. Something had to be done. He had been badly betrayed. Betrayed by the one he loved and betrayed by the one to whom he was blindly loyal. He thought and thought. He had gone for counselling. He had tried positive thinking but to no avail. Outside of seeking counselling he had spoken to a couple persons in the hope that his obsessive worrying would end.

He now contemplated something quite drastic. He was sure that his philosophy, way of life and attitude to others were such that he ought not now to be going through what he was being made to endure these past long twenty-four weeks.

He was sure that he had done no one any wrong.

"What did he do to deserve this? Nothing," Patrice thought.

He knew that he could not continue thinking and living the way he was. To say that he had become despondent and desperate, could not truly capture the dark gloom that afflicted his every thought. He was like a person who was haunted and constantly pursued by all the forces of evil.

At last an idea struck him. He had to find a way short of suicide to end the torment. He had thought and thought. He even had prayed, but found his prayer to be devoid of faith, trust and hope. He figured that the help he needed would come. But it would have to be external help. He had to seek help outside of himself. He continued to ponder on his plight and to try to locate a quick and rapid solution.

He knew that the vast majority of persons in his community and in the surrounding areas were law-abiding. Then the ways, past and history of two well-known characters—hoodlums in their prime—entered his thoughts. He remembered Packa-Wow and Matthias, both of whom he had not seen for months.

He had heard unbelievable reports that Matthias had undergone something of a personality change. In the unlikely event that this was true it would have been the irony—the paradox of the millennium—if Packa-Wow had turned his back on his past. Certainly Matthias and Packa-Wow could not have simultaneously transformed their way of life while being together resident on the same land mass. Known to be nomadic and erratic, Packa-Wow, if motivated sufficiently, could offer Patrice his very last hope. How would he find Packa-Wow and what would he have to offer him to induce the well-known thug to carry out his bidding?

Unknown to Patrice, Packa-Wow had been out of jail for close to thirty months. As soon as he had left jail, Packa-Wow had started selling water coconuts for a living and supplemented his income by selling coconut bread at street corners on Friday and Saturday nights. Packa-Wow had for close to a year made enough money to deposit it with the National Commercial Bank and eighteen months after leaving jail, he borrowed $6,000 from the bank to improve his house. The Loans Officer at the Bank had never invoked character when dealing with Packa-Wow. Indeed he had asked the convict very few questions.

Then all of a sudden Packa-Wow's circumstances changed. Many persons started to sell coconuts close to the very location where he conducted his business and the forces of competition started to divert business away from him in a dramatic way. He lost so much money that he was finding it almost impossible to meet his loan installments. In his panic Packa-Wow resumed drinking heavily and where and when he could, he did a liberal amount of stealing as well.

Having carefully compared Matthias with Packa-Wow and influenced considerably by what he had recently heard of the former, Patrice resolved that he would find Packa-Wow. For fear that his plans might not materialize, Patrice decided to trust no one to search for and locate Packa-Wow for him. He would find his man himself.

IT WAS NOW SATURDAY. Patrice set out from home about 10.30 a.m. and headed for the city. He was going to search every bar and rumshop until he found Packa-Wow. As he moved through various streets in the city it appeared to him as though most people were looking at him rather curiously. There were times when he felt all eyes were focussing on him. This definitely made Patrice feel more paranoid and confused. Did he look that awful, or could it be that many persons felt that he looked strange or was it that people had been hearing things? Amidst it all he felt in a sick kind of manner that some people looked at him and doubted his identity, for by now Patrice's decline in weight overall had become very pronounced. Yet his belly appeared large—in a contorted kind of way.

Some people who were assembled in the rumshops were astonished that a person would stand outside, measure each drinker from head to toe and leave without buying a drink or waiting for one to be offered.

After just about two hours moving from bar to bar in the city, Patrice was sure that he heard some persons singing loudly in Bryan's bar. He summoned sufficient courage to approach this place. The noise grew louder. It became clear that four middle-aged men, having belted down some white-rum were trying to sing Psalm 23 to the crimod while a heated argument about cricket took place close by among another three who also had been drinking. A lone figure dressed in a worn out pink short-sleeved shirt, sporting a pair of aged grey-blue jeans stood in the doorway as if waiting either to welcome Patrice or some good Samaritan who had enough cash and generosity to buy him a drink. Packa-Wow stood forlorn, looking both preoccupied and expectant.

"Garçon," Packa-Wow greeted Patrice.

"I cannot recall having ever seen you in a place like this. I believe some good soul has sent you to me to bring me a shot of white rum and two Piton beers."

"Of course, I shall buy you some drinks. To tell the truth I will have a couple of drinks with you too," Patrice said, summoning all the courage he could find.

Packa-Wow was definitely astonished. He had known Patrice for more than two decades and never believed that he would ever be seen drinking in a rumshop. Before ordering a flask of white rum and three Pitons, Patrice told Packa-Wow,

"My friend, we need to talk. I do not feel that we can do so in here. If you exercise patience and wait six or seven minutes we can chat, then we can have a couple of drinks together."

The two walked down a narrow alley which offered them enough privacy. Eye to eye with Packa-Wow, Patrice spoke softly, hardly able to hold back his pain. Packa-Wow told him that his request was most unusual and required the closest possible reflection.

"Whatever I do decide, garçon, what we just discussed remains between the two of us."

Packa-Wow then told Patrice that he too was having very serious problems and provided information as to how he could be contacted and gave Patrice an 'estimate'. Before returning to the bar Packa-Wow told Patrice that the two of them had to be careful, planful and always on the lookout. His last words to Patrice before going back into the bar were:

"We will trust no one."

The two wasted no time knocking off the flask of white rum and chased the hot chemical substance with Pitons; Patrice drinking one while Packa-Wow consumed two beers. They spotted an empty table with three chairs in the far east of the bar and decided to sit.

The argument about cricket continued heatedly while the spirited quartet brought together rather extemporaneously and inspired by the liquor they had been consuming, were now doing their third rendition of the crimod more loudly than ever. So as not to give away nor spill their secret, both Packa-Wow and Patrice feigned some valid appreciation of the Psalm that was being sung. Packa-Wow had heard it at a couple of funerals he had attended but the crimod started to bring mixed memories to Patrice. Were it not for the alcohol he was drinking, Patrice was sure that Psalm 23 bore the capacity to remind him of his role in the church, of his own naivety as a member of St. Gabriel's the Greater, and the experiences he was living in recent months. Packa-Wow was surprised at the capacity Patrice was exhibiting and the quantum he was devouring.

As they were parting company about 2.00 p.m. Packa-Wow reminded Patrice quietly how to contact him and realized that Patrice was gripping his right hand and placing something in it. As Patrice was about to walk out he held Packa-Wow's hand beneath the square red metal table. Patrice had deposited five hundred dollar bills in Packa-Wow's right hand inviting him to check what was in his hand. With this gesture, Packa-Wow thought he certainly meant business even though he had not verified how much it was.

Packa-Wow started to think. If the balance of the money could be paid in the very, very near future, he should be able to clear his debts and in the event that he changed his mind about wiping out his debt, he would have enough to meet the cost of his ticket to a far off place along with a considerable fund to take with him.

However, he did feel that he had to do two things first. Without any intention of quitting drinking forever, he had to keep a clear head and in accordance with the beliefs of his most significant peers, eat properly with some fasting in between. Secondly, he had to learn the ways of the detective. His own past and proclivities had never seen him abandoned by his cousin Leerone. Leerone had time for Packa-Wow though he had failed to get his wayward cousin to abandon his devious ways. George Smith was related to Packa-Wow but the latter had not seen George for months. This meant that in Packa-Wow's world he had but one reliable relative available to him.

Despite being a Police Officer and a very fine detective it was well known that Leerone was both able to walk the straight narrow road and yet always accommodate Packa-Wow when the latter visited him. Leerone had made up his mind: he would be law-abiding, but he was not going to ostracize or alienate Packa-Wow. Leerone Jacques-Bean had been a detective, for the better part of twenty years and was decorated. He took such pride in his many successes that he would boast to his family and friends about how many cases he had cracked and even took the risk of spelling out in detail the methods he used in his investigations. Packa-Wow was aware of some of these techniques but now felt that he needed to be as close to Leerone as could be, to listen to learn how to stalk persons, how to track down people and how to succeed in keeping persons under surveillance.

Over the next few weeks, Packa-Wow practised discipline in physical exercises and discipline in eating the right foods and discipline in fasting. Moreover he resisted any urge to drink. These forms of self-denial were practiced by some criminals just when they had something up their sleeves.

Leerone took note of the metamorphosis his cousin had undergone and without complimenting him, secretly hoped that his sudden change would usher in a new phase in Packa-Wow's life. Leerone was eager for Packa-Wow to find ways of avoiding jail, or better still, avoiding crime. Leerone did have some belief that Packa-Wow had not always been charged for crimes he had done. Packa-Wow's wishes to learn from Leerone did not suffer disappointment and the senior detective could find no reason to be suspicious of the increased visits which his devious cousin was paying him, nor the very real fact that in the many social gatherings in which the two were engaged, Packa-Wow was doing what appeared to be an inordinately great amount of listening. In any event, Leerone loved people to listen while he delivered interesting anecdotes about cases which he had probed.

Packa-Wow was learning fast. In an era when good listeners were diminishing in number simply because many preferred to talk than to listen, and notwithstanding his background of holding forth in rumshops, Packa-Wow became the perfect listener.

It was after four weeks of his being at Leerone's house that he met Patrice again. Patrice's weight had stabilized somewhat, but his face was still haggard. He remained lean and had come to pay Packa-Wow a further deposit. If he had to 'invest' all of his life's savings he was prepared to do so. Patrice's mind was firmly made up. For him to rescue his sanity, his problem could only be dealt with where the roots of it started.

"Garçon," Packa-Wow started softly.

"You have told me everything and I have been preparing to help. You have already shown that you are serious by paying a very small deposit..."

Whereupon Patrice frantically pushed his left hand in the pocket of his dark grey trousers and pulled out a wad of bank notes.

"This further deposit is six times what I have already paid you."

"Thanks," Packa-Wow said. Then he said to Patrice:

"Garçon you spoke to me in that alley that afternoon. You told me everything. Now I can say to you that is just what you believe, in fact, just what you said you know is definitely true. For I have seen them together in the night, and more than once."

"Did I tell you...." Patrice was not trusting his memory, "that she had moved out of my bedroom?"

"You did not but if she sleeps with just one man at a time I would know that she gives you nothing."

Then Packa-Wow stood before Patrice and put his right hand on the left shoulder of this man who was clearly suffering and who to his credit, had not committed suicide. Packa-Wow remembered that Patrice had said that the further deposit was six times the earlier one, but as Packa-Wow was rather unschooled, to use a litotes, he was happy but dared not ask Patrice what the exact figure was, for fear that he would be deemed greedy and too impatient.

"I think I can do the job within eleven days, so prepare yourself."

Patrice understood Packa-Wow very well. He sensed that Packa-Wow meant that the final payment would be due within the time just stated.

They parted company and Packa-Wow went to Leerone's house to find out when next he could have a soft drink with his cousin. Leerone was not at home, but his wife, who given her own way would have kept her distance from Packa-Wow, did tell him the exact time and hour at which she expected her husband.

"Should I tell him why you are coming?" she inquired.

"Mrs. Jacques-Bean," Packa-Wow decided to be formal, as formal as she was with him. "I enjoy the stories my cousin tells about his experiences as a detective. I like to listen to him."

As Leerone's wife thought to herself that it was rather late in life that Packa-Wow had decided to take lessons from a police officer, Packa-Wow told her.

"I have to go, but let him know that I will return about half hour after he comes home."

If the truth be told, it is incredible how people at Packa-Wow's level could spot egoists and work on lubricating their notions of self. Packa-Wow knew that Leerone was vain, so egotistical as to derive gratification from narrating accounts of his exploits. Therefore, in addition to the fact that Leerone had never rejected Packa-Wow, the latter knew how to provide esteem for the detective. In his mind Packa-Wow knew what he was learning from his cousin. Above all he was sure why it was necessary to stick close to a person with the expertise from which he could draw when the right moment presented itself.

So resolved was he that consistent with his deep belief that fasting, vegetarianism and abstinence from pleasure would prepare him that he actually increased the degree he was practicing these things and started a form of meditation, Packa-Wow's way. He felt sure how he would do the job, but where? He wondered. It was also a question of when.

The exact timing did not depend solely on how quickly Patrice would pay the last amounts of money, it was left also to two individuals with whom Packa-Wow would have an encounter.

Within a couple of days Patrice handed over the money

which he had come to expect. Then in light of the plans he had for his future, Packa-Wow decided that it was pointless paying his creditors. What he did do was to rent a motorcycle for eight days. Day by day he would change the registration number of it.

Now it was a Thursday night and he felt that the green car ahead of him was definitely transporting Linda and the man with whom she was having an affair.

Aaron had decided that on this night he was not going to take Linda to the Ranch.

"You know, Linda, variety is the spice of life. Instead of going to our usual hideout we will do it parking out tonight."

"Yes, dear, I love you. Whatever you want."

Packa-Wow had taken the precaution of travelling with a full tank of gasoline in the event that the couple ahead of him were going to adjust their plans. As he rode behind them he reflected on how he had failed in the past. He was not going to live in Helen Isle after the deal he was embarked on to perform. There was a time he had met a fugitive in Mayreau, one of the Grenadine Islands and the man provided advice as to the movements of the vessels which traversed the Caribbean sea. He had enough money to bribe any sailor or seaman. Then as he realized that the two in front of him had passed the Ranch, two things entered his mind. No one listens to a good detective and then goes ill-prepared and his cousin Leerone would no doubt be shocked on discovering the true motive behind his visits to the home of this sleuth.

But his mind was made up. He told himself that he was justified not just for the pay he had received, but that man who incidentally was now in open country, had wrecked a marriage. That man had posed as a religious leader. The woman with him was to Packa-Wow, no better than the evil man in whose company she was seen frequently at night. Packa-Wow's mind then raced onto how Georgie Smith's military career had been ruined. And he knew who had caused Georgie's fall.

The car was still visible. It was not very late. Dark clouds had positioned themselves low and close to the earth. It was supposed to be full moon. However, the moon was hidden behind the clouds.

Unaware that he was being followed, Aaron parked the car in an unpaved grassy road. The car was now between ten banana trees five on each side of the track. The occupants of the car were too caught up either to survey the scene or to sense the presence of a stranger.

Packa-Wow was sure that he had not been seen. He drew a deep, deep breath that could be heard by no one. All four windows of the car were down. Quickly he fired a shot straight to Aaron's chest. This was followed quickly by another to the head.

As Linda started to scream, he shouted, "Get away! You, run away fast!"

Screaming, she started to run.

More shots were fired. Not totally sure where she was, she ran south, then north. She was running in circles.

By now Packa-Wow, cocksure that he had not been seen, went back to where he had left the motorcycle and fled east.

A tourist stopped when he noticed a woman screaming and running along the lonely road. Hysterical, she screamed.

"Murder! Murder!"

The tourist, a repeat visitor, drove into the Police Station a full 10 miles away and reported in her presence what Linda had told him. Four Police Officers raced to the scene. The first thing that caught their attention was two 9 mm glocks lying close to the body of a man. The Sergeant in charge of the operation checked Aaron's pulse. He searched for other vital signs.

Using a cell-phone which he had recently acquired, he called the local Police doctor. He also called Simpson's Embalmers Morticians and Funeral Directors.

The doctor and undertakers' assistants arrived almost

simultaneously.

The doctor pronounced: "This man is dead."

Aaron's body lay reclined in the co-driver's seat.

Simpson's embalmers morticians and funeral directors lifted the lifeless body into the van in which they had come, and drove off north into the dark, along the lonely winding road.